DANCE WITH THE NIGHT

CITY OF VIRTUE AND VICE: BOOK 2

SUSANNAH WELCH

CONTENTS

Cover Concept and Design by Art Muse (Patricia E. Badalo)
Editing by Red Loop Editing (Victoria Basnuevo)

eISBN: 978-1-7365770-2-8
Paperback ISBN: 978-1-7365770-3-5

www.susannahwelch.com

ALSO BY SUSANNAH WELCH

City of Virtue and Vice Series

Dance with the Wind

Dance with the Night

Dance with the Dawn

For Jamal,
The Underneath...
because you would have definitely
been executed in the City

THE UNDERNEATH

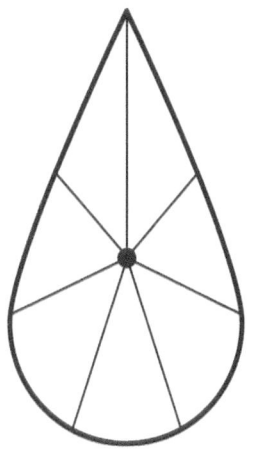

1

Ylena's brain felt sluggish, and she struggled to understand what was happening. Less than an hour ago, she had been singing and dancing with Caed in front of an audience of people. It was the most exhilarating, most transcendent moment of her entire life. And now, almost everyone she had met in the City was dead and she was in an underground city she had been living above with no knowledge.

Grandfather looked deeper into her eyes. "Ylena, I'm so glad you are safe. When Wilder came back without you, I was terrified that—"

"Wilder?" Her mind woke up with a jolt. The last she had seen Wilder, he was walking out the stage door and abandoning her and the rest of the cast without a way to finish the show. "You know Wilder?"

"Um ... Maybe it's best if we get you inside before we talk about this." Grandfather looked around at the people walking by. Passersby mostly ignored them, but a few people gave them glances out of the corner of their eye, sizing them up.

Grandfather stood and held his hand out for Ylena. She

used his strength to pull herself to her feet. Her body felt older than her eighteen years. Besides dancing for hours, she had also escaped the theater by climbing down the side of the cliffs. Every muscle in her body felt as broken as her heart.

Grandfather looped her arm through his and walked her down the street. Her mind only vaguely noticed the people and the buildings she passed. Everything was so strange and confusing that her mind faded around the edges until she only noticed the sidewalk under her feet. It was the same white stone as all the buildings in the City above, but in the purple light of the crystal spire, she could see that the sidewalk was stained and chipped.

She followed the dirty sidewalk until Grandfather stopped in front of a closed shop. Through the grimy windows, she could see shelves of glass jars filled with unidentified substances. He led her behind the shop and unlocked a heavy door, revealing the glow of a crystalline lamp inside.

He ushered her into a room that was modest compared to everything in the City but luxurious compared to the cave they had shared for her entire life. There was a wooden table with four mismatched chairs, a couch with a bright quilt covering some of the ragged spots, and a short bookshelf with a dozen books stacked haphazardly among more glass jars. He led her to the table and gently guided her into a chair, then walked over to a small wood stove and started a kettle of water to boil.

Watching him go through the familiar motions was soothing. They'd never had a wood stove, but he had made tea for her every morning over their fire pit. Her mind wandered back to a simpler time. When they lived in the cave behind the waterfall, she was happy. She could see the Shining City when she climbed the mountain, and except for Grandfather's cryptic warnings, she'd had no idea what it was like inside. It was so much more beautiful and sacred than she had ever imagined, but also so terrible and wrong.

He pulled two mugs out of a cabinet and scooped in tea leaves from a glass container. He brought the mugs to the table and poured in the boiling water. The familiar scent of tea caused a sense of calmness to settle over her. She hadn't had tea for so long. She'd been drinking coffee each morning with Pim ...

Her breath caught on a sob, and she covered her eyes with her hands. Sweet Pim. How could she be gone? She was singing and dancing and so full of life, and then ... nothing. Gone. Nowhere.

Grandfather's gentle voice broke through her thoughts. "Ylena. Please, talk to me." He sat in the chair next to her and took hold of one of her hands. "Tell me what happened. Are you hurt?"

She studied her tear-stained hand in his and chuckled darkly. "No, I'm not hurt. But Pim ... the other acolytes ... Madame Director ..." She choked back the sob and bit her lips to keep it from escaping. "A lot of people died tonight. It was my fault." The sob stayed inside, but her tears continued to fall.

He squeezed her hand. "Ylena, it wasn't your fault. There are a lot of things happening here that have nothing to do with you. I'm so sorry you were stuck in the middle. After you were cast in the Pageant, I didn't know how to get you out without compromising everything we have been working for."

She blinked her eyes and tried to make sense of his words. "What have you been working for?"

He rubbed his wrinkled forehead and sighed. "I don't think you are ready for that conversation tonight. How about you drink your tea, and I will figure out where you can sleep, okay?" He patted her hand and stood.

She sipped the tea with her eyes closed and tried to pretend she was seated near the fire in their cave and had never stepped foot off the mountain. Grandfather came back to the table and watched her finish the last sip. He helped her up and led her to the open door beyond the wood stove.

"You can sleep in here," he said. The room had just enough space for a narrow bed and a writing desk. "I'll sleep on the couch." He handed her one of his shirts that was soft and worn. "I thought you might want something else to sleep in besides ..." He pointed at her gown. She was still dressed in her costume of the Goddess.

"Thanks," she mumbled. She draped her cloak over the chair at the desk.

"Ylena?" Grandfather had his hand on the door when she looked up. "I am sorry this has been such a rough night. I hope you get some sleep."

She nodded and turned away as he silently closed the door. She let her Goddess costume fall in a heap on the floor, put on the soft shirt, and crawled beneath the covers. Her tears soaked the pillow, but they didn't cause any miracles.

When Ylena woke, she sat up in bed with a gasp and had no idea where she was. She saw her costume piled on the floor, and the previous night came back in a flash. Her emotions felt numb, and she didn't think she had any tears left in her body. To be safe, she used the pitcher of water Grandfather left to wash off any lingering tears from her hands and face. Her previously elaborate hairstyle was in complete disarray, but she twisted her long, black hair into a messy knot away from her face. She couldn't imagine putting her Goddess costume back on, so she stayed in Grandfather's shirt until she could find something else.

She walked out of the bedroom looking for Grandfather but found Wilder.

"Good morning, Ylena." He was sitting at the table with a notebook in his hands. His bright white shirt shone against his dark skin, and he looked clean and rested, unlike herself. "Your grandfather went to run a few errands and didn't want you to wake up to an empty house." His smile was hesitant.

Her numb sadness leapt to a dark fury. "You realize they are all dead, don't you?" She saw his quickly indrawn breath but didn't give him a chance to collect his thoughts. "Everyone in the show is dead. Madame Director is dead ... Pim. Is. Dead." She pushed the cold grief down even further and let the rage warm her. "You left us, Wilder. You left us all to die."

Wilder looked stricken. He stood and tried to take a step toward her. Ylena's hands moved up into the fighting position she had learned from the Discipline Priests. They both knew she was not an expert fighter, but her stance, plus the look in her eye, was enough for him to take a step back.

"Ylena? What's going on?" Grandfather was standing in the doorway with his hands full.

"It's okay, Brynn," said Wilder. "It's my fault."

Ylena sneered at him. "That might be the most honest thing you've ever said."

He flinched but tried to cover it by sitting back down.

Grandfather walked to the table and set down the bundles he was carrying. He held one out to Ylena. "This is for you."

She slowly relaxed from her fighting posture and took the bundle. "What is it?"

"I got you something to wear." He raised an eyebrow at her. His shirt was long enough to cover her, but just barely. "I thought you might want something a bit more appropriate to wear when we have visitors."

A part of her felt like blushing, but she pushed that down next to the sadness and let the rage continue to blossom. "I'm not worried about Wilder's opinion, Grandfather, but I do appreciate the gift." She turned on her heel and walked back into the bedroom with her head held high.

Once she closed the door, her back sagged against it. She clutched the bundle to her chest and took enough deep breaths to get her thoughts under control. She opened the worn linen bag and found a pair of soft, brown leather pants with a cream-colored sweater. The quality of the fabric wasn't as fine as what she wore in the City, but it was similar to what she used to wear on the mountain underneath all of her wool sweaters and fur coats. She laced up the boots she found at the bottom of the bundle. He had also given her a hairbrush, and she spent some time brushing her hair with slow strokes until it fell in a dark, glossy shroud around her shoulders. She picked up her costume from the floor, folded it carefully, and laid it on the chair by her cloak. When she felt like she had all of her thoughts neatly organized, she took a deep breath and opened the door.

Grandfather and Wilder sat at the table in silence, and it was up to her to break it.

"Do you have any coffee?" she asked.

Grandfather blinked but then jumped to his feet. "Yes. I have coffee. I'll make some."

Ylena nodded once. She sat down at the table next to Wilder but didn't look at him. Grandfather warmed up water in the kettle and took a glass jar filled with dark brown ground coffee out of the cabinet. She'd never watched anyone prepare coffee before. It was always waiting in a carafe in the mornings when she and Pim ...

She took a deep breath and focused on Grandfather's actions. He scooped the ground coffee into the bottom of a clear carafe and then poured the steaming water on top. He carried three mugs over to the table, along with a little bowl of sugar. Pim always laughed when Ylena added sugar ... Her breath hitched in her throat.

He set the carafe on the table and put on a lid with a lever that he pressed down to strain out the grounds. Ylena allowed herself to be fascinated with the process. When he finished slowly pressing the lever, he poured some coffee into her cup. She breathed in its comforting scent and took a sip.

She twisted her face and reached for the sugar. After she had dumped in several scoops, she closed her eyes and imagined Pim smiling at her over the top of her cup. She kept her eyes closed, pretending the illusion was real.

Grandfather cleared his throat. "Ylena." She opened her eyes slowly and looked at him. "Would you like to talk about what happened?"

She took a long sip and then set down her cup. "Almost everyone I knew in the City is dead. Sentinels would like to add me to that list. Wilder abandoned me and didn't care if we lived or died, and it turns out that the two of you know each other. It seems like I'm not the one that needs to explain what happened." She picked up her coffee again with a cool glance.

Wilder turned to look at Grandfather, who flexed his jaw before he spoke. "Ylena, I didn't want you involved! I wanted you to stay on the mountain and—"

She set her coffee cup down and stared him in the eyes. He sagged and took a gulp of his coffee.

"Yes, I've known Wilder for a while," he said. "He was specifically trained to get the role of the Companion in the Pageant so he would be on stage at that exact moment. You weren't ever in the plans. I still have no idea how you even knew to audition. Why did—?"

She crossed her arms and continued to stare.

"Well, um ... his only purpose was to pour the tears in and then leave. He did what he was required to do. You could have left with him! He would have brought—"

He stopped talking as her head snapped to Wilder. His eyes widened, but he didn't flinch this time.

"What else did you pour in besides the tears?" In their last scene together, they poured the tears collected from the infant Priests into the basin that bonded the babies to the City. "I saw you pour in something else from a bottle you had in your pocket. What was in that? What did you do?"

Wilder turned back to Grandfather. She looked between the two of them and realized how little she really knew either of them. They each had an underground city hidden within themselves that they had never shown her. A hole opened up inside of her, and she realized she had never felt so alone in her life.

"They were tears, Ylena. Only tears," said Grandfather. He took another gulp of his coffee. "I never told you about your mother becoming a Priest."

"The list of things you never told me gets longer by the minute," she said coldly.

He looked down at the dark liquid in his cup. "I was not a good person before your mother was born. I lived most days in a mindless stupor, and your grandmother kicked me out of the house time after time. But we were both fools, and she always let me come back. When your mother was born, something inside me sparked to life for the first time. Mae was so beautiful and small, and her little smile ..." His voice cracked, but he took a sip of coffee and continued. "When her Gift manifested, something inside me broke. This little child was the one good thing I had created, and she was going to be taken from me. Your grandmother wept for days on end. I think that the day we dropped your mother off at the temple is the day your grandmother started to fade away. She was gone within a year." He drained the rest of his coffee.

Ylena remembered the Sentinels being handed a baby through the mysterious door. "You gave her up?" she whispered.

"What choice did we have?" His voice was rough with emotion. "Once a child's Gift manifests, they have to be bonded to the City within a year or they will die. If a baby born down here has a Gift, the only way to save their life is to hand the child over to the Priests. The Goddess wants to keep all the power to herself." He sneered at the name of the Goddess. "The Shining City is not only built on our backs, but its religion continues to steal our children year after year." He leaned back in his chair. "We finally did something about it."

"What did you do?" she whispered.

He leaned forward and his hands were clenched into fists on the table. "We are keeping our Gifted babies from now on. Wilder poured their tears into the basin, and now, they will stay down here with us."

2

___

Ylena followed behind Grandfather and Wilder as they walked through the dark streets of the Underneath. The underground city looked exactly the same way this morning as it had when she arrived last night. The same number of people roamed around or slept in dark corners. She was glad she grabbed the black cloak before they left. She pulled the hood closer around her face and avoided looking anyone in the eye.

Grandfather and Wilder talked privately to each other a few steps ahead of her. Ylena got the sense that she was the topic of their conversation based on the concerned glances they would each shoot her way. She used the hood of her cloak to avoid looking at them. Her grief was barely contained behind a wall of anger, and if she leaned into the compassionate look on their faces, she was afraid her heart would shatter.

She glanced up at the top of the cave high above. She tried to imagine the people of the City walking around in the bright sunlight. Had Caed made it back to Temple Discipline? Would the High Priests blame him for participating in the failed Pageant? She couldn't imagine what he would be doing at this moment. Then, with another flare of anger, she realized she never knew what he was doing because he kept so many secrets from her. She was walking around in a secret underground city as a prime example.

She could tell by the brightening of the streets that they had arrived at the crystal spire. She looked up to the top of the cavern, where the glowing crystal continued through the stone and eventually up through the middle of Temple Purpose above them. The area surrounding the spire was the brightest in the whole cave. She thought people might gather around the light, but other than the three of them, it was empty. On the other side of the bright, open area was a building carved directly into the wall of the cave.

A few buildings and sidewalks in the Underneath looked like Purpose Priests had shaped the stone, but someone carved this structure using more conventional means. A rough-hewn door was carved into the wall, surrounded by jagged stones pieced together in a random but interesting pattern. Shadows formed when the purple light struck the uneven texture of the stones. The rough surface of the building was in direct contrast to the smooth stone temple up above.

She followed Grandfather and Wilder into the building and down a great hallway that caused her to reevaluate how far back they had tunneled into the stone. They arrived at a doorway guarded by a man and woman who both stood with the intimidating stance of Sentinels. They noticed her grandfather and opened the door to let them inside.

Ylena grew up in a cave, but this room built in the rock was completely unlike her home. Luxurious rugs covered the floors, and lamps filled the room with a warm crystalline glow. An enormous fireplace was carved into the stone, and

Ylena tried to imagine how the smoke was vented out. There were shelves filled with books and more glass jars like at her grandfather's house. A mahogany table with a dozen matched chairs was on the far side of the room, but Grandfather led her to the leather couch and chairs near the fireplace.

A woman with dark red hair set down a book and rose to meet them. "Good morning, Brynn. It's good to see you." She was wearing a tight, white dress and matching high heels, and she bent to kiss him on both cheeks. "And Wilder, I'm glad to see you are well after last night." He bowed his head in thanks.

She stepped closer, and Ylena realized the woman was almost as tall as Wilder. "This must be your granddaughter." Her warm, deep voice was soothing, but her eyes were sharp. The woman took Ylena's chin in her hand and tilted her face up to study it. "She's fortunate she didn't get her looks from you, Brynn." She chuckled and released Ylena. "Come sit down. Let's discuss."

The woman sat back down in her chair, and Grandfather took the chair opposite her, leaving Ylena to sit on the couch with Wilder. He didn't relax into the cushions, but sat up straight, staring at the woman with a reserved expression.

The woman shifted to face Wilder. "I've heard reports you were successful in your task. The children have been bonded to the City. Their hair has returned to its natural color, and they will survive for a full year because of your success."

"Thank you, Warden." Wilder bowed his head graciously.

"I also heard that your performance was stunning as usual."

Wilder didn't look up, but Ylena caught a hint of his usual cocky smirk.

"Brynn." She turned her sharp eyes to Grandfather. "I have heard many theories on what happened to the spires last night. I'd love to hear yours."

Ylena stopped breathing and leaned her head down further into her hood. During the Pageant, one of her tears fell into the crystal basin, and when it did, every spire in the City went dark. Icy wind and snow blew into the City for the first time since its creation. That's what caused the Sentinels to storm the stage where Pim and the others … A sob threatened to burst from her throat at the image of Pim lying dead on the stage. She caught a worried glance from Wilder, so she focused her mind only on Grandfather's words.

"I'm not sure, Warden." Grandfather tightly gripped the arms of his chair. "We knew there was a risk that placing our children's tears into the basin would have an unexpected effect, but no one knows enough about the creation of the crystal spires to know exactly why they would react that way."

The Warden pursed her bright red lips. "I don't like unexpected events, but I do love how the poor, weak City folk panicked." She threw her head back and laughed. "Yes, the crystal flickered off down here, too, but we are accustomed to the dark. I can't help but laugh every time I think about how terrified the people above must have been."

Grandfather echoed her smirk, but Wilder's face was unreadable.

The Warden leaned back comfortably in her chair. "This new purple light will take some getting used to, but if that's the worst we have to deal with, then I count the night as a complete success."

Ylena pictured the cast lined up dead across the stage, and a feral anger flared inside her chest. She opened her mouth to speak, but Wilder caught her hand in a firm grip. He pressed his mouth into a thin line and gave one quick shake of his head. She willed her furious breathing to come under control. She turned back to the Warden, and luckily, the woman was still looking at Grandfather.

"To celebrate this success, we have decided to hold our own sort of 'Pageant' in a fashion unique to the Underneath." She had a wicked glint in her eye. "How could we not? We need to gather up some more performers, but we already have our two stars!" She turned to Ylena and Wilder and laughed again.

"A Pageant?" asked Ylena. "You can't be serious." The words escaped her mouth before she thought better of it.

The Warden turned the full force of her penetrating eyes on Ylena as she addressed Grandfather with a cool voice. "I'm surprised you didn't teach your granddaughter that it's impolite to question a Warden."

Grandfather leaned forward in his chair. "I apologize for her, Warden. She is new to the Underneath."

Ylena turned fierce eyes on him at the understatement. He never mentioned the Underneath existed even though she asked him about the City daily. She was a breath away from saying she had no idea what a Warden was either when she felt Wilder squeezing her hand even harder.

The Warden leaned back in her chair and studied Ylena. "I thought you might be as naturally obedient as Wilder, but I guess I can find other means of motivation."

"That's not necessary, Warden. I guarantee Ylena will do what's necessary." Grandfather's voice was subservient, and Ylena cringed at the sound.

"Yes, you will guarantee it, Brynn. If Ylena fails to do her job in any way, you will be the one to pay the price." She turned her narrowed eyes back on Ylena. "You understand the cost of a failed performance, don't you, dear?" The dancing firelight in the Warden's eyes proved that she knew exactly how many friends Ylena had lost in the unfinished Pageant.

Ylena struggled to breath, which reminded her of the Sentinels' poisonous dust. She imagined the Warden killing Grandfather without a moment's hesitation.

She bowed her head. "I understand, Warden."

3

The Warden dismissed them, and the guards ushered them into a dusty room off the main hallway. Mountains of paper were haphazardly stacked on every surface. A shell of a man stooped over a pile of papers on his desk. He squinted at the three of them in the dim light of his single lamp, then waved them inside impatiently.

He held out a scrap of paper to Wilder. "That has the names of each of your contacts, including the time of your first rehearsal." He dug in a drawer in his desk and pulled out two small pouches. "This is a portion of the honorarium you will receive for your performance. The amount of your next payment will depend on your skill in securing extra talent for the show." Wilder picked up both pouches and handed one to Ylena.

"The Warden expects you to represent her interests wherever you go. I trust you understand what interests the Warden?" He raised a ragged eyebrow.

"Yes, we understand," said Wilder. Ylena was glad that at least someone understood.

The old man looked back down at his papers. "You may go now."

The three of them walked down the dark hallway and out into the bright light surrounding the crystal spire. Grandfather jerked his head at Wilder, who moved off a few steps to give them a moment alone.

Grandfather rubbed his eyes. "I thought that after the Pageant was over, I could protect you. I'm sorry I was wrong."

"I don't understand ... What is going on?"

"Wilder will have to explain it as you go. They won't want to wait long to hold this celebration. This is the biggest victory, the only victory, we have ever had in the Underneath. We need this celebration to unite us." He reached into his pocket. "Take this." He put a shiny medallion into her palm. "If you need to get out of the Underneath, give this to the Sentinel at the temple door to let you out." She never saw what the people at the secret door handed the Sentinels, but now she knew. "Guard that medallion carefully. People down here work their entire lives trying to earn enough to get one of those."

She studied the cool, silver medallion. On one side was a picture of a temple with the towering crystal spire running through the middle. The other side showed the tall crown the High Priests wore.

"You are the one who needs this, Grandfather. She threatened your life!"

"It's not the first time, Ylena." He sighed. "I know you will do what is required. But if you get into trouble, use that to get out. Don't worry about me. I'll be fine."

This time, she knew he was lying. She was glad she could see through at least one deception. Even though she swore not to use it, she slid the coin inside the pouch from Wilder.

"I thought this would happen much differently, Ylena." He gently took her hand. "I'm sorry that you are still in the middle of this."

"But why me? Just because I was in the Pageant?" She still didn't know why Lady Erenne tricked her into auditioning for the Pageant, and once again, Ylena was stuck in the middle of a performance with deadly consequences.

"They know that you have the power to heal, Ylena." Grandfather looked ashamed.

She inhaled sharply. "What do you mean?"

"Wilder saw you try to heal that Priest. He knows that is your power. Your white streak of hair was a clue." He looked at her hair. "I'm glad to see that the streak went away after the Pageant. That's a good sign." He gave her a small smile.

She reached up and touched her hair. She hadn't noticed that the streak was gone.

"I'm grateful that healing is your power and not something else that they might try to twist. Let's hope there's no need to use that Gift on this adventure." He smoothed back her hair. "I know you've been just fine on your own in the City, but I guess I will always worry about you. Take care, Ylena."

Ylena watched her grandfather leave, as Wilder slowly walked back to her side. His steps were tentative, and she looked up at him with hard eyes.

His shoulders sagged. "I'm sorry for all of this, Ylena. I wish that—"

"I'm not in the mood for apologies right now, Wilder. I'd rather know what is going on."

"I'm caught up in the Warden's game again, and unfortunately, this time, you are in it, too."

"But why? What is this all about?"

Wilder's voice cracked with a harsh laugh. "I don't know,

Ylena! Do you think I was expecting this? Do you think any of this is what I want?"

"I have no idea what you want, Wilder." She spat out the harsh words. "Everything I knew about you was a lie."

His shoulders sagged even further. "What do you want to know? I have nothing left to hide."

She considered the strange question. She wasn't sure what to do with someone who actually offered her the truth.

"How did you get involved with the Pageant in the first place?" she asked.

"I auditioned for the chance to play the role of the Companion. I was told that a private group wanted their own performance down here. It wasn't until I won the part that I found out I was going Upstairs as a spy to add the babies' tears into the basin."

She was surprised at the readiness of his answer, so she pressed further. "What did you think would happen after you poured in the tears?"

He avoided her eyes but answered, "I wasn't sure. I knew it was a risk."

Her voice turned to steel. "But you took that risk, and as a result, they are all dead now."

"They were my friends, too, Ylena!" Wilder's voice crackled with emotion. "I never wanted them to die. I knew it was a risk I had to take to save the lives of the Gifted children down here, but I didn't want any of the cast to get hurt." His voice dropped to an unsteady whisper. "I never wanted Pim to die."

"Don't you say her name!" Ylena whispered harshly.

He looked at the glowing crystal. "I had no idea the tears would cause that. I never expected it to go that terribly wrong."

Ylena looked at the purple crystal, and an awful thought whispered its way through her mind. She tried to push the idea away and hold on to her anger, but it slipped past her defenses and wrapped itself around her heart.

Wilder didn't kill Pim.

She did.

Wilder walked out, and it might have been a disaster, except Caed stepped in to fill the role. The show would have turned out fine, if not for Ylena's tear falling in the basin. She's the one who broke everything. Not him.

She wanted to run from the knowledge of what she had done. She could take the coin and escape Upstairs and find her way out of the City and back to her cave on the mountain. But if she left, the Warden would kill her grandfather. She couldn't let that happen. No one else would die because of her.

There were so many layers of her own secrets involved that she couldn't speak the words out loud. Wilder was looking at her with concern, so she wiped all of the grief and guilt off her face.

"Where are we going?" She tried to make the leap in conversation feel natural, but her voice was shaky.

Wilder gave her one more concerned glance, then turned back to the crystal. "That is the spire that leads up through Temple Purpose. You entered through the staircase that runs next to it." She nodded. He gestured to the dome of the cave that extended from the spire. "All of this is Grotto Delirium. Its goal is to be everything that the Virtue of Purpose is not."

He pointed to the cave wall far away to their right. "There is a tunnel that leads to the next Grotto. That's where we are going."

"The next Grotto?" she asked.

"There are seven different Grottos like this under each of the seven temples."

She looked back into the soaring cave that was filled

with buildings and houses and people and babies and dogs. Her mind was trying to calculate the sheer number of people who lived in the Underneath. "There are six more caves this size?"

"Yes."

She turned from the cave to study Wilder. His flirty smile was gone, and his eyes were troubled.

"The seven Wardens of the Grottos make their plans and force people like your grandfather and me to follow them." He stepped closer to her and dropped his voice. "But if you want out, say the word. I will find a way for you to escape. I don't know if you can find somewhere safe to stay in the City or outside the walls, but I will get you out if you ask me."

His dark brown eyes were so intense she had to look away. "If I escaped from here, what would happen to Grandfather?"

"They will kill him."

She flinched at his matter-of-fact tone.

"I'm done keeping secrets from you, Ylena. I don't expect you to ever forgive me for what I've done, but someday, I hope to gain back your trust."

He believed he was responsible for Pim's death. And she couldn't say otherwise without revealing all of her own secrets. She didn't trust him or anyone else with that information. She swallowed her own guilt and did what Pim had taught her.

Pretend everything was okay.

She straightened her cloak around her shoulders. "It looks like you will have plenty of time to do that while we prepare for this Pageant." She turned toward the tunnel. "Let's go."

PECULIARITY

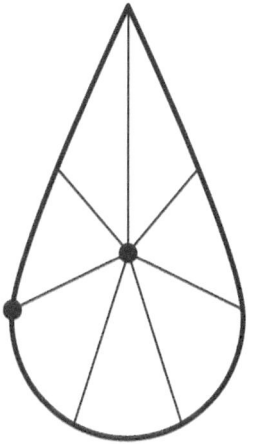

4

———

Ylena wasn't sure how much longer they had until they reached the end of the dark tunnel, but she was ready to be out of it. She could see the next few glowing lamps in the distance, but the gentle curve of the tunnel meant she couldn't see the end. The spaces between the scattered, crystalline lamps were disturbing. She had been alone in the deeper part of the cave behind the waterfall, but this cave was different. It had other people.

They met a few people coming from the other direction. Most of them did the same as Ylena and Wilder—try to time their passing until they were in the brightest part of the tunnel and pretend to ignore the other party. There were a few who slowed their steps, forcing Wilder and Ylena to cross them in the darkest parts of the tunnel. In those cases, Wilder crossed on the inside and glared at whomever they passed. She wasn't sure what would happen if someone attacked them. She wanted out of the tunnel as quickly as possible so she wouldn't find out.

She eventually saw a purple glow in the distance and heard Wilder sigh in relief. They both hurried the last few steps and stepped out into the open cavern.

This Grotto had the same purple crystal spire driving up through the stone overhead and further down into the stone below, but she noticed differences from Grotto Delirium.

All the buildings and houses were brightly colored, almost garishly so. They were teal and orange and fuchsia and sepia and lilac. Sometimes, all the colors were on the same building. She saw what she thought was a house, but it was smaller than her grandfather's bedroom. It was next to a building that was four stories tall, with floors all different sizes and shapes. She wasn't sure how it was standing.

The people were as brightly decorated as the buildings. That wasn't unusual compared to the elaborate fashion in the City, but down here, the people's bodies were just as decorated as their clothes. She thought she saw a woman wearing sleeves with a flower print, but then she realized the flowers were drawn on her skin. She noticed people with vines looping around their forearms and feathers shooting out between their shoulder blades and butterflies resting on their cheekbones.

She turned around to see the back of a man whose entire face was decorated like a snake. He had metal rings through his nose and ears, and the snakeskin pattern covered even the back of his shaved head. Wilder followed her stare. "A little different from up in the City, huh?"

She started walking again. "Is it paint? How do they have time to put that on every day?"

"It's not paint. It's a tattoo. Something like that takes a long time to get done, but once it's finished, it is permanent."

She stopped again. "Permanent? He wants to look like a snake forever?"

"Not everyone is quite that committed, but this is Grotto

Peculiarity. He is the Underneath's version of a true believer."

"Peculiarity..." She traced a mental map of the City in her mind. "We are under Temple Perfection. So, this is one way they try to be as unlike the world up there as possible?"

He nodded. "You're getting it."

"This doesn't seem that bad. I think this would be extreme fashion up there and that they would love it."

"Of course they would. And the High Priests know that. That's why they have a very profitable business letting the people Upstairs come down here and play, then charging them exorbitant amounts of money to get back out."

Wilder continued walking toward the crystal, and Ylena hurried to catch up. "Money? The people up there pay to come down here? I never saw money in the City."

"Upstairs, there isn't an actual need for money. If you want to eat, there is plenty of food. If you need a place to live, there are a lot of houses standing empty. And if you don't work, they execute you. If you hoard food or clothes, they execute you. People only take what they need because if they don't, then ..." He mimed blowing the poisonous dust the Sentinels carried. She shivered.

"It doesn't work like that down here. The High Priests set up their own currency in the Underneath so they could control it. If you want to come down here and play and then get back Upstairs, there are only a few ways to do that. Secretly hoard enough food or other essentials that you can trade for money here in the Underneath and hope you keep enough to get back out. Or get a medallion that lets you pass by the Sentinels by doing a favor for a High Priest."

Her eyes widened at the thought of the medallion her grandfather gave her. "What kind of favor?"

Wilder didn't meet her eyes. "Even if it means escape from the Underneath, the cost is always much too high."

She wondered what cost her grandfather paid to earn the medallion in her pocket.

They arrived at the far edge of the Grotto and stepped into the glow surrounding the purple crystal. Here, there were rows of carts with bright, patterned clothes and black leather skirts with matching chokers and bottles of shimmering liquid used for dyeing hair. Vendors called to her as she passed, trying to get her attention.

Ylena's natural curiosity lay muted in her chest. The hair dye reminded her of Pim. The jewelry reminded her of Pim. Everything fascinating or beautiful reminded her of Pim. The Underneath was filled with wonders, but Ylena's heart was empty.

Wilder walked to an entrance cut into the side of the cave, similar to where they had met the other Warden, but this building was painted in gaudy colors with swirling lines and polka dots and stripes. She blinked several times at the strangeness, then hurried after Wilder.

5

ilder had given their names to a guard at the door, and they were quietly waiting in the long hallway when the double doors flew open.

"Look at the two of you! Aren't you just adorable?" The Warden had her dark hair pulled up into two knots on the top of her head. She was wearing a bright purple dress covered in peacock feathers, and a trail of glitter followed her as she walked. "Come in here right now and entertain me!" She laughed and walked back into the room.

Ylena and Wilder followed her and stepped inside. The walls of the room were painted just as flamboyantly as the outside, and a turquoise carpet stretched from one wall of the room to the other. The Warden seated herself on a sparkling golden throne. There was nowhere else to sit, so Ylena and Wilder stood.

Ylena wondered how the eccentric woman in front of her could be part of a scheme that resulted in Wilder auditioning for the Pageant. She didn't look like a master strategist. Although, Ylena never suspected Lady Erenne of the political maneuvering involved to become a High Priest, so maybe she wasn't the best judge.

The Warden wore a wide, odd smile and pressed her hands together at her chest. "Of all the Grottos, Peculiarity is the one who knows the most about putting on a good show."

"Yes, of course, Warden." Wilder's voice sounded sincere. Ylena looked at him out of the corner of her eye. She knew he was a skilled actor in his role, but she wondered if this was how he sharpened his skills.

"We have a lot of talented performers to contribute. My assistant will hand you a list after you finish with your first rehearsal."

Wilder bowed his head. "You are too kind, Warden."

"It's not just kindness, boy." Her voice snapped across the room, but the smile stayed plastered on her face. "I don't want anyone thinking less of my Grotto than the others. We are the ones who will give this spectacle its flavor! Mmm ..." She made a sound like she was tasting the word. "Spectacle. Yes, that's what we'll call it. It's not a Pageant. It's a Spectacle." Her eyes lit up, and she stared off into the distance.

Wilder didn't reply, and Ylena thought it was best she kept her mouth shut.

"Did you get that?" Her eyes snapped back to the two of them. "It will be called The Spectacle." She smiled, but it didn't reach her eyes.

"Yes, Warden," said Ylena. "The Spectacle."

Her smile stayed frozen in place. "You may go now."

Wilder bowed his head and turned to leave before the woman's words caught up to Ylena. She quickly bowed her head and followed Wilder out.

Ylena and Wilder exited the Warden's inner room and found the guards waiting. The taller guard led them to the door on the right, which led to a hallway with an open doorway on their left and a staircase in front of them. The guard stepped in front of the staircase and pointed them through the open door.

They entered a training room of some sort. Furniture and equipment were pushed to the edges of the room, leaving an open space big enough to dance.

"So, I guess you are the two I am waiting for?" The man was leaning back in his wood chair, one arm resting on the rough-looking table. He drummed his long fingers in a nervous pattern, then ran them through his silver hair. "The two of you look like children."

"She's eighteen and I'm nineteen," said Wilder.

The man sighed. "So, yes, children. At least you are a year or two older than the other performers. Hopefully, you have at least a year's worth more sense than they have." He sat up in his chair and ushered them closer. "Come here and show me what I have to work with."

They walked forward and stood awkwardly in front of him while he evaluated them in silence. He spoke suddenly. "I'm assuming you are both skilled. They wouldn't have picked you for the Pageant unless you were."

"We are more than qualified." Wilder's cocky voice had more edge than usual.

The man stood and circled around them. He was dressed in bright colors like the rest of the Grotto, but his well-fitted polka-dot shirt and pinstriped pants suited him. "That's good. We have little rehearsal time, so I will need you both to pick this up quickly. We will repurpose some choreography from the Pageant, so we at least have a place to start."

"So, this is like the Pageant?" asked Ylena.

He laughed. "No. The Wardens want it to be a story about the founding of the Underneath and how the Goddess wasn't a part of it."

Ylena and Wilder exchanged looks. "But I thought that was why Wilder and I were recruited? I thought we were playing the Goddess and Companion in this?"

"You are," the man said. "But you have a small role this time and are not the stars."

Ylena sighed with relief. "That sounds much better. I never wanted to be the star."

The man cocked his head as he tried to understand her words. He turned to Wilder. "I guess you never wanted to be the star, either?"

Wilder smirked. "I always knew I'd be a star."

Ylena rolled her eyes.

"Terrific." The man's low voice was sarcastic. "The Wardens have cast other young people to play the roles of themselves. I shouldn't be surprised that the Wardens would put me in charge of a cast of teenagers. They are fond of torture." He sighed dramatically. "You can call me Maestro. I guess we should get started—"

"How can you start without me?" A teenage girl skipped into the room. She looked exactly like a younger version of the Warden. She was wearing a copy of the Warden's purple dress with peacock feathers, and her dark hair was similarly knotted into two buns on top of her head.

The man blinked in confusion as the girl walked in. "I did not intend today to be a costume rehearsal, but I appreciate your enthusiasm, Jerra."

Jerra gave him a slightly unhinged smile that reminded Ylena of the Warden. "Thank you, Maestro. I take my role seriously. I hope everyone else will be just as dedicated." She glanced at Ylena and Wilder, her low opinion of them clear.

Maestro's lips stretched into a fake smile. "Jerra, this is Wilder and Ylena. They have practiced a lot during their rehearsal for the Pageant, so I believe they will fulfill their role in this performance. Wilder and Ylena, this is Jerra. She will play the role of the Warden of Peculiarity."

The three of them each mumbled a half-hearted greeting.

The Maestro clapped his hands together. "I guess we can begin. We will run through the part of the Pageant that introduces the Grotto of Peculiarity and figure out Wilder and Ylena's placement during Jerra's solo. For everyone's sake, let's hope this doesn't take long."

After several hours of rehearsal, they were each familiar with their parts. Jerra had obviously been rehearsing her lines for weeks, maybe months in advance. Ylena initially thought they might have picked Jerra based on her looks alone, but she was actually a talented singer. Her song was strange compared to the Pageant's music, but Ylena found it intriguing.

Maestro adapted some of Ylena and Wilder's choreography, and they picked it up pretty quickly. When Wilder moved to hold her in one of the standard dance positions, Ylena stepped away from him. "No. Find another combination." Wilder looked at her with a pained expression.

The Maestro narrowed his eyes at her. "I'm not sure what is going on here, but it won't affect the performance, will it?"

"No, Maestro," said Ylena. "I'd just like another combination."

"Fine." He showed them an alternate move where she wasn't touching Wilder, and Ylena copied it quickly. Wilder tried to hide the hurt look on his face, but Ylena could still see it. She couldn't blame him for Pim's death, but he still abandoned them. She would perform in the Spectacle beside him, but she didn't want him close enough to touch her.

They rehearsed their small portion, then waited in their pose while Jerra performed her solo. Ylena finally realized the reason Lira always had so much time to glare at her. When you weren't the star, you spent a lot of time holding a pose and waiting for your next exciting moment. Ylena didn't feel like glaring at Jerra, but she definitely got bored.

Eventually, Maestro called a halt to their rehearsal. "I think you all have it. Now don't forget it! Wilder and Ylena, you will learn a new portion in each Grotto. We won't run through the entire show until we meet together in the Heart of the Grottos for the actual performance. I trust that the two of you can rehearse on your own if necessary?"

"We will be ready," said Ylena.

"Good. And Jerra, you are obviously well-prepared. You are clearly the Warden's treasure." Something about Maestro's voice felt forced, but Ylena wasn't sure Jerra noticed. "I will see you when we reach the Heart. And Ylena and Wilder, I will see you in the next Grotto."

6

As they stepped out the door, a man in a purple suit with peacock feathers matching the Warden's dress handed Wilder a small sheet of paper. Then, he turned on his heel and strode off. Wilder put the piece of paper in his pocket and walked out of the Den.

Once they were in the bright area around the crystal, Ylena asked, "What did that man give you?"

Wilder opened his mouth to answer but then glanced at the vendors surrounding them. He shook his head and kept walking. Ylena grunted and tried to keep up.

Wilder passed the carts with merchandise and walked down a narrow alley between brightly painted buildings. He was silent as he turned in a twisting pattern down street after street. He would occasionally glance behind him, but Ylena had also been watching and had seen no one suspicious. At least, no one more suspicious than anyone else in the Underneath.

He stopped in front of a tiny house painted vivid yellow. The purple glow wasn't as bright this far away from the spire, but the yellow paint shone in the light of the crystalline lamps lining the street. He took a deep breath and knocked on the door.

The door flew open, and a young woman stood outlined in the bright light coming from within. She breathed out, "Wilder!" She grabbed his face, pulled it down to hers, and gave him a full, passionate kiss. Wilder didn't move to embrace her, but he didn't pull away. She finally removed her lips but kept her hands on his cheeks. She licked her lips and sighed, "Oh, Goddess, I've missed you."

Wilder raised his head back up with a bit of his usual smile. "Good to see you, too, Rev." He took a step to the side. "This is Ylena."

The young woman hadn't noticed Ylena standing behind him and now stopped to size her up. Ylena noticed Rev cocked her head strangely to the side to look at her. When Ylena stepped closer into the light, she realized it was because Rev was wearing an eye patch and could only see out of one sparkling blue eye.

Rev bounced over to Ylena. "Aren't you just a lovely thing?" She twirled her blond ponytail around her finger and bit her rosy bottom lip. "Wilder, you bring me the nicest gifts!" A blush sprung to Ylena's cheeks, which only caused Rev to smile wider.

Wilder cleared his throat. "Rev, may we come inside?"

She turned and saw his serious expression, but she held to her light-hearted tone. "Of course! Follow me!" She flipped her golden hair over her shoulder and strolled inside.

Rev flopped down on a bright pink velvet couch with an eager look, but Ylena took the fluffy armchair instead. Wilder sat down beside Rev on the couch, and she happily curled up next to him.

"What do I owe the pleasure?" She spoke the last word slowly.

"Ylena and I have been assigned to take part in the upcoming celebration for the Grottos."

"Oh! I've heard about that! It's like our own special Pageant," she purred.

"It's now called the Spectacle, I guess," said Ylena with a shrug.

Rev turned her glittering blue eye on Ylena. "The Spectacle! How titillating!"

Ylena focused her attention on Wilder in the hopes he would rescue her. He saw Ylena's face and smirked. "Rev, Ylena is from Upstairs, and she's new down here. Can you please refrain from trying to seduce her?"

Rev sat up taller so she could see Wilder properly. "Are you telling me you've spent time with this stunning young woman and have not tried to seduce her yourself?"

Ylena thought back to countless moments during their rehearsal when Wilder smiled and winked and whispered, and her cheeks flared red again. He appeared to have the same memories and turned his usual smile upon her.

Ylena looked at the two of them sitting side by side on the couch. Wilder was tall with dark brown skin and long, coiled, raven hair, and Rev was petite and curvy with pale skin and bright gold hair. They looked nothing alike, except for matching flirty smiles. Ylena shook her head. "If I hadn't seen that kiss earlier, I would swear the two of you are twins."

Wilder and Rev looked at each other and burst into laughter. She sighed in relief to know that the same trick worked with Rev as it often had with Wilder. If she could make him laugh, she could get past the flirting facade and see below the surface.

Although, she now realized, below his smile was just another facade. She was once again trying to figure out who he really was.

The two of them recovered from their laughter, and Rev curled herself into a position where she could see them both. "So, you are looking for some performers for this Spectacle, are you?"

Wilder pulled out the list of names the Warden's assistant had handed him. "Any names on here I should be wary of?"

Rev examined the list. "You know you should always be wary around here. But I think the last two names are especially worrisome. They each recently received a more prominent role because some of their costars had mysterious accidents." She handed the list back to him. "Or so they say."

He put the list back into his pocket. "Thanks, Rev. Do you mind if we crash here a night or two?"

"It's no trouble at all!" She got a wicked glint in her eye. "There's plenty of room in my bed for all three of us."

Ylena blushed, and Wilder and Rev burst into laughter again.

7

___

When Rev found out they had eaten nothing since breakfast, she talked them into going out for dinner. Ylena had only ever eaten dinner in the cave with her grandfather or in a temple, so she wasn't sure what it really meant to "go out." But to Rev, it meant that Ylena needed to find some better clothes to wear than the boring outfit she was already in. Rev dug through her closet and threw several options at Ylena to try on. She took a break from her flirtatious teasing and was staring at Ylena as seriously as one of the costume designers from the Pageant. Ylena felt a sudden flash of fear and wondered if the costume designers were still alive. The High Priests might have killed everyone by now. The feathered dress she held slipped out of her hands.

"What's wrong?" Rev dropped an armful of clothes on the bed and hurried to Ylena's side.

Ylena shook her head and tried to smile. "I'm fine." She picked up something sparkly. "This is pretty."

Rev crossed her arms and frowned. "I might have only one eye, but it sees clearly. You are obviously not fine."

Ylena tried again to smile and pretend everything was

okay, just like Pim had taught her. Pim … Her breath caught, and she dropped to sit on the edge of the bed. "Last night was … a really bad night." She had to talk slowly to choke out the words without crying.

Ylena could see Rev's brain working, and then her eye widened. "You were in the Pageant with Wilder."

Ylena nodded.

Rev studied her face. "You and Wilder escaped."

Ylena nodded again.

Rev touched her gently on the arm. "Your friends didn't escape."

Ylena shook her head and covered her eyes with her hands.

"Oh, honey, I'm so sorry." Rev gathered Ylena into her arms and stroked her hair. Ylena tried to hold the tears back but failed. She wept in the arms of a complete stranger like she had never wept before. Rev held her and rocked her back and forth, murmuring comforting sounds and letting her cry.

After a time, Ylena's sobs quieted into sniffles. Rev reached into the pile on the bed and pulled out a soft handkerchief and handed it to her. Ylena wiped her nose and realized there were tears drying on Rev's shoulders. Ylena's eyes opened wide, and she tried to wipe off the tears.

Rev brushed her hand away. "It's okay, honey. The tears didn't hurt me."

Ylena opened her mouth to speak but then shut it again.

Rev studied her face. "I was right. Wilder really did bring me a gift." She smiled, but not as flirtatious as before. "I had a pounding headache earlier. I get them frequently when I strain my eye to read, but I've learned to live with it. But as you cried on me, my headache melted away. What a beautiful Gift."

The implications of healing Rev clicked in Ylena's mind, and she looked at the eye patch.

Rev realized what she was thinking and chuckled quietly. "Not that. Just the headache." At Ylena's frown, she continued, "Gifts can't heal injuries like that. And honestly, I don't know if I would ask, even if it were possible. I lost my eye when I was a small child, and it shaped me into who I am. I believe the Goddess not only loves me as I am, but celebrates my Peculiarity."

Ylena wiped the last of her tears. "You believe in the Goddess? Even here in the Underneath?" Ylena realized her question might be extremely rude, but before she could apologize, Rev answered.

"Not everyone does. I assume we are like the people Upstairs in our varying levels of belief. But I believe." She rubbed her temples and sighed peacefully. "Thank you for sharing one of her Gifts with me."

Ylena ducked her head in embarrassment. "You're the one who deserves thanks. I've been choking back tears all day. Thank you for letting me cry like that."

Rev patted her hand. "You suffered a loss, and it won't be the last time you cry. But when you get the chance to cry with a friend instead of all alone, take it."

Ylena met her eye with a hesitant smile. Even though she had just sobbed on her shoulder, she wasn't sure how ready she was to trust one of Wilder's friends.

Rev grabbed something sparkly and something feathery and handed them both to Ylena. "Now, we need to get dressed and go out. It's time you learned what that means."

~

Ylena ended up wearing the sparkly dress. Since the dress was Rev's, it was both too short and too big in the chest for her. She covered the top with the feathery wrap, but the shortness of the skirt led to a competition between Wilder and Rev on who could come up with the most provocative line about it. After crying on Rev's shoulder, Ylena had stopped her blushing and resigned herself to rolling her eyes.

Rev led them to a restaurant a few blocks from her house. There were several crystalline lamps glowing within, and tendrils of music drifted out through the open windows. The tables filled with such a variety of people fascinated Ylena. And there were children! She had only seen the babies in the temple nursery, but here, she saw older children eating dinner with their parents. After watching some of them, she realized why the people Upstairs kept them at home. Kids appeared to be pure chaos, which didn't fit well in a City holding the Virtue of Order.

In the City, food was everywhere and in large quantities. They didn't have as much food in the Underneath, but Rev told them what to order, so the little they had was delicious. It was spicier than Ylena was used to, and she wasn't exactly sure what the meat was, but she enjoyed it.

The musicians started playing an upbeat song, and Rev clapped her hands. "I love this song! I'm going to dance! Want to join me?" Ylena and Wilder both shook their heads. "Suit yourself!" She walked to the dance floor with an exaggerated sway to her full hips and blew a kiss at them over her shoulder.

Ylena watched Rev walk onto the dance floor and immediately be surrounded by multiple dance partners. "After my first night in the Underneath, I was not expecting to meet someone like her."

Wilder looked at Rev with a soft smile. "She's one of a kind. The rest of our trip won't be as pleasant, but it's good to enjoy it while we have her."

Ylena let the silence fall between them for a while before she spoke again. "She let me cry on her shoulder."

Wilder gave Ylena a small nod before he looked back at Rev. "She's let me do that before, too."

She turned to look at him. "Really?"

"She's actually had a lot of people cry on her shoulder before. She's like the Underneath's versions of a Priest, except without all the powers." Rev twirled into the middle of the dance floor and threw her head back and laughed. Several of the other dancers laughed along with her. "She helps people who are hurting and scared and confused."

"She helped you like that?" asked Ylena.

"Yes."

He didn't elaborate, so Ylena just watched Rev dance and tried to savor the feeling of being out.

8

Ylena slept better than she thought she might. Wilder slept on the couch, and Ylena shared the bed with Rev. She teased Ylena a bit before they got into bed, but Ylena fell asleep almost the moment her head hit the pillow. She dreamt about dancing with Caed and their final kiss before she escaped to the Underneath. His last look at her both warmed her heart and broke it in two. When she woke, she found Rev and Wilder drinking coffee on the couch.

"Good morning, honey," said Rev. "There's coffee in the kitchen."

Ylena rubbed her sleepy eyes. "Rev, you are definitely my favorite." She heard the two of them laugh as she walked into the small kitchen and poured her coffee.

She brought her mug to the chair she sat in the night before. "So, where are we going today?" She looked at Rev as she took a sip. "And are you joining us?"

"Wilder, I told you she couldn't get enough of me." Rev's voice was sultry, and Wilder rolled his eyes. "You won't be here long. I have to get as much time with you both as possible. So, yes, I will follow you wherever you go today!"

"And where is that exactly?"

Wilder drained the last of his coffee and said, "Today, we are going to the circus."

Ylena didn't know what the circus was, but when she saw it, she fell in love. They walked inside the brightly colored tent in the middle of the Grotto, and ushers led them past the wood benches where the rest of the audience sat to a roped-off area with red velvet couches and a table set with tea and a variety of snacks.

They didn't have Priests who could control the stone surrounding the crystalline lamps, but they had people who threw levers to cover all the lights in the tent and dropped the room into darkness. A single spotlight appeared and illuminated a man in a bright red coat. "Ladies and Gentlemen! Welcome to Peculiar! Welcome ... to the Circus!"

At his cue, music echoed through the tent, and the full lights sprang to life. Around the room was a show that reminded Ylena of the Pageant. Animals performed stunning tricks, although she wasn't sure if the animals learned their skills from Priests or long training. The stage design and set pieces were beautiful, although instead of living plants and fountains, they had built elaborately constructed trees out of twisted wires and fluttering ribbons. Dancers twirled on fabric high in the air, but these were not Discipline Priests who could tempt a breeze to catch them if they fell. Everything they did was without the benefit of the Priest's Gifts, and yet it was still beautiful.

It was also different because the Pageant was extremely orderly. The script had remained unchanged for centuries. Every line had its perfect order and timing. At the circus, everything happened at once. She tried to follow the horses as they circled the ring with riders on their back, but she got distracted watching the man swallowing a sword, but she didn't see him finish because the clowns all knocked each other down, but then she saw the woman walking across a wire stretched at the top of the tent.

She saw a bearded lady. There was a man with no arms strumming a guitar with his feet. Then, she saw a woman whose arms and half of her face looked like they'd melted. Grandfather had a burn scar on his ankle, and Ylena gasped at what fire had done to this woman. The woman was smiling, but Ylena knew from experience that people could smile despite the pain. Rev looked at the woman with the scars with a narrowed eye and a slight frown.

The show ended with thunderous applause and cheers from the crowd. Ylena was standing and clapping when she noticed Rev cut across the rows to go speak to the woman with the burns. The ringleader walked up to Ylena and Wilder and gave them a bow with a flourish.

"Welcome to the Circus!" The ringleader's voice boomed like he was still in the center ring. "It's an honor to have such esteemed guests join us today. I've heard that the two of you are touring the Grottos?"

Wilder handed the list of names to the ringleader. "The Warden has tasked me with gathering performers for the upcoming Spectacle at the Heart."

"Yes, of course! We are looking forward to it!" He looked at the list of names with a slight frown. "Are these the only ones you need?"

Ylena looked at the list in his hand and could see that Wilder had rewritten the list and left off the last two names, as Rev had suggested.

"Only those on the list. You've got high-quality performers here. I can tell you've trained them well!" Wilder gave the ringleader his most winning smile.

The ringleader puffed out his chest. Ylena bit her lips to hide a grin. Apparently, Wilder's smile worked on other people, too.

Rev caught up with them as they exited the tent and began the walk back to her house. Ylena gave her a questioning look, and Rev stepped close to whisper. "Some parts of the circus are complicated, Ylena." She sighed. "Grotto Peculiar and its circus celebrate those of us who don't fit the norms. But sometimes, there are people who take advantage of those who are born differently and use them for their own purposes. And there is an extreme worship of Peculiarity that causes people to take radical measures to make themselves unique." Ylena's eyes widened at the thought of the woman inflicting that much pain on herself. "She made the choice for herself, but I thought it might be worse. Sometimes, it's the child's parents that are the believers."

"Parents would do something like that to their child?" Ylena whispered.

"Yes. Like that and more." Rev sighed. "The longer you stay in the Underneath, the more beauty and terror you will discover."

9

On the way back to Rev's house, they passed a tattoo parlor, and Ylena begged them to let her stop and watch. A woman covered in drawings of fantastical creatures was tattooing a young man stretched across a table in front of her little shop. He had a few friends gathered around who were giving him a hard time about the strained look on his face.

"Does it hurt?" asked Ylena.

Rev lifted her blond hair to reveal a crescent moon surrounded by a circle of seven stars behind her ear. "If you enjoy getting stabbed repeatedly by a needle, then no, it doesn't hurt at all," she said with a smirk.

Wilder laughed. "The pain varies depending on where you get the tattoo."

Ylena turned to him. "You have a tattoo?"

He unbuttoned the top few buttons of his shirt to reveal a seven-pointed star inside a teardrop above his heart.

"The symbol of the Goddess..." she said. "I didn't notice you had that before."

He raised an eyebrow. "And exactly when have you seen me without my shirt on?"

Ylena remembered looking at Wilder one night through his bedroom window in the temple, and her mind worked furiously to find a reasonable explanation. Rev faked a dramatic gasp and covered her mouth with her hands.

Wilder's laugh let her off the hook. "You know I would have let you look anytime you asked." His wink left her relieved and exasperated. "The High Priests don't like people in the City showing off items they can only get in the Underneath, so I had to cover it when I was up there."

"Why did you pick the symbol of the Goddess?" she asked.

He seemed a little embarrassed. "I follow the Goddess in my own way."

Ylena didn't understand his reaction, but before she could ask him more, Rev stepped in. "Some people pick tattoos that are pretty or scary or funny, but some people choose tattoos that are meaningful to them."

"And the moon and stars are meaningful to you?" Ylena asked.

Rev's shining blue eye seemed to look through her. "I've never seen the moon or stars before."

Ylena sucked in a breath and stared up at the stone cavern high above her. "I'm so sorry. I never considered that..."

Rev gave her a small smile. "There was no sin here. You and I have lived very different lives, and I don't expect you to know everything about mine." She touched delicate fingers to the tattoo on her neck. "Yes, this is meaningful to me. I hope to see the moon and stars someday. And even the sun." She closed her eye and tipped her head back as if the sun was shining on her face. "I hope. And I believe." She opened her eye and smiled at Ylena again. "It's a small piece of art that helps me remember that."

A tear threatened to fall past Ylena's lashes, but she

blinked it back. "Thanks for sharing that with me." She looked over at the boy as he stood up from the table and stared at his upper arm with a wide grin. "There's someone I need to remember like that, too."

Getting stabbed by needles was about as painful as it sounded, but she distracted herself by remembering the past. Ylena had asked the woman to tattoo a bright blue bird on her wrist. She remembered the day she stood with Pim in the park. Pim was so happy to be in her home Diocese of Harmony with all the animals. That day, a blue bird had landed on Ylena's wrist and Pim told her to make a wish. Ylena decided that whenever she looked at the tattoo, she would remember Pim as she had been on that day, smiling and hopeful.

When the woman finished, Ylena paid and thanked her for the beautiful art. Wilder and Rev stood from the bench where they had been talking. "Thanks for waiting," said Ylena. She gingerly touched the blue feathers.

Rev rapped Ylena's hand. "Don't touch that yet! You were just at the circus with animals. I'm sure your hands are filthy."

Wilder shoved Rev and laughed. "You are always so bossy!"

Rev crossed her arms at her chest. "I'm bossy because I'm right." She turned to Ylena. "Come on, let's get back home so we can get you cleaned up."

They walked the last few blocks back to Rev's house in the constant purple glow of the spires. As they turned onto her street, Wilder pulled them both to a stop. Someone had broken into the yellow house. Only pieces of the wooden door remained. She covered her mouth to stifle her gasp.

Rev's eye narrowed, and she assumed a fighting stance Ylena had seen at Temple Discipline.

Wilder whispered, "I'm going to go look. Both of you stay here."

Rev grabbed him by his sleeve and growled. "Not a chance. We all go look, or we all leave now. Those are the only options."

Wilder ground his teeth together, then sighed. "Fine. We all go." Rev nodded once. "But if I say 'run,' everyone runs. We will meet back up at the tattoo parlor if we get separated. Got it?" Rev nodded and ushered him to take the lead.

He hurried to the other side of the street and hugged the shadowed side of the building. Ylena tried to remember what it had been like sneaking through shadows in the City, but this felt distinctly different. Wilder hesitated outside the shredded door, and Ylena strained to hear any sounds inside. The silence was enough for him to hurry inside quietly, and Ylena followed with Rev bringing up the rear and watching behind them.

Inside, everything was chaos. Rev's pink couch had been ripped apart with stuffing littering the floor. Books had been thrown off the shelves and the pages ripped out. In the bedroom, all of her clothes had been dumped into piles on the floor, and the kitchen floor was covered with the little food she had.

It shocked Ylena that someone would cause such needless destruction. Rev had collected beautiful and peculiar things over the years, and now it was all destroyed. Ylena tried to catch Rev's eye to see her reaction. She wanted to comfort Rev like Rev had comforted her. But Rev did not look sad. She looked focused and intense. Each step was intentional and careful, and she moved as smoothly as Wilder did through each room.

Wilder caught her eye and gave her a nod. Rev appeared

to understand. She lifted a rug covered with ashes dumped from her wood stove. She pried up a piece of the wooden floor and removed a leather pouch and a small wooden box. After she put both in her bag, she nodded at Wilder. He moved to the door at the back of the house and led them both out into the quiet street. They moved on a winding path through the City, and Ylena noticed the purple glow fade as they moved farther away from the crystal spire. They stopped in front of the entrance to the tunnel that led out of the Grotto.

Wilder spoke for the first time since they had entered the house. "Are you sure about this, Rev? It's not too late for you to turn back."

Rev smirked. "Now, Wilder, it looks like you and Ylena have gotten yourselves into something quite peculiar. You don't expect me to miss out on that do you?"

Wilder rubbed his forehead and sighed.

Ylena's eyebrows pulled together as she tried to understand what they were talking about. "Are you saying that someone destroyed your house because of Wilder and me?"

Rev nodded. "Without a doubt! Can you think of anyone who is looking for the two of you?"

Ylena shrugged. "Um ... seven High Priests and a legion of Sentinels?"

Rev threw her head back and laughed. "Lead on, Wilder. I can't wait to see what kind of adventure the Goddess has planned!"

Indulgence

10

_____

After a harrowing trip through the tunnel between Grottos, they emerged into another large cavern glowing with purple light. They stayed quiet through the tunnel, so it felt strange when Ylena broke their silence. "So, where exactly are we going?"

Wilder pointed toward the purple crystal. "I thought we should check in with the Warden of Indulgence now. We are a bit earlier than scheduled, but it's probably best to keep our movements unpredictable."

As they walked closer to the purple glow, Ylena noticed that this Grotto wasn't as brightly colored as Peculiar was, but it still had a more festive air than Delirium. There were little shops lining the streets, with colorful glass covered crystalline lamps inside. She could see people laughing and groups of people dancing. Friends walked down the sidewalk with their arms around each others' necks, singing loudly and off-key.

Wilder, Ylena, and Rev approached the crystal spire and walked beyond it to the massive building carved into the cave wall. They walked down the long hallway to similar wide doors that had contained the Wardens in the other

Grottos. The guards waved the three of them to the right, into the small office of an assistant.

The office was neat, without a single piece of paper out of place. The room shone with a sterile light, and the three of them stood awkwardly until the woman at the desk raised her head.

"You're early." Her voice was as sharp as her lacquered red nails.

"We had some unexpected visitors." Wilder gave her a wide smile, but her irritated expression didn't waver.

"You can meet the Warden later tonight at the Central Tavern. Maestro and Greyson are rehearsing. Go find them." She bent her head back down to her paperwork as a dismissal.

They crossed the hallway, and the guards watched them as they entered the door on the left side of the hallway into the rehearsal space.

Maestro relaxed in his chair, barely watching the performance in front of him. A young man in a fedora spun out of a turn and slid across the floor to a stop in front of Maestro's chair. The young man's bright tenor reverberated through the room, and Ylena felt it in her bones. After his echoing last note, Maestro clapped lazily.

"Not bad, Greyson," said Maestro. "I think the second verse could use a bit more work. Let's try—" He noticed the three of them standing near the door. "Well, look who joined us. I guess we can get this part over with now."

"Don't sound so enthusiastic," said Greyson with a sarcastic grin. He crossed the room and removed his fedora with a flourish. He took Rev's hand and kissed it. "It's a pleasure to meet you. Are you the Goddess?"

Rev chuckled. "I like this one."

Wilder reached out to shake hands, which broke Greyson away from Rev. "I'm Wilder, and this is Ylena. We are the ones who will be in the Spectacle. Rev is just here to watch."

Greyson looked back at Rev. "Here in Grotto Indulgence, we encourage full participation, but I guess we can allow you to only watch. As long as you promise to fully savor the performance."

"I'll savor it, you tasty little morsel." Rev had a wicked glint in her eye. Greyson seemed to take it as a challenge.

Maestro sighed dramatically. "All right, young people. I don't have the energy to deal with your enthusiastic libidos, so please, can we just rehearse?"

Maestro led Wilder and Ylena through several combinations that they added to Greyson's number. Greyson's steps were smooth, and his rich voice even smoother. Rev was leaning back in her chair with a satisfied expression on her face. Ylena whispered to Wilder while holding their pose at stage left. "Is Rev always so ... friendly?"

Wilder chuckled quietly. "She knows how to be serious when necessary, but most of the time, she likes to experience life to the fullest."

"What do you think about him?" Her eyes flicked to Greyson.

"I assume we will meet performers like him and Jerra in each of the Grottos. It looks like the Wardens have cast younger versions of themselves in each role. The Wardens are extremely vain, so that isn't surprising. I'm not sure if Greyson is a willing participant here or not."

"He's definitely good at what he does. And so was the last girl in Peculiar. I'm glad the show will be good, even if our roles are boring this time."

"The Underneath still demands the same level of quality, but you don't have to worry about Sentinels killing you if you make a small mistake. Here, you might be rewarded by a Warden for unintentionally hurting someone they were angry with. Or if you look at a Warden the wrong way, your entire family could be tortured. I have no idea how high the expectations are for this Spectacle, but I know we have to meet them."

"Do you think my grandfather is okay?"

Wilder shrugged. "I don't know. He knows a lot of people, so he's got connections if he gets in trouble. And he appears to know the Warden well. That's good because it means that she must need him for something and will want to protect him. But it's also bad. If a Warden knows your name, it rarely ends well."

Ylena felt guilty for how little she had thought about her grandfather since she had entered the City. Finding him was the whole reason she had come down the mountain, but once she was in the City, it seemed like her world expanded and he was a much smaller part. But she couldn't imagine a world without him in it. She had to do whatever she could to keep him safe.

11

They left the Warden's Den and walked back into the well-lit area. Ylena looked around and realized she didn't know what time it was. She remembered waking up earlier and drinking coffee, but without the sunrise, she couldn't be sure that had been morning.

She realized she had fallen behind Wilder and Rev. They were both walking with confident steps in the same direction. "Why do I get the feeling that the two of you have plans I don't know about?"

They stopped abruptly and turned around. Rev and Wilder looked at each other, and the same unspoken communication she had seen before passed between them. Their silent conversation ended with Rev speaking first.

"There is a lot going on here, and even Wilder and I are out of our league. We need to gather a few friends."

Ylena still wasn't sure she trusted the two of them, so the thought of more of their friends joining her wasn't very comforting.

Rev noticed Ylena's hesitation and grabbed her hand. "You aren't alone in this."

She remembered Rev's destroyed home and decided that they could use a few more people on their side, even if they just kept watch.

They walked through crowded streets with buildings packed with people who were laughing and yelling and singing. Wilder and Rev walked up to a door that looked like all the others. They ushered Ylena inside as they both looked up and down the street for anyone following.

A strong, brown hand gripped Ylena by the front of her sweater. "Entrance is by invitation only." Ylena looked up to find that the hand belonged to a young woman with hair that floated like a dark, lush cloud. Her brown eyes drilled into Ylena's skull.

"Is that the way you greet our new friend, Tayeh?" drawled Rev.

The young woman kept her hold on Ylena's shirt, but her hard eyes slid to Rev. "What in the Abyss are you dragging in here, Rev?"

"Hi, Tayeh." Wilder stepped to Ylena's other side. "It's good to see you."

Ylena was close enough to the woman's face that she could detect a brief pleased expression behind her eyes. She recovered quickly and acknowledged him with a word. "Wilder."

Rev wiggled a little closer to the woman and purred, "So, are you going to let us take a seat?"

She rolled her eyes. "Make yourself at home."

Rev smiled and nodded her head toward the woman's hand still clenching Ylena's shirt. Tayeh sighed and released her. Rev took Ylena's hand and said, "Come with me. There is someone else you need to meet." She led Ylena away, but Wilder remained with the young woman.

Rev led Ylena through a maze of tables filled with people talking quietly enough she couldn't hear them over the sound of the guitarist playing a melancholy tune. Ylena took a seat next to Rev across from someone hidden behind a stack of books. Rev rapped her knuckles on the wood table. "Knock, knock! Can Quinn come out to play?"

Ylena saw dark and artfully tousled hair over the stack of books. Shining blue eyes behind glasses widened in surprise, and he pushed the books out of the way. "Hi, Rev! It's good to see you."

His smile was sweet and honest, unlike Wilder's cocky grin. He turned his open gaze onto Ylena, and she felt an unexpected jump in her heartbeat. "I'm Quinn. A pleasure to meet you!"

Ylena coughed but found her voice. "I'm Ylena. It's nice to meet you, too."

Rev patted Quinn's hand fondly. "I've missed you, Quinn! Has it been boring here without me?"

He grabbed a book off the stack. "You won't believe what I've been working on, Rev! I'm using some of the ancient books from the City to create my own code language. It will be so advantageous to have a new code! Although, sometimes, I get distracted by attempting to translate the original language." He started flipping through the pages of a book and soon appeared to forget about the two of them.

Rev leaned close to Ylena and spoke in a low voice. "He is beautiful and brilliant but quite distractible." She sighed. "Quinn, dear, can you join the two of us again?"

He pushed his glasses up and looked at Rev with clear eyes. "Of course! What do you need?"

"Our sweet Ylena here seems to have gotten herself into a bit of trouble, and Wilder and I are looking for a few people who can keep an eye on her for a while. Do you have any availability?" Ylena turned to look at Rev with raised eyebrows. *She got herself into a bit of trouble?* She sighed. If the first step off the mountain counted, then it was true.

"I'm always available to help a friend!" His smile was so sincere and good-natured that Ylena had to grin back.

"Thanks, Quinn." Rev looked over at the door where Wilder was talking to Tayeh, who stood with her arms crossed. "I'm not sure that Wilder is having as much success."

"Don't worry! I'll talk to Tayeh. I can convince her." He smiled and looked between Rev and Ylena. "So, where are we going?"

"To the Central Tavern." Ylena wasn't sure if it was a secret, but she dropped her voice anyway. "To meet with the Warden."

"That sounds intriguing!" He pushed his glasses up and started stacking his books. "I'll grab my supplies and be right back!"

As he walked through a door at the back, Rev turned to Ylena. "I'm not exactly sure what we are up against, but at least we now have a proper crew."

12

Ylena wasn't sure if it was Quinn or Wilder that convinced Tayeh to come along, but soon, the five of them were headed toward the center of the enormous cavern. Quinn had left most of his books somewhere, but he was carrying a large bag that held what he called "supplies." Tayeh walked near Wilder at the head of their group. She flowed through the streets with predatory grace and a glare for anyone who looked their way.

"So, what exactly are we doing at the Central Tavern tonight?" Tayeh finally asked.

Wilder answered. "Ylena and I are coordinating the contributions to the Spectacle that will take place at the Heart of the Grottos."

Tayeh turned to look at Ylena with a raised eyebrow but never stopped her smooth stride. "Why are you in the middle of all of this?"

Ylena thought of the previously amber spires going dark and then relighting in purple. "Um ... I guess I was just in the wrong place at the wrong time."

Tayeh grunted but asked nothing further.

They arrived at a large, circular building, whose shape seemed to be an intentional mockery of the circular temples up above. They walked up the stairs that went around the building and found themselves in a courtyard filled with people and loud music. Glowing, multicolored lamps lined the walls, and people stood laughing in the light or snuggled up together in dark corners. Tayeh strode over to a woman carrying multiple glasses in her hands and asked her an unheard question. The woman nodded her head toward a doorway, then hurried off.

The five of them walked through the door into a cozy lounge with leather couches and a long bar that stretched the length of the room. Ylena looked around for the Warden, but she didn't know what he looked like. They moved closer to the bar, and the man on the other side removed his fedora with the same flourish Greyson did. Ylena blinked in surprise when she noticed how similar he looked to the young singer they met earlier that day.

"Welcome to Indulgence! Thanks for meeting me here at the Central Tavern." His deep voice sounded kind, but Ylena didn't feel it was wise to let her guard down.

"Thank you, Warden," said Wilder. "This is Ylena, my costar from the Pageant, and a couple of our crew. We look forward to hearing what you want to contribute to the Spectacle."

The Warden gave a deep laugh. "Oh, you will do more than hear! Tonight, you will drink to your heart's desire." At this, Rev and Quinn both smiled, but Wilder's face remained impassive. Tayeh looked like she wanted to strike, but Ylena thought that might just be what her face looked like.

"Step up to the bar, young friends!" He set out a line of six small glasses and poured a clear liquid into it with a flourish of the bottle. "This is a little something special I whipped up for the occasion." He grabbed a glass and drank the liquid in one gulp, then closed his eyes with a satisfied smile and chuckled. "I really outdid myself on this one."

Rev was the first one to reach for a glass of her own. She tossed the liquid back and then licked her lips with a wicked grin. "Now that's just lovely, Warden. I really appreciate the hospitality."

"There's plenty more back here!" He waved to the bottles of various colored liquids lined up along the wall. "Go ahead! Drink up!"

Wilder picked up the small glass and drank it in one gulp. Ylena picked up the glass in front of her and swallowed the liquid that looked like water.

It wasn't water.

It was fire.

The liquid burned her throat all the way down and the fumes rose to burn her nose. She immediately started coughing, and her eyes watered. Wilder looked at her with pity, and Rev clapped her on the back as she continued to cough.

The Warden laughed and poured her another glass. "The only thing that helps a reaction like that is a second shot!" His dark eyes shone with a predatory gleam.

Ylena was still coughing, and she turned to Rev with wide eyes.

"Oh, Goddess," sighed Rev. "This is going to be a long night."

Ylena wasn't sure why Rev had looked so concerned earlier. After Ylena drank the second little glass filled with fire, the Warden brought her something else he said wouldn't burn

64

her throat as badly. The drink was sour and had sugar lining the edge of the glass, and she thought it was delicious. She drank several glasses and decided she definitely preferred it over what he called shots.

She saw Quinn across the room playing a game of darts with a glass of dark brown liquid in his other hand. Tayeh was standing near the door with a grimace. She had respectfully tasted the first shot, but after that, she moved into a watchful position and didn't move. Rev was laughing and dancing with the younger version of the Warden. Ylena thought it looked like fun, so she stood from her tall seat at the bar. Her knees buckled strangely, and she gripped the stool until the room stopped spinning.

She reconsidered and thought she might wait on the dancing. Perhaps she would just drink another glass while she waited for her head to settle. She licked the sugar off the rim of the glass and turned to see Wilder staring at her.

She giggled. "Did you try one of these? They are soooo good!" She licked off the rest of the sugar and took another sip of the sour drink.

"Um ... Ylena, you probably shouldn't drink any more of those." He only drank a few shots and had been drinking water since the Warden left.

Why would she choose water when she could have this sour juice drink? It was even better than coffee! She signaled for the server to bring her another.

Wilder sighed and rubbed his forehead. "I probably should have explained to you what we were getting into tonight. I forget how little you know about all of this."

Anger flared up in Ylena at just how accurate that statement was. "You never tell me any ... anything, Wilder!" She poked him in the chest. His very muscular chest. "If I want to know something, I have to fi-fighur it, figerr ... learn it myself." The server returned with the drink, and Ylena started licking the sugar again.

"Ylena, I'm serious. You should stop drinking those. You are going to feel terrible tomorrow."

She snapped her head around to look at him, and after the dizziness cleared, she said, "Wilder, I feel terrible every day! Maybe you've forgotten that my best friend was recently murdered? Along with everyone I knew in the City? Well, except for you, of course. You ran away and left us all to die. So, ya know what? I'll drink whatever Goddess-damn thing I want, and you can run off and leave me alone while I do it." She picked up the glass and drank every drop. She had to focus on her hands as they set the glass down because the bar sloped strangely and the glass kept trying to tip over.

Wilder's voice was quiet, and it was hard for her to focus on the words. "I know you might not believe me, Ylena, but none of this was my plan. I'm glad I poured the children's tears into the basin, because I saved their lives. But I couldn't stay. My orders were to get back to the Underneath as soon as I poured in their tears."

"Your or-orders?" She hiccupped. "You always do what you are ordered to do? Even if it involves killing people?"

He looked down at the bar and traced the scratches in the dark wood. "You don't understand what it's like, Ylena. It's different in the Underneath. Those of us who live down here don't have choices like they do Upstairs."

"Pim doesn't have any choices now." She felt tears spring to her eyes. "I'm going to the ladies' room." She stood on wobbly legs and clung to the sloping bar. "Your orders are to stay right here." She tried to walk away with as much dignity as the shaking room would allow.

She made it into the dark hallway and felt her way along the wall, looking for the correct room. She just needed a quiet place to cry in peace. A hand reached out from the darkness and pulled her into a shadow.

She opened her mouth to scream, but Caed put his hand softly against her lips. "Ylena, it's me."

"Caed!" she breathed.

He staggered back a step and coughed. "Wow, Ylena. You have been ... seriously drinking." He blinked his eyes several times as if they burned like hers had when she drank the shot.

"Yes! They have such good sour drinks here!" She reached out and hugged him. "Oh, Caed! I've missed you so much! It's awful here. I want to go back to the City with you." She clung to him because he was steadier on his feet than she was.

He gently took hold of her arms so he could look at her. "Ylena, you can't. You have to stay down here. It's not safe up there."

"It's not safe down here!" Her voice was raising, and he kept shushing her. "Someone broke into Rev's house and ripped everything apart! Someone was looking for me and Wilder. There is nowhere safe for me to go." The tears were back in her eyes. She felt a moment of panic about that but couldn't remember why.

"I'm so sorry, Ylena. I thought your grandfather would keep you safe." He brushed his dark, wavy hair away from his face. She realized he wasn't wearing his silver Priest circlet. But he wore all black like usual, and his tight pants looked really good ...

"Maybe you should escape out of here and go back into hiding on the mountain," he said.

Her head snapped up, and she had to steady herself with a hand on his chest. "What did you say?"

"You could go back to the cave you lived in with your

grandfather. I don't think anyone would try to hurt you there."

She growled. "Are you tryna get rid of me?" Her eyes narrowed, which actually seemed to help the spinning room slow down.

"No! I don't want you to go. I just want you to be safe." He brushed a sweaty bit of hair away from her forehead, but she shook him off.

"Safe? No one is safe. Not me. Not Rev. Not Pim. No one. And you can't do anything about it." She spat out the words as the tears fell down her cheeks.

Caed's eyes widened in hurt. She stood taller in triumph. She was glad she hurt him. There was so much he could have told her about the Underneath, but he kept the information to himself. There had been an entire world beneath her feet, and he had never once mentioned it. He was just as guilty as Grandfather when it came to secrets. She was alone once again, and no one could save her but herself.

"Ylena, I don't think you are feeling like yourself. Let me take you home." He took her hand gently.

A cool breeze ruffled through her sweaty hair. She took hold of the wind and wrapped it around Caed until it pushed him against the wall. The wind pressed his back flat against the battered wood panels, and his wavy hair blew away from his startled eyes.

She grabbed the front of his shirt and whispered harshly, "I have no home, Caed."

He looked at her with pity. "I know. I'm sorry." A tear hung on his dark lashes, and she stared at it in fascination. His breathing was labored. "Please, Ylena ... You're hurting me."

The wind was holding him so tight that he struggled to breathe. She gasped, and the breeze floated away. She stepped away from him, horrified at what she had done.

He bent forward, pulling in deep breaths. "It's okay, Ylena. I understand. Let me help you."

His gasping breath made her think of Pim struggling to breathe as she died. She stumbled back down the hallway, beyond the bar, and past Tayeh keeping guard at the door. She vomited in the courtyard and curled up in a dark corner until her gasping breath melted into snoring.

13

Ylena woke to someone smashing her head between two boulders. Her sticky eyes opened, and she found herself in a strange bed. She tried to sit up, but her head swam, and she thought she might vomit. Her mouth tasted like she already had. Her head thrummed with each heartbeat, and she held her temples between her palms and tried to heal herself, but it didn't work. She had a vague memory of someone crying but wasn't sure if it had been her or a dream. She slowly swung her legs out from under the covers and realized she was only wearing her shirt. Someone had removed her pants and her boots, and she had no memory of it.

She panicked, imagining what possibly could have happened during the time of her missing memory. She had felt afraid several times recently, but she had never felt so out of control. Her mind was sluggish, and her body didn't seem like it was working properly. She found the rest of her clothes draped over a chair in the tiny room, so she put on her pants and laced her boots up tight. She hoped that slight action would help her feel more like herself.

She opened the bedroom door and peeked out. Rev was

sitting at a narrow table, drinking coffee and reading a stack of papers. She looked up when Ylena stepped out of the room.

"Good morning, dear." Her voice was quiet and soothing. "There's coffee."

Ylena nodded but wished she hadn't. She stood still for a moment as her head floated back into place, then she poured herself a cup of coffee and sat down gingerly.

Rev didn't speak for a while. She just watched Ylena drink her coffee. After she took a few sips, Rev brought her a plate with a large piece of crusty bread. The thought of eating made Ylena's stomach protest, but the look she received from Rev was pretty clear. Ylena ate a couple bites before Rev finally spoke.

"Ylena, I'm so sorry we didn't warn you what to expect last night. We should have prepared you. Each of us has felt what you are feeling at least once, but we always knew what we were getting ourselves into. I promise to share what I know sooner next time so you don't have to pay the price."

"If you actually do share information with me, you would be the first one to do that since Pim." She took a quick sip of coffee to hide the emotion in her voice.

"Pim was the friend you got the tattoo for?" Rev looked at the bird on Ylena's wrist.

"Yes. She knew there was something odd about me, but she always answered my questions honestly. And she was kind." She stared into her cup. "I only wish I had been as honest with her as she was with me. She never really knew who I was."

Rev reached across the table and rested her hand on Ylena's. "She might not have known where you were from, but she knew you. I haven't known you long, but I already know that you can't help but reveal your heart with everything you do, Ylena."

Ylena panicked at the thought of unintentionally revealing all her secrets. She looked up when Rev chuckled. "See? I can tell you are thinking about whatever secrets you still hold." Ylena's eyes widened. "Don't worry. I don't need to know what they are. But that proves my point. I know your heart. And so did Pim."

Ylena silently considered Rev's words as she ate the last few bites of toast.

"So, what are you doing here, Ylena?" asked Rev.

Ylena choked on a bite. "What do you mean?"

"I'm here because Wilder asked for my help. Wilder is here because he is deeply entrenched in the game the Wardens are playing. But what are *you* doing here?" Her blue eye pierced Ylena's heart.

"I don't want Grandfather to be punished if I leave."

Rev raised the eyebrow above her eye patch. "I'm sure he's made it through tough situations before and knows how to take care of himself. If you knew he would be okay, would you still be here?"

"Yes." She didn't realize the answer until she said it out loud.

There was something about Rev that drew out honest answers. Rev didn't say anything else, but she leaned back in her chair to listen.

"When I was Upstairs, I had so many questions. I felt that each step on my journey to the Pageant was leading me to the answers I needed. But when the Pageant ended, I was left with more questions than before. I'm not sure what I'm looking for down here, but I can't leave until I find it."

Rev nodded as if she understood, even though Ylena wasn't sure if she understood herself. Ylena considered asking Rev to explain when the back door opened and Wilder peeked inside. When he saw the two of them at the table, he opened the door for Quinn and Tayeh to come in, too.

"Good morning, Ylena!" said Quinn. "How are you feeling?"

She winced at his exuberant voice. "Just fabulous."

"How do you like Tayeh's place?" he asked. "She's a good decorator, isn't she?"

Ylena took a moment to look around and realized the house wasn't what she would expect from the gruff young woman. The walls were pale blue, and someone had painted graceful, navy whorls along the ceiling and over the doors. Shelves of delicate pottery stood on either side of a gray sofa covered in bright pillows.

She looked at Tayeh, dressed in a dark leather vest with metal grommets and thick straps pulled tight around her waist. More straps and buckles looped around her thighs, where she carried several weapons. Her ebony coils floated like a voluminous crown on her head. Ylena widened her eyes, trying to reconcile Tayeh and the beautiful room. She opened her mouth to ask a question, but Tayeh folded her arms and glowered. Ylena's mouth snapped shut.

Wilder walked toward Ylena like he was approaching a wild animal. "We brought you some breakfast." He set a paper-wrapped item on the table, and Ylena could smell some kind of sausage and cheese. It smelled both amazing and awful. "They have a lot of supposed cures for hangovers in Indulgence, but this is one of the best."

She was going to refuse, but when she saw Rev's expression, she unwrapped the sandwich and slowly began to eat.

14

After Ylena finished her breakfast, Tayeh pulled a chair up to the table and motioned for Quinn and Wilder to join them. "I think it's time we discuss our strategy for whatever it is we are doing." She looked at Wilder. "I don't know how you convinced me to join another one of your schemes, but I need to know what I've gotten myself into before I go any farther."

Rev poured each of them a cup of coffee as Wilder explained how he and Ylena played the parts of the Goddess and her Companion in the Pageant and how he poured the tears of the children from the Underneath with powers into the basin. "No one knew exactly what would happen when we poured their tears in, but no one could have predicted that all the towers would go dark and then light up purple like they did."

Ylena took a sip of her coffee and hoped that no one looked at her face, because she thought Rev might guess that Ylena knew more about that than she was telling.

Wilder continued, "The Wardens want to celebrate this victory against the High Priests by throwing their own anti-Pageant they are calling the Spectacle. I'm sure that, by including Ylena and I after we were in the Pageant, they feel like they are solidifying this event as the first step of their independence."

"What do you mean?" asked Ylena.

"The Underneath completely depends on the High Priests for food and other necessities that come from Upstairs. With the ability to have our own Priests who can make food, we can eventually become self-sustaining and not under their control."

"But the children who manifested their Gift this year are only babies," said Rev. "How long will it take until they can actually make enough food for us all?"

"I've heard whispers about a revolution." Tayeh's voice was matter-of-fact, but her eyebrows furrowed. "Nothing distinct enough for me to take it seriously, but I wouldn't be surprised if the Wardens are planning a war and expect us all to follow along obediently when the time comes."

Wilder nodded in agreement. "The Wardens don't share their plans with anyone, so it's hard to say for sure. They don't even like to share their plans with one another. When they joined to get me into the Pageant, it was the first time they have worked together."

"So then what's our plan?" asked Rev. "We can try to keep Wilder and Ylena safe as they travel from Grotto to Grotto, but how much do we really want to help the Wardens with their plans? I'd love to believe they are planning a revolution for the benefit of all the people in the Underneath, but I'm not sure that's the case."

"I think we need to investigate and see what the Wardens are planning," said Quinn. "Having Wilder and Ylena on the inside could make that job a lot easier."

Tayeh leaned forward in her chair. "The two of you will get closer to the Wardens than the rest of us have managed in a long time. This could be a great opportunity."

"I agree," said Wilder. "I thought I might retire from this job after the Pageant, but since the Wardens forced me back in, I don't mind taking advantage of it." His usual flirty smile was now a wicked grin.

"What sort of job do you mean?" asked Ylena.

He looked at her with serious eyes. "The same job I had during the Pageant. Being a spy. But now, I can use those skills for myself."

"Then we are all agreed?" asked Tayeh. "We will protect Wilder and Ylena as they prepare for the Spectacle and work together to discover what we can."

Everyone nodded except Ylena. "But what do we think we will discover? What can the five of us possibly do with any information we actually find?"

Rev grinned. "Information is one of the most lucrative businesses in the Underneath. The four of us have gathered information together before, and we've earned enough to make ends meet."

Quinn nodded vigorously, and Tayeh raised a single eyebrow, which seemed like an enthusiastic response from her.

"I'm skilled in code-breaking, picking locks, and discovering secrets," said Quinn with a smile. "Tayeh here is the one you call when you need a firmer touch—as in someone to break down a door or to rough someone up." Tayeh leaned back in her chair with a proud grin. "And Wilder and Rev can charm the pants off anyone. They literally have done it! One time, Wilder—"

Wilder cleared his throat. "I'm sure Ylena doesn't need to hear that story."

Ylena very much wanted to hear that story, but she had a bigger question. "What will I do?"

Wilder looked at her with his dark, piercing eyes. "Are

you telling me that, during your time in the City, you never learned skills to help you uncover secrets?"

She opened her mouth to protest but then shut it quickly. In the confusion of discovering the Underneath, she had forgotten who she had become in the City. "I can sneak around in the dark without being seen. And I can climb almost anything."

Wilder nodded. "I've seen her climb. I know that's a skill we can put to use." He looked at her again. "Will you share the other secret you have?"

"What secret?" Her words came out too quickly.

"You already shared it with me." Rev smiled and touched her temple.

"Oh ... you mean healing?" Ylena asked with a careful glance at Quinn and Tayeh.

"Yes. Being able to count on someone for healing is a luxury we've never had before," said Rev.

The four of them stared at her with curious eyes. Healing was the only Gift anyone besides Caed knew she had, and she thought it best to keep it that way. "Sure. I think I can manage that." They all relaxed back in their chairs.

"Good!" said Wilder. "I propose we spend today gathering supplies and then head to the next Grotto tomorrow." Rev, Tayeh, and Quinn stood and started discussing where they would go to get what they needed.

Wilder said quietly to Ylena, "I thought you might need a day to recover from last night. I'm really sorry that none of us thought to warn you what you should expect."

At his words, Ylena remembered a fuzzy conversation with him while they sat at the bar. "I think you tried to warn me, but it was too late."

He smiled. "Well, you aren't feeling anything that we haven't felt ourselves at least once, and because of that, I know you must feel awful. You were in pretty rough shape last night when we carried you home."

A blush rose to her cheeks. "You had to carry me?"

He laughed. "It was quite a walk from the Central Tavern, so Tayeh and I took turns."

"Who put me into bed?" She couldn't meet his eyes.

Wilder softened his voice. "Rev got you into bed and made sure you had privacy. She forced us to leave this morning so you could sleep as long as you needed."

Ylena looked over at Rev where she stood talking to Tayeh and Quinn. "That was very considerate of her." She turned back to Wilder. "I honestly don't remember everything I said to you last night, but I'm—"

"You didn't say anything that wasn't true. I can explain to you the reasons that I did what I did, but that doesn't remove the fact that, because I poured in the tears, all the crystals failed and, as a result, they killed everyone on that stage but the two of us. I am to blame for that, and I know there is no way for me to make that right."

She felt the anger toward him stir back up, but it wasn't based off the truth. The Pageant carried on fine with Caed in his role. Everyone would have survived the night if her tear hadn't fallen into the basin. She broke the crystals, not him.

She looked at the shame written on his face and wanted to tell him the truth, but she couldn't. Her own guilt froze the words in her mouth.

All she could do was nod. He gave her a sad smile and joined the others in the conversation about their supplies.

～

Ylena spent most of the afternoon with a pillow over her head, blocking out the light from the crystal that was spilling into her otherwise dark room. She was grateful that the others had gone to run various errands and left her with the quiet house. She had time to close her eyes, but since the room was still spinning, she wasn't able to sleep.

She eventually got up and explored Tayeh's house. There were three small bedrooms, and they had been kind enough to give her a room to herself. Or perhaps, considering how bad she smelled, they were acting in their own best interest. There was a bathroom, but it was nothing like what she'd had in the temples Upstairs. The Underneath appeared to have running water, but the pipes were a lot more complicated, and there was no hot water. She considered heating some water on the stove and taking a long bath but settled for a quick cold shower. Afterward, she felt slightly more alive. She found a shirt and pants in the closet, and judging from the size, they weren't Tayeh's. She didn't feel like sliding into the stiff leather gear that Tayeh wore.

The crew returned together, and this time, they weren't concerned about being quiet. They came inside with several bags each and dropped them in various places around the living room.

"Did you miss me?" asked Rev with a big smile. "I brought you some gifts!" She handed Ylena a bag filled with clothing. She grimaced at the baggy shirt and rolled up pants Ylena was wearing. "It looks like I got here just in time. You look tragic!"

Ylena stuck out her tongue, then looked into the bag with a smile. "I hope you found things that actually fit me and aren't way too short and tight!"

Rev gave her a wicked grin and set one of her other bags on the kitchen table. "I also got us some dinner. I hope you are hungry!" Ylena was still a little hesitant to eat, but it smelled good. "It's a curry that they say is another hangover cure. I'm not sure about that, but it definitely helps Grotto Indulgence live up to its name!"

Wilder, Quinn, and Tayeh were in the other room, dividing up little pouches and metal tools that Ylena couldn't identify, but at the smell of the food, they hurried into the kitchen. The five of them sat around the table, dipping the flatbread into the spicy sauce, and Ylena felt one small piece of her soul relax.

15

A fter dinner, they discussed their plans for the next day and then each moved on to separate activities. Quinn was engrossed in a book, Tayeh sharpened a knife, Wilder wrote in a little notebook, and Rev delicately folded the pile of clothing she had picked for herself. Ylena told them goodnight and slipped back into her room.

She locked the door and tried on some of the new clothes Rev had picked out for her. The sleek emerald pants and cropped navy shirt fit her perfectly. Ylena thought Rev might be a little too familiar with the size of her body, but the clothes were well made, so she decided to not complain about it.

She laced up her boots, grabbed her cloak, and quietly unlatched the lock on the window above the bed. Her arms shook as she pushed herself up and out the window. Her feet landed quietly on the ground, and she pulled the window closed behind her without letting it latch. She wrapped her cloak around herself and headed out to find Caed.

When she pieced together her fuzzy memories and

remembered what she did to him last night, she was horrified. She used a Gift of the Goddess to hurt him. She wasn't in her right mind at the time, but that wasn't a good enough excuse to ease her guilt. After mapping the location of this Grotto in her head, she knew Indulgence was underneath Temple Discipline, his home. She had to find him now before they moved on to another Grotto.

She had three ideas about where to look. She could leave the Underneath and try to find him in the temple, but that would use her one medallion, and she liked the idea of holding on to it for an emergency. She could go back to where she had seen him last night, but the Central Tavern was the last place she wanted to go. Or she could go toward the crystal spire and hope that she could catch him as he exited the stairway leading down from the temple.

She moved from shadow to shadow, and her cloak helped to hide her. The farther she moved away from Tayeh's house and toward the crystal, the stronger she felt. She had forgotten what it was like to have this sense of independence. No one was pulling her along. She chose to search for Caed, so she went.

As she moved through the Grotto, she saw streets full of bars and taverns. She heard people laughing a bit too loud and wondered if that's what she'd sounded like the night before. She remembered laughing and having fun, even though she found the missing parts of her memory disturbing.

She made it to the crystal spire and found an alley where she could watch the entrance to the staircase. A group passed her, carrying one of their friends who could barely walk, and there were people passed out in the streets, alone. She thought about Wilder and Tayeh carrying her and realized she must be one of the lucky ones.

Several people exited the staircase, but she could tell by

the way they walked that they weren't Caed. She was dreaming about the way Caed walked when he stepped into the alley beside her.

"What are you doing here?" he asked.

She was proud of herself for not flinching, even though her heart was beating wildly from the surprise. "I was looking for you. How did you find me?"

He looked embarrassed and couldn't meet her eyes. "I followed you from the house where you are staying."

"How did you know where I was staying? I didn't even know where I was staying until I woke up there this morning!"

"I followed you home last night. I wanted to make sure you made it there safely."

Now it was her turn to be embarrassed. "That was kind, especially considering how I treated you. Thank you."

"Not that I was especially pleased to see that it was Wilder who got to carry you home, but I was glad to know that you had a safe place to stay. You were not yourself."

Her embarrassment turned to shame. "Caed, I'm so sorry that I used a Gift against you. I could have seriously injured you. I came to find you because I need you to know how sorry I am."

His lips quirked up in a sweet smile. "Even though I do always love the surprise of you apologizing to me, Ylena, there isn't a need. I'm fine. And I probably deserved worse for cornering you in a dark hallway."

She raised a single eyebrow. "You realize you also just cornered me in a dark alley, right?"

He laughed. "It's a nasty habit, and now, I apologize to you." He reached down and took her hand. "Can we go sit somewhere that's not an alley and talk? The polite thing for me to do is to offer to buy you a drink, but I'm not sure if you'll think that is a good idea."

She laughed, and the sound echoed loudly in her head. "Definitely not! Maybe somewhere with dessert instead?"

"I know just the place." He took her hand and led her out of the alley.

Since they were in Indulgence, the location was still a bar, but they also served dessert. Caed ordered several of his favorite types of dessert for Ylena to try. She was licking the creamy chocolate mousse off her spoon when his voice turned serious.

"I had to find you to make sure you are okay. Your last night in the City ..."

"It was the worst night of my life." She studied the apple tart to avoid his eyes. "My soul alternates between stabbing pains and a dull ache."

"I'm so sorry, Ylena. I can't imagine what you've gone through. I wish I could help."

She put her spoon down and looked at him. "You can. You can tell me what I need to know."

He grimaced and tried to hide it by taking a bite of cheesecake.

"I'm serious, Caed. You could have told me the Underneath existed on the first day that I discovered the doors leading down here, but you didn't. Why?"

He set his spoon down and wiped his mouth with his napkin. "When I found you watching the entrance to the Underneath that night, so close to the Sentinels, I knew how dangerous it was for you to be there. You had already demonstrated the Gift of Discipline when I saw you dance, and I knew you were in danger because of that. But that night, you touched my hand and accidentally used your Gift of Knowledge on me. You showed me the moment when your grandfather walked away and left you all alone on the mountain. I could feel how betrayed you felt. How lonely you were."

She looked down at her plate. That moment was so clear in her mind, and she felt exposed knowing she had revealed that to him.

He gently reached for her hand. "I realized you had more than one Gift. I realized you were something special. Something I didn't expect." He sighed. "I'm sorry I'm not very good at handling surprises."

"But why didn't you tell me later? Did you think I wouldn't find out about an entire hidden city?"

"I hoped that once the Pageant was over, you wouldn't be under the eyes of the High Priests and would have a bit more freedom. I never imagined the Pageant would end that way."

They sat in silence for several minutes. Eventually, Caed stood and offered her his hand. "I know you don't need me to walk you home, but do you mind if I do?" She chuckled softly and took his hand.

They walked through the streets in a comfortable silence. When they reached Tayeh's house, they walked together to the back window she had left unlatched.

She turned to face him and looked up into his eyes. All of her thoughts seemed to float away as he leaned toward her, her lips parted. He was so beautiful with his serious eyes and his dark hair with a white streak ...

She stopped his forward movement by twisting her fingers around his white streak of hair. "How did you get this?"

He caught his breath and ducked his head. "Ah yes ... I was definitely going to mention that."

Ylena crossed her arms and narrowed her eyes.

Caed's voice was reluctant. "You know that the babies who manifest their Gift have one year to become bonded to the City, otherwise their hair turns completely white and..."

"And they die." Her voice was hard as stone. "Yes. Go on."

"The tears of those new Priest children were in the bowl you and Wilder poured into the basin during the Pageant." She nodded, and he continued. "At the end of every Pageant, every adult Priest in the City drops their own tears into the basin to be bonded to the City for another year. And well ... this year, the Pageant ended before we could put our own tears in. Several Priests have tried to bond themselves to the City the last few days, but no one has succeeded."

She stared at his white streak, trying to understand.

"It means that unless we find some way to bond to the City, every time a Priest uses their Gift, they get one step closer to death."

Ylena's eyes widened. "Oh, Caed! There has to be some way to fix this!"

He gave a smug grin. "I'm not upset about it. In fact, I think it's the best possible result from the whole terrible night. If Priests can't use their Gifts, the High Priests will lose the control they have over everyone. This will tear down the entire system better than I ever planned."

She looked at him with horror. "But you'll die!"

"I just can't use my Gift anymore. The babies don't have enough control to stop themselves, which is why it is so critical to get their tears into the basin each year. As long as I stop using my Gift, I'll survive."

"But you'll never be able to dance true again."

"It's a small sacrifice, but it's worth it if the High Priests are overthrown."

"So, there's no risk that you will accidentally use your Gift? None of the other Priests are in danger?"

"Um ... I'm sure we will all be fine."

She narrowed her eyes, and her voice went cold. "You could have mentioned this at any point tonight, but you didn't. You were going to kiss me goodnight and then walk away saying nothing. I can't believe after everything that has happened, you are still keeping secrets from me."

"I would have told you, Ylena, but—"

"Good night, Caed." She turned on her heel and climbed back through her window. She looked at him through the glass for a moment before pulling the curtains shut.

RIVALRY

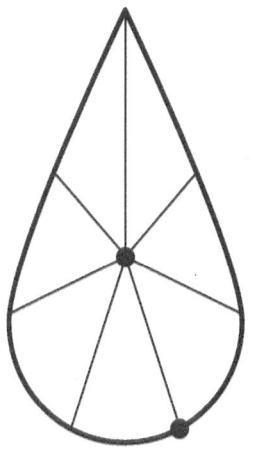

16

———

Ylena woke the next morning physically recovered, but her conversation with Caed the night before severely affected her mood. Luckily, her attitude fit in well for their next stop in Grotto Rivalry. Everyone in the Grotto seemed coiled and ready to spring, which was completely different from the laid back feel of Indulgence. Walking down the street, the crew encountered conversations that were argumentative at best, violent at worst.

The guards at the Warden's Den said they could find the Warden at the arena. On their way, they talked little, concentrating more on where they were walking. Several strangers had already yelled at them when they thought one of their crew was walking a bit too close. Quinn had accidentally bumped a man on the elbow, and the only thing that had stopped a full brawl was Tayeh stepping forward and staring the man down.

Ylena thought it might be less stressful when they arrived at the arena, but that was because she didn't know what an arena was. When they arrived at the towering stone structure in the middle of the Grotto, she realized that one of them could have warned her about this as well. The rows of stone benches reminded her of the amphitheater where they had performed the Pageant. Her anger flared up again when she realized Priests had built the building.

Tayeh led the rest of their group through the hallways of the arena, and she seemed familiar with the location. Outside of a stone doorway, she spoke to the guards, who then ushered their crew inside. The room was lavishly decorated in leather and fur rugs. At the front of the room, a wide door led out onto a balcony. A petite, dark-skinned woman stood alone with her arms resting on the balustrade, surveying the sandy pit down below.

She turned as they approached. "You must be the stars of the upcoming Spectacle. Welcome to Grotto Rivalry."

Tayeh took a step to the side to let Wilder talk. "Yes, Warden. Thank you for meeting with us."

The Warden looked Wilder up and down with a predatory grin. "It's a pleasure to meet with someone with your ... skills."

Ylena saw Tayeh's shoulder blades twitch. Wilder seemed a bit thrown off guard but recovered. "We heard you have some performers to recommend for the Spectacle."

"Grotto Rivalry has a wide range of performers. I'm sure you can find a few of them in your old stomping grounds, Wilder." She gave him a wink. A tremor passed through Tayeh's right hand.

The Warden gestured out to the sandpit. "You are in time to watch the next performance. These two will be a welcome addition to the Spectacle."

They all stepped closer to the balustrade. Down below, Ylena could see two young girls dressed in what appeared to be short, lacy nightgowns. Their hair was in pigtails, and they looked like sisters. They walked out into the center of the arena to cheers from the people seated on the stone benches. They each carried a long wooden staff, which they spun in a circle and then planted into the sand.

From another entrance walked a group of five large men. They were dressed in a mismatch of leather armor and dirt, and they strutted into the arena with cheers from another group of people in the stands. The men didn't appear to have any weapons other than their massive arms and fists, but Ylena could see them eyeing the wooden staffs at the girls' sides.

A bell rang, and the girls fell into a stance that looked similar to a kata Ylena learned in Temple Discipline. Their small bodies held the pose, waiting for the attack.

They didn't have to wait long. One man lunged forward to grab a girl, but she shot past him. He slid to a stop in the sand and turned to face her. The girl at his back picked up a staff and cracked him in the head. The sound of wooden staff against skull echoed through the arena. He crumpled to the sand. The crowd burst out in cheers.

The other four men looked like they were unsure what happened. It happened so quickly that even Ylena was shocked from her lookout above. The men shook off their surprise and reformed their line. Two of them signaled each other and headed toward the unarmed girl. The girl with the staff launched it into the air, and it landed in the waiting hand of her sister. She whipped the staff in front of her and spun it in a pattern that caused the men to slow their attack.

The next two men split off to advance on the other girl, but she had already grabbed the second staff and spun it in a similar pattern. Soon, there were two separate fights happening, and Ylena struggled to watch them both. The men warily eyed the girls as they whirled their staffs, but each man took turns trying to advance. Each time they got close, the girl would smack a wrist or an elbow or give a rap on their backside. The girls could have aimed for more debilitating areas, but Ylena got the sense they were playing with the men, like a cat with a mouse.

The crowd was cheering and laughing uncontrollably, and the men grew furious. Their attacks became frenzied, and they looked winded. One guy got lucky, and instead of getting smacked, he grabbed hold of the staff. He seemed surprised his attack had succeeded. He grinned and used his significantly greater weight to pull the staff toward himself.

As he pulled, the girl sprung up, allowing his weight to pull her forward, and her heel connected with his jaw. He dropped.

Ylena looked over at the other girl. She had knocked out one man who had been fighting her. The two girls swung their staffs and backed up toward each other.

The two remaining men were now full of rage and ran toward the girls, who stood back-to-back. As one, the girls spun apart, and the men stumbled to a stop side by side. The girls slid to opposite sides and rapped the men hard on the knees. As they stumbled off balance, the girls lunged and thrust the ends of their staffs at their chests. The men doubled over, and the girls twirled behind them and smacked them hard on the head. The men slumped forward in unison.

The girls stuck their staffs in the ground again, then turned toward the balcony to look up at the Warden. They held the edges of their lacy nightgowns and lowered into sweet little curtsies. The Warden nodded in approval. The girls grabbed the staffs out of the ground and skipped to exit the arena.

Ylena stared after them in shock. Their graceful moves

were choreographed with more precision than anything she had ever done in the Pageant. Their skills were a work of art. And yet she couldn't believe the violence that flowed from their small hands. Two men in the pit were sitting up slowly and trying to piece together what happened. But three men were not moving. Not at all.

She tried to imagine the number of hours, the number of years, that had gone into that sort of training. She couldn't imagine the girls had been alive that long. This training must have taken their entire life. She remembered herself at their age, living a hard life on the mountain, but she still enjoyed building snowmen in the winter and chasing butterflies in the summer. She was trying to imagine the girls' childhood when she realized the others were talking.

"They will be an entertaining addition to the Spectacle. Thank you, Warden," said Wilder.

The Warden stepped closer to him and rested a dark, manicured nail on his chest. "I look forward to you entertaining me soon, Wilder. I hope I don't have to wait until the Spectacle for you to perform for me."

Tayeh's eyes flashed, and she took a single step. Before her second step, the Warden twisted Tayeh's hand behind her back and slammed her against the wall. The rest of the crew stood frozen in place.

The Warden leaned forward and whispered into her ear. "You wear your emotions too clearly, my dear. You should spend more time in this Grotto so we can beat your telling behaviors out of you."

Tayeh's cheek was pressed up against the stone wall, and her thick, gossamer hair trembled with each furious breath. Her eyes burned with a dark fire, and she looked like barely contained violence. Wilder didn't move a step, but he whispered, "Please stop."

The Warden smiled and released Tayeh. "Since you asked so nicely, Wilder." She kissed her lips together as she walked back to the balustrade.

As they left, Ylena studied Tayeh's fierce eyes and knew it wasn't the Warden that Wilder had begged to stop.

17

They left the arena in silence. It wasn't until they had walked several blocks that Wilder spun on Tayeh and growled. "I can't believe you did that. You could have gotten us all killed!" Ylena held her breath. Other than some tense moments with Caed, Ylena had never seen Wilder angry before.

Tayeh chewed on her lip and couldn't meet his eyes. "You asked me to protect you."

Wilder's body was tense like he wanted to scream, but his voice came out in a harsh whisper. "If you ever have to protect us from a Warden, it means we are already dead, and you know it."

She blew her breath out in a sigh. "I know, I know. I was stupid, okay?"

"Yes, you were. The vibe you give off is kerosene to the people in this Grotto, Tayeh." He rubbed his forehead and took a deep breath. "You know where we are headed next. Can you handle this?"

Tayeh closed her eyes and shuddered. She opened her eyes and nodded.

Wilder led the silent crew down the street as Ylena wondered what would terrify Tayeh more than the arena.

～

Ylena spent the long and awkwardly silent walk peeking inside the buildings they passed. Almost every window she looked through showed people fighting. She saw boxing gyms, dojos, and signs advertising more types of fighting than she knew existed. The Grotto seemed to be filled to the brim with sweating and bleeding people.

Wilder surprised Ylena when he finally stopped. He took a deep breath and pulled open the door. The five of them stepped into a common room with people lounging on couches and sprawled on the floor.

The squealing started soon after.

Tayeh hovered in the doorway with Ylena, but a giggling crowd surrounded Wilder, Rev, and Quinn. "Wilder! We've missed you! ... Rev, I love what you are wearing! ... Quinn, are those new glasses? Did you miss me?"

The group was both male and female, and every one of them was beautiful and flirty with a sharp gleam in their eye.

A tall guy maneuvered his way to the front of the group. He swept his blond hair to the side and smiled, but his eyes narrowed slightly. "Welcome back, Wilder. I thought you had outgrown this place. What can we do to help a big star like you?"

"Hello, Kieran." Wilder smiled, but his voice was strained. "It's good to see you again."

"Oh, I'm sure it is." Kieran smiled and flipped his hair out of his eyes. He studied the rest of their group, and his gaze stopped on Ylena. "Who do we have here?" He took

Ylena's hand and raised it to his lips. "I'm Kieran. And you are?"

Her eyes were darting from person to person, trying to understand what was happening. She received a few angry glares at this attention from Kieran. "I'm Ylena." He seemed to wait for her to say more, but she felt that fewer words were probably safer at the moment.

Wilder stepped in to rescue her. "We're looking for the headmaster. Where is he?"

Kieran let go of Ylena's hand and turned back to Wilder. "You didn't get enough attention from the headmaster while you were here, so you came back for more?" He laughed like they were having fun together, but it was a forced laugh.

Wilder's smile was painfully fake. "You are the best, Kieran. Thanks for reminding me how much I loved my time here. I don't want to interrupt your serious work, so if you don't mind, I'll go find the headmaster myself." Wilder moved to step around him, but Kieran slid back in front.

"The headmaster is busy right now, but I will leave him a message and let him know you stopped by. Is there somewhere I can tell him you are staying? Or are you living on the streets like when you were younger?"

Several people behind Kieran giggled, and Wilder's face froze. Tayeh stepped forward, but Wilder gripped her hand to hold her in place. Ylena looked to Rev for help, but her eyes were darting around the room looking for someone. She turned to look at Quinn and realized he was gone.

"So, what's your message for him? I will pass it on." Kieran flipped his hair back again and folded his arms over his chest.

A bit of life seemed to escape Wilder, and he relented. "We are putting together a group of performers for the upcoming Spectacle being held at the Heart of the Grottos."

98

"And why did they pick you to do this?" Kieran's eyebrow raised in doubt.

"Ylena and I starred in the Pageant in the City, so it's a bit of revenge, I guess?" Wilder shrugged his shoulders.

At his words, the eyes of every girl in the group snapped to Ylena. She realized then exactly why this moment felt familiar. She wanted to growl at him when she heard Quinn's cheerful voice.

"Good news! I found the headmaster!"

The swarm broke apart at this news. Their crew passed between them and walked down the hallway to the headmaster's office, followed only by angry glares. Ylena walked beside Wilder and whispered furiously, "You said you'd prepare me if there was anything else I should know!"

"I'm sorry, Ylena. I should have warned you before I dropped you into an entire room of Liras, Goddess rest her soul." He glanced at Kieran, who was staring at him. "Believe me, I know what it is like." He continued down the hallway, and she followed with an angry grunt.

Lira wasn't the worst thing she'd had to deal with in the City, but she had definitely made Ylena's life miserable. The girls with Kieran knew what it meant for her to star with Wilder in the City, and she had seen murder in their eyes. And considering the sort of competition she had already seen in Rivalry, she thought that murder wasn't off the table.

"Wilder! It's so good to see you!" The headmaster came forward and kissed Wilder on both cheeks. He was gray-haired but looked a lot younger than Grandfather. He turned his sparkling eyes toward Ylena. "And this must be your Goddess." He gripped her with powerful arms and kissed both of her cheeks. He stepped back and looked at them both side by side. "I would have loved to see your performance. I bet it was phenomenal!"

"It started out great, but the ending left a bit to be

desired." Ylena regretted her words as soon as they left her mouth.

The headmaster's kind eyes dropped, and his smile fell. "That was insensitive of me. I don't know all the details, but I've heard rumors about how the night ended. I apologize."

Ylena bit her lips and nodded. Wilder cleared his throat. "Thank you for meeting with us, headmaster. Ylena and I are traveling to each of the Grottos to find performers, and we've brought along a crew to help with any unforeseen ... difficulties."

"Quinn mentioned that. I told him he could take Tayeh and Rev to the kitchen to see if there was anything to eat while the three of us talked." He ushered them into the chairs in front of his messy desk. "You know all the performers here, so I don't expect it will take you long to round them up. Although, I have a feeling that you could use my help with more than that."

"Have you heard any rumors about the Spectacle? It seems out of character for the Wardens."

The headmaster leaned back in his chair. "When the Wardens sent someone up to the Pageant, that shocked a lot of us. They had never worked together before that decision. No one knows what convinced them to work together."

"How did you get picked for the Pageant, Wilder?" Ylena had always wondered, and she felt like she was finally close to the answer.

The headmaster gave Wilder a fond smile. "Wilder joined our school to study with me several years ago. He's a natural talent, but I'm sure you already know that." Ylena nodded, because Wilder truly was an amazing singer and dancer. "He picked up a lot of valuable skills before he came to study here." At this, Wilder seemed embarrassed, even though he was usually cocky when he received compliments. "He learned everything I could teach him and then some. When the Wardens looked for the right person to audition for the Pageant, they came here. Rivalry is about competition in all forms, and in this challenge, Wilder was the victor."

"I'm guessing that Kieran was one of the other competitors?" she asked.

"Yes, he was! Among others. But Wilder has always been outstanding, so it wasn't surprising when he came out on top."

Ylena expected it was surprising to Kieran, but she kept that thought to herself.

"You asked about rumors," said the headmaster. "I have heard nothing definite. Just whispers. It surprised everyone that the Wardens worked together like this. That they chose you to be in the Pageant was a closely guarded secret, so most people believe this Spectacle is the first time the Wardens are working together. Many people assume this is the first step toward an uprising and that maybe at this Spectacle, the Wardens will explain their plans."

Wilder frowned. "The Wardens aren't known for explaining anything."

"No, they aren't," said the headmaster. "But there is a general sense of hope that the Spectacle will be the way to get the people of the Grottos excited about a revolution."

"So, if this performance has never happened before, what is this 'Heart of the Grottos' where it is taking place?" she asked.

The headmaster slipped into a teacher's voice. "The Heart is directly in the center of all the Grottos. Each Grotto has three tunnels leading from it: two lead out into the Grotto on either side and one tunnel leads to the Heart. Sometimes, people will conduct business there between Grottos, but not as often as you might think. The location is a little … creepy."

Ylena widened her eyes at this. Everyone in the Underneath was locked in an underground cave with no access to the sun, and there was a place that all of them thought was "creepy"?

"So, the Wardens are planning for all the people of the Grottos to meet there?" she asked.

"The place is like the amphitheater we performed in." Wilder's voice was a little sheepish at reminding her about that night.

"The people will risk the unsettling environment to finally hear some news about revolution." The headmaster's voice dropped to a whisper. "Promise me you will be careful, Wilder. I have a bad feeling about the Spectacle. I think the Wardens are planning something, and I'm worried you are stuck at the center."

Wilder frowned and looked at Ylena. "That's what we're worried about, too. I appreciate the warning, though. I do have a favor to ask. Would you mind letting us stay here a few nights? I'd love to spend an extra day or two in Rivalry, seeing what we can discover."

"Of course! We have several open rooms upstairs. You are always welcome here, Wilder."

"I should warn you as well. We think that there is someone looking for us. They destroyed Rev's house and sent us on the run. I don't want to put you at risk."

The headmaster laughed. "I'm not worried about that. We've got precautions in place. I'm more worried about you and any threats from within. I'm curious to see how some of your old rivalries play out." He smiled a wicked grin. He clearly cared about Wilder, but Rivalry was in his blood.

18

Ylena and Wilder left the other three at the school while they went to the Den for rehearsal. Considering how distracting Rev was at their last rehearsal and Tayeh's altercation with the Warden, they thought it might be best to limit the number of personalities in the room.

They entered the familiar rehearsal room and found Maestro reading alone at the table. "Hi, kids. The Little Warden isn't here yet, so have a seat." He lowered his silver head back to his book.

As they sat down, Wilder said, "Where did the Wardens find these performers? I am surprised none came from the school here."

Maestro shook his head. "I don't know where they found them. Thank the Goddess they're good, or I'd be even more fearful of my life than usual. As it is now, I don't have to do much to whip you kids into shape. They have clearly been rehearsing on their own for some time. I just have to tie all these pieces together in the end."

"You seem to know every little piece of the Pageant. Does everyone in the Underneath know it so well?" asked Ylena.

Maestro snorted. "Hardly. Most people in the Underneath have never heard a single song from the Pageant. My familiarity with the Pageant is the reason I was, shall we say … recruited … for this position."

"You aren't excited to be doing this?" asked Ylena.

Maestro looked at Wilder. "She really is new down here, isn't she?" Ylena ducked her head in embarrassment. Maestro continued, "No, I am not excited. I, like everyone else, wanted to live far removed from any of the Wardens' plans. Just the fact that they know my name puts me and my husband both at risk. I don't know who told the Wardens about my previous life, and they better hope I never find out."

Ylena would not get shamed for asking another question, so she kept her mouth shut. Luckily, Wilder had the same question she did. "What was your previous life?"

Maestro narrowed his gray eyes at Wilder and considered him a moment. He seemed to make some internal decision, because he sighed and sank back into his chair. "I'm from Upstairs. And I've starred in and directed the Pageant before."

"What happened?" Ylena breathed out the words before she could stop them. Luckily, he was caught up in storytelling mode, so he answered.

"I was born in Order Diocese, but when my parents saw I was a natural performer, we moved to Discipline so I could train with the Priests who taught singing and dancing. I soaked up everything they taught. And I'm not ashamed to say I was brilliant. I starred as the Companion twice, and then I became the youngest person to direct the Pageant. That year was particularly dazzling, if I say so myself. I was on track to direct for years to come, but I ran into a problem … Ty. We were always in the same dance classes, and he was jealous of me. He just lacked the spark.

And you maybe don't know this about me yet ... I can be a bit catty."

Ylena and Wilder tried to give innocent expressions.

"I never said anything that wasn't true. And he was just as vicious. When I took the role of Director for the second year in a row, I thought I had won, but Ty wasn't content to let me enjoy my success. One day, I was drinking my morning tea, and the next thing I knew, I woke up on my kitchen floor. Ty had broken in to my house and put something into my tea that caused me to pass out and miss a full day of rehearsal. That kind of 'laziness' is not tolerated Upstairs. I was frantic and started throwing all of my belongings into a bag. The Sentinels burst in the front door as I escaped out the back. I ran to Temple Perfection to avoid the Sentinels from Discipline. The Sentinels in Perfection let me through the doors, and I've lived down here ever since."

"I'm sorry," said Ylena.

"Why are you apologizing? The Priests are the ones to blame. You aren't a Priest, are you?"

Ylena tried to blink away the tears that had sprung up at his story. "Um ... no?"

"It doesn't matter now anyway. That was so many years ago, and it feels like a different life. I made a new life down here with Pierce, and that's what I have to protect. There isn't anywhere to run beyond this."

Ylena was going to ask him more, but a young performer who looked like Rivalry's Warden walked in. She was petite with glowing dark skin and close shaved hair.

"Let's do this. I'm ready to perform."

"It's good to see you too, Aminah." Maestro sighed. "Let's take your number from the top."

Ylena and Wilder learned where they would stand, and it was farther away than usual. Part of Aminah's song would include a fight scene with the two girls from the arena, and they needed plenty of room to move. The girls wouldn't be there today, but Aminah was clearly trained in a similar style of fighting. She practiced her portion of the choreography, and even without the other two girls, Ylena felt a sense of danger in the room. She was glad when Maestro said they had rehearsed enough.

"I will see you at the next Grotto, children. Be safe out there, okay?"

Ylena looked at the tiny yet dangerous body of the Little Warden and nodded.

19

R ev, Quinn, and Wilder had all studied with the headmaster at what Ylena understood was a type of performing arts school. She wanted to hear the stories of how they met and what they had studied, but Tayeh pulled her aside as the other three were catching up with the current students.

"I think you'd like to come with me to do some training." Tayeh mumbled the words.

"What kind of training? Shouldn't we stay here with the others?"

Tayeh was fidgeting with a buckle on her leather vest. "You know ... training." She shrugged. "I am guessing you don't have much fighting experience."

"I don't have any experience." Ylena looked at the others sitting on couches and laughing at old stories. She really wanted to stay. But Tayeh seemed more uncomfortable than Ylena had seen her before, and she took pity on her. "I guess it would be nice to get out of here for a while." Tayeh gave a relieved sigh and led her out of the school.

They didn't have far to go since there was a gym on every corner. When Tayeh walked inside, Ylena saw her strong shoulders relax. Tayeh looked around the gym and actually smiled.

"Come on, Ylena. Let's go hit some stuff." Tayeh led her inside.

They walked to a corner of the room, where a thick canvas bag hung by a rope from the ceiling. "Have you ever hit one of these?" Tayeh asked her.

"The only type of fighting I've ever done is learning some katas from Temple Discipline." She remembered flipping Wilder on his back that afternoon, but she was pretty sure she couldn't replicate that move if she tried.

Tayeh snorted. "The Priests study the different styles of fighting, but they don't get a chance to use them in a practical way like we do down here. What you learned is the basis for the type of fighting the girls in the arena used. I assume it was obvious how different that was from Upstairs?"

"The demonstration I saw from the Priests was beautiful and looked more like dancing than fighting. Those girls ... Some of their moves resembled choreography, but they were vicious. I think they killed several of those men." Ylena was still shaken by the thought that the young girls were trained to murder.

Tayeh nodded. "I'm glad you picked up on the viciousness. That is exactly what it takes to survive down here. Those girls learned what they needed in order to survive. You need to learn the same."

Ylena thought about the sound of the wooden staff cracking against the first man's head. She whispered, "I don't think I can do what they did."

Tayeh laughed. "Of course you can't! Those girls have been training since they were infants. I only have a few days with you."

Ylena frowned. "That's not exactly what I mean."

"I know what you mean. You don't know if you could hurt another person like that." Tayeh slapped the hanging bag with an open hand. "Even if someone was threatening your life, you think you might freeze." She balled her hand into a fist and threw it into the side of the bag. "You worry you'd hesitate and end up injured." She gripped the side of the bag and thrust her knee upward. "You aren't sure you could consider the weakest part of a human body and hit there." She kicked the heavy bag, and as it swung, she stepped close to Ylena. "Those things might happen to you. Or they might not. You won't know for sure until that moment."

Ylena grabbed the bag and stopped it from swinging. "What do I do?"

"Prepare for what you can." Tayeh smacked her hand against the bag again. "Imagine this is a big, scary guy coming at you. What's the first thing you should do?"

Ylena stared at the bag. "Umm ... I guess try to hit him?"

"No. The first thing you do is run. Run as fast and as far as you can."

"Oh. I guess that makes sense."

"You aren't a trained fighter, and you probably won't ever be. Your first response should be to escape. Especially down here, where you are surrounded by fighters. You run, okay?"

"I've run before." Her voice trembled as she remembered running on the night of the Pageant. She wanted to help her friends, but she just ran and hid.

"I assume that the reason you are alive right now is that you ran, correct?" Ylena nodded, and Tayeh continued. "Then you made the right choice. Sometimes, running is the last thing you want to do, but you have to know when to escape and live to fight another day." Tayeh smacked the bag again. "Let's say they grab you so you can't run. What do you do?"

"Hit him now?"

"Sure. Hit him anywhere he is weak. Poke him in the eyes. Kick him in the crotch. Bite him until he lets you go. And then what?"

"Um ... run?"

Tayeh smiled. "You are a quick learner. I can work with that." She pulled Ylena forward until she was standing right in front of the bag. "Put your hands into fists." Ylena did, but Tayeh took hold of her fingers and folded them the correct way. "Good. Now give this bad guy a hard punch to slow him down so you can run."

Ylena punched the bag. She grimaced at both the pain of her knuckles and the fact that the bag didn't budge at all.

"You definitely aren't getting away with a weak punch like that. Haven't you ever been angry enough to want to hurt someone?"

Ylena took inventory of her life and realized that no, she had never been angry like that. "In dangerous situations, I've been scared, not angry."

Tayeh nodded. "That's understandable. But you can shape your anger into a weapon." She blew out a breath. "You maybe noticed today that my anger almost got us all killed by the Warden." Ylena gave an innocent look like she didn't know what Tayeh meant, but she remembered the moment vividly. "The hardest thing is to control that weapon without it controlling you. Close your eyes. Think back on one of those times that you were afraid and wanted to act but couldn't."

Ylena didn't want to remember the night of the Pageant, but it was the clearest example. She thought about how she ran away with Caed and hid. She could hear the heavy boots of the Sentinels stomping on the stage below her. Then, the screams and the sounds of the falling bodies of her friends.

"You remember how afraid you were?" Ylena nodded

with her eyes closed. "Dig beyond that feeling of fear to the anger. Do you know who you were angry at?" Ylena nodded again. "Then open your eyes and punch again."

Ylena saw the masked face of a Sentinel and punched him. She was terrified and punched him again. She was angry at the High Priests too, so she imagined punching each one of them individually. The fear seemed hidden beneath the anger. She punched Lady Erenne for betraying her. And Wilder for abandoning her. She punched Caed for leading her away instead of helping her rescue the others. And her grandfather for lying to her about her parents and leaving her alone on the mountain. She was angry at all of them, and she kept punching until she realized who had made her the most angry.

Herself.

She punched herself for going along with Lady Erenne's secret plans. She punched herself for not seeing that Wilder was hiding something from her. She punched herself for allowing Caed to lead her away. She punched herself for abandoning Pim to die. She punched herself for being born to parents who died because of her. She punched herself for ever walking down the side of the mountain.

She punched until her hands fell limply at her sides and took a shuddering breath in.

"You are definitely a quick learner," said Tayeh with a soft voice. "Your moves weren't pretty like anything you would learn Upstairs, but if you learn how to tap into that when necessary, you will do what it takes." She pointed at a bench along the wall. "Go sit over there. I'll get you something to take care of your hands."

Ylena looked down at her heavy hands and realized they were cut and bleeding. She hadn't felt her hands at all when she was punching, but now, they felt stiff and sore.

Tayeh sat down next to her on the bench. She cleaned

Ylena's hands with a liquid that burned, but Tayeh's hands were gentle as she wrapped Ylena's knuckles with bandages.

Ylena felt the tears drying against her cheek at the same moment she felt the pain throbbing through Tayeh's shoulder. She wasn't moving any differently, but Ylena could feel Tayeh's injured shoulder like it was her own. She gasped and looked into Tayeh's eyes. "What happened to your shoulder?"

"You were there. I let my anger get the best of me." She winced as she tried rolling her shoulder. "The Warden is a lot stronger than she looks."

"Why didn't you say something? You know I can ..." She looked around nervously. "You know."

Tayeh frowned. "I deserved what I got. It's a good reminder for me to be more strategic with my anger."

Ylena felt the pain of her shoulder shooting down Tayeh's arm and into her hand. She couldn't let her continue like that. "It's your job to protect me, right?" Tayeh nodded slowly. "I don't think you can do that job effectively while injured. I'd rather you were at the top of your abilities."

Tayeh stared at her through narrowed eyes.

Another tactic. "Are you afraid of being healed?" She said it with a teasing voice, but by the look on Tayeh's face, she thought she made a direct hit.

"I'm not afraid!" Tayeh whispered harshly.

Ylena gave her a comforting smile. "It won't hurt. In fact, it will be quite the opposite."

Tayeh growled. "Fine. Do what you want. It's no big deal." She angled her shoulder toward Ylena and looked away.

Ylena touched her fingertips to the bare skin of Tayeh's arm. She spoke to muscle and tendon and blood and told them to return to their proper places. Tayeh's eyes widened slightly, and she shivered. She rolled her shoulder around several times and sighed.

"Thanks for letting me help," said Ylena with a small smile.

Tayeh's expression didn't change, but Ylena could see the laughter in her eyes. "I will beat up lots of people on your behalf to repay you for that."

20

Ylena finally escaped to the small bedroom that had been assigned to her. There wasn't much in the room other than a bed, but she crawled out onto the little balcony and admired her view of the soaring crystal above the neighboring buildings. She had hoped that the air out on the balcony would help her feel less trapped, but there wasn't much wind in the Underneath. The breathable air must come from hidden vents, but it wasn't enough to cause any noticeable wind currents.

She leaned her head back against the building and tried to remember the feel of the biting wind coming down from the mountain when Wilder stepped out onto his balcony next door.

He smiled when he saw her and asked, "Mind if I join you?"

She considered the distance between their balconies and said, "I'm curious to see you try."

He grinned as if she had challenged him. The balconies were narrow platforms with an iron railing. Wilder climbed to the outside of his railing and turned his body to face her. Then, he let go.

He leapt across the expanse and caught himself on the bars of her balcony. The platform shook under the impact, and her hands automatically reached to the bars to brace herself. He smiled a wide grin and stepped easily over her railing and lowered himself to her side.

"Let me guess. You've done that before."

He grinned. "A time or two."

"Are you glad to be back?"

He leaned his head against the wall. "It's complicated."

She didn't know what else to say, so she waited for him to talk. She leaned her head against the wall and closed her eyes.

"I grew up alone on the streets. Kieran wasn't lying about that." Wilder's voice was quiet. Ylena opened her eyes but didn't turn to look at him so as not to startle him from his tale. "There are a lot of kids who grow up on the streets down here, so I wasn't unusual in that way. My father wasn't interested in being a parent. When I was five years old, he did a good enough deed for a Warden to earn his own medallion, and he escaped up to the City. He left me with my mother. She was ... She never should have been trusted with a child." He paused long enough that she wasn't sure he would continue. "I was eight when I escaped."

She turned her head and looked at him. "You had to escape?"

He shrugged. "They were both terrible people. Even as an orphan, I was better off without them."

Ylena was still upset with her grandfather for keeping so much from her, but she couldn't imagine what her childhood would have been like if she didn't have him. Or if he had hurt her.

Wilder continued, "It's usually easier for an orphan to survive if they stay in the same Grotto where they were born, but my father made several enemies before he left, so it wasn't safe for me to stay. I traveled from Grotto to Grotto for a while, but I never had a place I could call home. Until I met the headmaster. He heard me one day as I was trying to earn a few coins by singing. He convinced me to come study with him here. I met Rev and Quinn and found the first friends of my life. We found Tayeh one day at the gym across the street. Those years before the Pageant audition were the best of my life." He sighed. "This school has the sharp edge of Grotto Rivalry, but it really has been my home."

"I found the arena pretty disturbing, but I admit, some kids in this school are terrifying." They both grinned.

He stood up. "I should go. I want to spend some time tomorrow checking in with my other contacts in Rivalry to see if they have any idea what the Wardens are planning for the Spectacle. Maybe they will know if there are any rumors about the Underneath's new child Priests or whatever they are calling them. And hopefully someone can tell us what is happening in the City. I haven't heard what's happened up there since the Pageant, and it would be helpful to know how the High Priests are reacting."

Ylena realized she knew a piece of critical information from the City. The Priests couldn't use their Gifts without risking their life. But she'd learned that piece of news from Caed. She wasn't sure if she wanted to share with Wilder that she had been in contact with Caed. They didn't exactly get along. Plus, she wasn't sure if anyone in the crew would trust the words of a Priest.

"Yes, that would be helpful to know. I can ask some random people tomorrow, if that would be useful?" Maybe she could pretend to get the information from someone else.

"Thanks, Ylena." He climbed over her railing. "I'm glad you are here." He smiled and jumped back onto his balcony.

Her platform shook again, and she reached out a hand to steady herself out of instinct.

She scraped her injured knuckles on the balcony, and it caused her eyes to water. She was glad Wilder had already climbed back through his window, because she was embarrassed to admit how bad her hands still hurt from her fight with the punching bag earlier.

It had felt good to get angry instead of living in the fear and sadness that had trapped her for days. She thought of all the people she was angry with, but her mind got stuck on Caed. How could he continue to keep so many secrets from her? His hair was turning white because he had used his Gift without bonding the City. She wondered how often the Priests could use their Gifts before they died. She was still angry at Caed but wished there was some way she could find him to ask him more questions.

She sighed and leaned her head against the wall again. A gray cat was sitting on the windowsill beside her. She looked over the side of her balcony and into her locked room and tried to figure out where it had come from. The cat hopped down from the windowsill and walked lazily to the edge of the balcony and looked over the edge. Then, it looked back at her.

"Um ... are you trying to get me to follow you?" The cat sat down and looked at her with a condescending glare. She couldn't tell if it was trying to communicate with her or if that was just his regular cat face. She stood up. "I'm free. I guess I can go with you."

The cat gave a purr like a grunt and jumped off the edge of the balcony to the street below. Ylena grabbed her cloak from her room. She stepped over the edge of the railing closest to the building and lowered herself from the edge until her feet grazed the top of a large trash bin. She jumped down, and the cat ignored her by licking his backside.

"I'm sorry I took so long. Was there something you'd like to show me?" The cat stretched lazily and trotted down the road.

She felt ridiculous following a cat to a location unknown; however, she had once followed a mouse and that had turned out well, so she thought she'd try. The cat turned down dark roads and even darker alleys. When he got too far ahead, he would sit down in the road to bathe himself like he was out for a leisurely stroll. They turned down another alley, and suddenly, he stopped directly in front of a door.

"So, there is something special here?" The door looked like almost every other door that led into the alley. "Okay, I'll try it." She put her hand on the doorknob, but the cat was licking himself again right in front of the door. "Um ... excuse me? Can I ...?" The cat finished his bath on his own schedule and sauntered away.

Ylena opened the door and found herself in a room packed with yelling people. She couldn't tell what they were yelling about, so she pressed her way further into the crowd. She came to a stone railing that surrounded a pit similar but much smaller than the arena. Two men were grappling along one of the far walls, and as they spun around, Ylena recognized Caed.

He was shirtless, and his lean body shone with sweat. His dark hair with the white streak was tousled delightfully. He threw a punch, and she saw each individual muscle along the right side of his body in perfect definition under the glowing crystalline lamps. She raised an appreciative eyebrow and thought she owed that cat a nice saucer of milk.

Caed was wrestling with a hairy man who had more bulk but nowhere close to Caed's amount of muscle. Caed's body was refined by years of dance training and, judging from his skill against his competitor, years of fight training as well. She was fascinated by his movements. Every dodge as precise and each punch as strong as his dancing.

She shook herself out of the trance of watching him move to ask herself what he was doing here. Why was he sparring in a random fight pit in Rivalry? What did this have to do with anything?

Caed maneuvered his arms around the man's neck. The man was already winded, so it didn't take long for him to fall limply to the ground. Caed stepped over him and shook out his muscles as the crowd around the pit cheered and groaned in equal measure. He walked over to the stone ledge and pulled himself up and out of the pit.

Ylena cut through the crowd until she was close enough to see that he was at the edge of the pit talking to a tall woman with bright red lips. The woman put something into his hand, but Ylena couldn't see what it was. The woman's hand lingered on Caed's, and she bit her red lips and smiled.

Ylena's eyes narrowed. All of Caed's secrets were piling up around her, and she wished she had a punching bag available at that moment. The woman withdrew her hand from Caed's and gave him a lingering glance over her shoulder as she sauntered away.

Caed turned around to leave and caught Ylena's eyes across the pit. She assumed he saw the anger in her eyes, and she was glad about that. She hoped he was too far away to see the hurt.

He opened his mouth like he could speak to her across the entire fighting pit, then pushed through the crowd in her direction. She spun around and slipped out the door she had come through. Outside, she saw the gray cat sleeping on top of a pile of wooden crates beside the door. She climbed up the crates and pulled herself on top of the roof. She crawled into an overhang and waited.

Caed came out the door and ran to the end of the alley, looking onto the side streets to see where she had gone. Eventually, he gave up and walked back to the door. She saw him brush his white-streaked hair out of his eyes, and she narrowed her eyes in anger.

The cat reached out and scratched Caed's hand before running away.

21

Ylena awoke again with no idea where she was. She shook off a bad dream and could eventually place herself mentally in Grotto Rivalry. The glow from the crystal was shining through the window in exactly the same way as it was when she finally had crawled into bed last night. She wasn't sure what time it was, but she smelled coffee coming from somewhere and decided it was possibly morning.

She was on her second cup when Wilder wandered into the dining hall. He grabbed a cup for himself and joined her at a table.

"I'm going to check out a few places in Rivalry today. Would you like to come with me?" he asked.

"Sure! I'd love to look around." She wanted to find out what Caed was doing last night, and maybe she could find out more if Wilder was with her.

"Well, don't you two look cute together?" Kieran slid into the seat next to Ylena and smirked at Wilder. "I'm sure the two of you drank coffee together a lot when you were performing up in the City. The two of you performing as Goddess and Companion, it's just so … quaint."

"Can we help you with something, Kieran?" Wilder's voice was polite, but only just so.

"Can't I just catch up with an old friend?" His mocking smile grated against Ylena.

Wilder was silent and drank his coffee.

"I hope we will get to see the two of you perform for us at some point?" Kieran blinked his wide, innocent eyes. "Since the other students and I are auditioning for the Spectacle tonight, it would be helpful for us to see what kind of performance you actually put on in the City. I'm sure it was simply adorable."

Ylena blinked slowly and tried to imagine words she could say to fight back, but her brain only thought about punching.

"I know they had to pick you, Wilder. You were the only one here that could pull off something so pedestrian and contrived." Each statement was an obvious attempt to get Wilder to react, but his face was completely calm.

Kieran shifted his attack. "Ylena, I hope we get to hear you sing. I'd love to watch you perform for me." He gave her a look that made her feel distinctly uncomfortable.

Wilder didn't react in the competitive way he normally did around Caed, but Kieran could see that he had found a weak spot.

"If you've only ... performed with Wilder, you don't even know what you are missing yet." He was leering at Ylena, but his eyes kept flicking to Wilder to see his reaction.

Wilder opened his mouth to respond when Tayeh rescued them. "Come on, you two. We have somewhere to be."

They hadn't made any definite plans the night before, but Wilder and Ylena followed her out the door like they had been expecting it.

Once they made it outside, Wilder said, "Thanks, Tayeh."

"No problem. That guy is a jerk."

"So, where are we heading?" asked Ylena.

"I want to check in with some people I know," said Wilder as he led them down the street. "Someone has to have a clue what the Wardens are planning at the Spectacle."

"I didn't bring enough coin to buy that sort of information," said Tayeh.

Wilder's lips curled in a slow smile. "Now, Tayeh, you know I have always been able to get information I want without resorting to bribes." Ylena rolled her eyes, but she was secretly glad to see some of the old Wilder back.

Tayeh grunted. "We'll see if you lost all your skills while you were Upstairs."

Wilder swaggered inside a building similar to the one where she had seen Caed fighting. There was a raised stage where two people boxed. A crowd surrounded them, cheering and yelling. Wilder cut through the crowd, but Tayeh pulled Ylena over to a bar along the wall.

Tayeh called the bartender over, and Ylena got a panicked look in her eyes. "I'm not sure I'm ready to drink anything they serve down here!" She just woke up and didn't feel like passing out again.

Tayeh gave her a flat stare. "Order one drink and hold it. You look suspicious if you linger in a place like this without a drink in your hand. Or I guess you could stand over there screaming for one of those guys to win?"

Ylena looked at the sweaty crowd packed closely around the stage. She ordered a drink.

Tayeh leaned back against the bar. "You can always count on Wilder to show off, and it looks like he's going to perform for us." Ylena turned to see Wilder across the room talking to a beautiful woman.

His wide smile was back, and he stood close enough to the woman to create an intimate moment between them. The woman twirled her blond hair in her fingers, and she bit her lip coyly as she stared up into his dark eyes. Wilder looked at her like she was the only woman in the world. He had caught Ylena in that stare before, and she felt a little sorry for the woman. Wilder tucked a strand of the woman's blond hair behind her ears, and Ylena felt an unexpected emotion flare up inside.

Tayeh laughed. "Looks like he's still got it. That girl will tell him everything she knows."

Ylena tossed back the drink in her hand and ordered another.

Tayeh and Ylena watched as Wilder worked his way around the room, gathering information while leaving a trail of swooning women behind.

"So, are we just going to stand here drinking while he does this all day?" asked Ylena.

Tayeh raised an eyebrow. "You don't find this entertaining?"

"I assumed you'd rather be doing something more active. Can't we gather information, too?"

Tayeh grunted. "My method of gathering information usually ends with someone bleeding. I try to do that only when necessary."

"I just didn't expect my entire day to be spent watching Wilder seducing a room full of women."

"You get used to it." Tayeh signaled the bartender for another drink.

"Maybe there is some way for me to gather information." Ylena tried to speak casually. "If I could talk to the people I knew Upstairs, maybe I could find some information about what is happening up there."

Tayeh narrowed her eyes. "I thought that everyone you knew except Wilder died."

"I ... uh ... I also knew a Priest."

"A Priest?" Tayeh spit on the floor. "What good would that do us? Do you expect a Priest to be honest with you?"

Ylena opened her mouth, but then shut it again. "You've got a point there."

"Obviously. A Priest will only tell you what is in their best interest. You can't trust a single word that comes out of their mouth."

Ylena nodded absently. Tayeh's words struck a little too close to home with her experience with Caed. The other Priest she knew was Lady Erenne, who didn't even tell Ylena she was a Priest until Ylena realized she was the next High Priest of Purpose.

Ylena saw Wilder slide into a chair across from a woman whose low-cut dress strategically highlighted her cleavage. The woman's eyes lit up, and she reached her hands across the table to put her hands possessively on his arms.

Ylena left her empty glass on the bar. "I think I'll wander around and see if I overhear anything interesting."

Tayeh shrugged and settled back against the bar.

Ylena threaded her way through pockets of cheering fans. She avoided couples hanging on one another and tried to listen to anything that sounded like gossip. Eventually, she realized the only way you could hear anyone speak was to stand as close as Wilder stood next to each woman he approached. She frowned and headed back to the bar.

"Ylena? Is that you?" She turned to see who had called her name but couldn't find a face she recognized.

Someone grabbed her from behind and twisted her arm behind her back. Every thought of defending herself fled, and her mind was blank with panic. A man's hand clamped over her mouth, and the unknown attacker pushed her toward a door in the back of the building. Her feet skidded on the ground, trying to slow down, but the man twisted her arm further, and she moved forward while trying to squirm out of his grip.

The man released Ylena suddenly, and she stumbled away from him. She was about to run when she realized Tayeh had an arm clamped around the man's neck. His hands fumbled on her arms, trying to break her hold. When he realized he wasn't strong enough to pull her arms away, he slammed back into the wall, smashing her against the stone.

Tayeh's breath escaped in a rush, and she released him. He rubbed his throat and turned to face her, but she was already moving. She kicked him in the knee, punched him in the ribs, and struck him on the jaw in quick succession.

Tayeh turned to Ylena and yelled, "Why aren't you running away?"

Ylena stood frozen, but the man took Tayeh's advice and ran out the back door. Tayeh took a few steps to follow him, but after she realized Ylena was still unmoving, Tayeh returned to her side.

"I couldn't run, because I couldn't move at all," said Ylena numbly.

Tayeh sighed and put her arm around Ylena's shoulder. "It happens to the best of us sometimes. Let's rip Wilder away from his lady friends and get back to the school, okay?"

Ylena nodded and let herself be led away.

～

As they walked back to the school, Tayeh told Wilder about the attack. "I shouldn't have let her wander off by herself. She's not used to all the weirdos that roam around the Underneath."

"He knew my name." Ylena's voice was quiet, but Tayeh and Wilder both stopped walking.

"You knew him?" asked Wilder.

"No. But he knew me. He called my name and grabbed me when I turned around."

Tayeh and Wilder exchanged looks and then continued walking. Wilder spoke first. "The High Priests must have sent him. They know our names and what we look like. They are still furious about what happened at the Pageant, and they won't stop looking for us. We just have to be more careful from now on."

Tayeh frowned. "Please tell me you learned something helpful in there. Surely one of those women surrendered all her secrets to you."

Wilder was subdued after the attack on Ylena, but a bit of his cocky smile surfaced. "They told me oh so many secrets. Unfortunately, not all of them apply to us. I learned that fighters in places like that are being recruited for some special tasks for the Wardens."

Ylena wondered if that was what Caed had been doing when she had seen him the night before. Maybe he was trying to get recruited by the Wardens to see what they were planning. He could have saved her the speculation if he told her what he was doing. But once again, he chose to keep his plans to himself.

"No one has any word about the children whose tears I poured into the basin. If there are any toddlers roaming around with powers, no one is talking about it." He frowned. "And no one has any information about what is happening

Upstairs. Apparently, the High Priests have locked down every entrance, and no one is going up or down."

Ylena furrowed her brow and wondered how Caed was getting in and out. Or maybe he was only living in the Underneath now? She wanted to reveal to Wilder and Tayeh what she knew about the Pageant failing and how the Priests' Gifts would slowly drain their life away, but she didn't want to explain how she found out. And there was a part of her that felt like revealing that information would be a betrayal of Caed. Even though she still felt betrayed by him, she didn't want to reveal his weakness to the others.

"I didn't find out everything I wanted, but gathering the information was a real pleasure." He smirked, and both Tayeh and Ylena groaned.

22

After their time gathering information, Wilder, Tayeh, and Ylena returned to the school to make plans with the rest of the team. Rev said that they would hold an audition later that night to decide who from the school would perform at the Spectacle. By the look on Wilder's face, Ylena could tell he was not looking forward to it.

Their crew was invited to eat dinner in the common room with the rest of the students. Ylena tried to eat her food quietly without drawing attention to herself. It was clear this was a group of performers. They each took turns trying to top each other with the most outrageous story. It felt familiar to her time with the cast of the Pageant, except with a sharp edge running through the center.

They told stories about Rev that poked fun at how flirty she was. She laughed along, but some stories were about failed relationships and clearly intended to wound. They told stories about how brilliant Quinn was. How brilliant, and yet so hopelessly unaware. They told stories about Wilder. About how he was always so talented! Which was so surprising considering the headmaster found him on the streets as a dirty orphan.

With every humorous yet terrible story, she felt the injuries inflicted. The dinner table felt as dangerous as the arena. She wished she had the skills to fight back, but instead, she ran away by sitting quietly. Rev, Quinn, and Wilder weren't defenseless, though. They had their own stories to fight with, but she felt like they were currently losing this competition.

The storytelling was still going strong when the headmaster came to the rescue and lead them to the school's theater, where they would hold the audition. Wilder's face was still grim, and Ylena realized they were taking a deeper step into the competition.

"Welcome to the audition!" The headmaster stood on the stage and looked out onto Ylena's crew and the non-auditioning students sitting in the audience. "Our school is contributing performers to the Spectacle, and here in Rivalry, a competition is the only way to decide who is worthy enough to be selected. Let's begin!" He moved to a seat in the audience.

One of the first things Ylena realized during the audition was that the Underneath had a wide variety of songs, but the only songs she knew were from the Pageant. Some lyrics caused Ylena to blush furiously. Some songs were so hilarious she couldn't control her laughter. And some lyrics were so violent they sent a shiver down her back.

She also understood exactly how skilled these students were. She had performed with the best singers and dancers the City offered, and every single student on the stage could have joined them. The students were just as skilled as the Pageant team had been, and they performed with a level of intensity Ylena and the others only had when they were being stared down by Sentinels.

Ylena was trying to decide how they would pick who should go to the Spectacle when Kieran walked onto the stage. She noticed Wilder tense slightly in the seat by her side.

"Good evening, ladies and gentlemen." His commanding voice carried through the theater. "For my audition piece, I would like to perform something from the Pageant. I could use a skilled Goddess at my side. Would you consider joining me, Ylena?"

She heard a few of the girls in the crowd whispering furiously, and she blinked her eyes, trying to understand what was happening. The headmaster clapped his hands. "That's an excellent idea! You will assist him, won't you, Ylena?"

Wilder's mouth drew into a thin line, and Rev growled softly. Ylena stood up slowly, walked down the aisle, and climbed onto the stage.

Kieran brushed his blond hair out of his eyes and gave her a smug smile. "I thought we could perform the first scene of Act Three, if you remember that one."

That was the scene when Wilder had abandoned her. The scene when she believed the High Priests might murder her. The scene when she danced with Caed in the most thrilling moment of her life, right before her tears broke the City and led to the death of her friends.

"Yes. I remember that one."

He walked to stage left, and she remained at center stage. The low drone from the strings began, and she heard the note in her mind a moment before she sang it. She heard the note for what it was.

A weapon. And one she finally knew how to use.

She pulled the note down from where it floated above the theater and plunged it into the hearts of everyone in the crowd. The melody shivered through the air and blew a frozen breeze down their necks. Her song filled every nook of the theater until there was no air to breathe except for what she allowed. She was the music, and she knew this was a battle she could win.

She was ready when she felt Kieran's hand at her back, and she spun away from him and allowed him to pull her back. His voice was warm and strong, and he moved through all the steps flawlessly. She wasn't sure what he hoped to gain by choosing something from the Pageant, but in this, he had made a critical error. In the Pageant, the Goddess was the only star.

Ylena ruled the stage. Kieran looked at her at all the right times, but his role as the Companion was to stare at her adoringly, which only strengthened her melody. He never dropped a line or missed a step, but Ylena could tell that he realized his mistake. He tried to recover by directing his charming smile at the audience, but that only caused him to look ridiculous.

Their dance together wasn't playful like when she danced with Wilder or as passionate as her dance with Caed. With Kieran, each step was a contest. Each note, a duel. And they both knew from that first note that she would emerge the victor.

When they hit the final climactic note, she sensed his relief even though he revealed nothing but a smile. She gave him a courteous bow and walked back to her seat in the crowd with a casual stride. She was back in her seat before the crowd had fully realized what happened.

Rev, Quinn, Tayeh, and the headmaster broke out in applause and cheers. There were mixed reactions from the students in the crowd. Some sat with mouths open, and some joined in the applause. Wilder turned to look at her with calm, dark eyes. He nodded his head a single time and turned back to the stage with head held high.

~

After Ylena's performance with Kieran, their crew spoke to the headmaster about who should go to the Spectacle. Based on the performances, they agreed on six students, which didn't include Kieran. The students agreed to work on their respective pieces and show up prepared for the Spectacle.

The crew agreed to leave early the next morning to travel to Grotto Instinct. Wilder caught Ylena before she made it to her room.

"Thanks for what you did on stage tonight. Your singing was beautiful as always, and it was so satisfying to watch Kieran realize he wasn't the star." He gave a wicked grin.

"I've felt a little useless lately, so it was nice to find something I could actually do for once."

"It's easy to feel useless living in the Underneath. I've spent most of my life being pulled from one scheme to another by people who want to use me. Grabbing hold of anything in your control is the only way to stay sane."

"Well, you spent most of the day grabbing other things." She felt pretty proud of her quick reply, but his smile was subdued.

"Yes, that's another skill I picked up to stay alive. Sometimes, I live in that personality so long that I forget who I really am."

"The real Wilder isn't a shameless flirt?" She winked, trying to coax a playful smile out of him.

"Maybe. I'm not sure."

She frowned. His rare lack of confidence surprised her. "When we first met, Pim told me you were a rascal who knew exactly what your smile could do to unsuspecting young women. I agree, because I saw it multiple times today. When you smile at a woman, she feels like she is the most beautiful woman in the room. You could choose to flirt in a way that reminds her you are attractive, but instead, your eyes tell her that she is captivating. You might have picked up some tricks along the way, but I believe that at your core, you truly enjoy seeing the delight on her face."

A soft smile crept across his lips. "Thank you. That means a lot to me."

"Just because I said that does not mean I will stop calling you a shameless flirt!"

"I would expect nothing else." His smile lit up the dark hallway, and her breath caught in a way that it hadn't for some time.

She backed toward her door. "I should get some sleep since we are leaving early."

His gaze was steady as he said, "Good night, Ylena."

INSTINCT

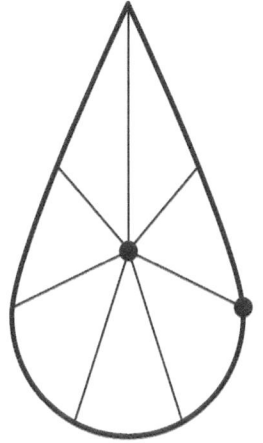

23

_____

Ylena awoke from bad dreams again. She couldn't stop worrying about the babies with Gifts in the Grottos, and the sound of a baby crying filled her dreams. She was powerless, and it set her on edge. They still hadn't heard a single rumor about the children, so she had to tuck the dream away and focus on what she could do.

She was glad to be leaving Grotto Rivalry. The others gave a fond farewell to their friends and an even fonder farewell to the students who would happily stab them in the back. The five of them said goodbye to the headmaster, and headed off to the next Grotto.

Their crew was formidable enough to be fairly safe walking through the tunnel between Grottos, but they still walked in watchful silence. Once they stepped out of the tunnel, Ylena stopped walking.

"Before we go any further, I'm just wondering if there is some terrible thing I'm going to discover in this Grotto. How about we try something new, and you can warn me about it in advance?" She crossed her arms and waited.

Rev laughed. "That's a fair request. We are in Grotto Instinct. It's not as violent as Rivalry, but you will still find a fair amount of alcohol. If you hold on to your coins, you should make it through here pretty easily."

Ylena wasn't so sure she believed that, but she followed the others from the tunnel into the Grotto. The buildings here weren't as colorful as in Peculiarity, but they were close. Crystalline flowed into contraptions that caused the light to flash on and off in different colors. Men and women stood underneath the lights, calling to passersby that their establishment was the luckiest in the Grotto.

Tayeh had taken the lead again, and she brought them in a straight path to the Warden's Den built into the side of the cave near the glowing crystal. Ylena squinted as they approached the purple light and realized her eyes had finally adjusted to the constant night of the Grottos. Once they arrived at the Den, Rev, Quinn, and Tayeh waited near the crystal while Wilder and Ylena entered the building. The guards at the end of the hall led them into the Warden's room.

The Grotto outside was colorful, but this room was stark black and white with clean lines. A large man rose from the long, silver table and walked to meet them. The glow from the crystalline lamps reflected off the dark skin of his bald head. He looked intimidating until he broke into a broad smile.

"Welcome to Grotto Instinct!" Laughter filled his voice, and it echoed through the room. "I can't tell you how excited I am about the Spectacle. It'll be a show like we've never seen!"

"Thank you, Warden." Wilder had slipped into his respectfully charming voice. "We appreciate the recreation you will provide."

"Of course! Of course!" His wide hand slapped Wilder on the back enthusiastically. "Take your time sampling everything we have to offer, and figure out what we can contribute." He reached into the pocket of his suit jacket and pulled out a stack of colorful coins. "Take these as my guest. Don't spend them all in one place!" He laughed loudly. "Or do! That's usually the most fun."

Wilder thanked him and took the coins. They turned to leave when the Warden stopped them.

"You didn't think you'd leave here without a little wager, now did you?" His mouth was still smiling, but his eyes had a manic glow. He reached into another pocket and pulled out a medallion.

Ylena's eyes widened, but Wilder's face remained smooth. A medallion was a ticket out of the Underneath, and even though Ylena still had the one from Grandfather in her pocket, she knew how valuable they were.

The Warden grinned and spun the medallion along the tops of his fingers. "How about a classic coin toss? Choose temple or crown correctly, and you win the medallion."

Wilder spoke carefully. "And if I choose incorrectly?"

The Warden's eyes glittered.

Wilder's eyes hardened. "Crown."

The Warden flipped the coin up into the air and caught it. He opened his palm to show the crown of a High Priest facing up. He laughed loudly and tossed the medallion to Wilder, who caught it out of the air. "I have a great feeling about this Spectacle. I bet the two of you will put on exactly the show we need."

Judging by the look in the Warden's eyes, Ylena wasn't sure they would win that wager.

They met up with the others by the crystal. Rev asked, "So? How did it go?"

Ylena said, "Wilder won, I think?"

Quinn's face perked up. "Really? What did you win?"

Wilder held up the handful of colorful coins. Ylena opened her mouth to speak, but Wilder spoke over her. "I won these on a coin toss. Thank the Goddess, because the terms for a loss weren't really clear."

Quinn shook his head. "I thought I taught you better than that."

Rev smiled at Quinn fondly and told Ylena, "Quinn is a pro at this."

"At what?" asked Ylena.

Quinn got an eager look in his eye. "How about the three of you take some time checking with your contacts in the Grotto, and I take Ylena on a bit of an educational tour?"

Wilder snorted. "Why do I get the feeling you've had this plan in mind for a while?"

Quinn chuckled. "That's a safe bet." He reached out and grabbed the coins from Wilder's hand. "I appreciate your contribution to Ylena's education. We'll meet you in our usual safe house later. But don't wait up. We are headed to the casino!"

24

Quinn led her inside a casino lit up with colorful, flashing lights. He was kind enough to walk slowly, so she had plenty of opportunity to look around. They entered a large room filled with dozens of tables surrounded by people who were laughing and cheering. Quinn wove through the tables until he found one that had room for them both.

He turned to her with a serious expression. "I know that your experience in Indulgence was not ideal." She raised an eyebrow at the understatement. "I am determined that this will not end poorly for you. Let's start with the simplest example of gambling we have around here."

He stepped up to the table and pointed at the colorful numbered squares on the table. They matched the numbers on a spinning wheel beside a woman wearing a short, glittery dress.

Quinn pulled a yellow coin out of his pocket and handed it to Ylena. "Pick a number."

She saw the other people at the table put their coins onto different numbers, and she put her coin on the number nineteen. Quinn nodded. The woman in the sparkly dress reached over and spun the wheel. A silver ball bounced over the different numbers, and it stopped on the number nineteen.

Quinn cheered, while everyone else at the table groaned. The woman slid two yellow coins over to Ylena, and Quinn gestured for her to pick them up.

"That's a fun first lesson!" he said cheerily. "Want to try again? You can use both coins if you want."

"Should I pick the same number?"

Quinn smirked. "That is the question everyone at this table is asking right now."

She frowned and put both coins onto nineteen again.

The woman spun the wheel again, and the ball bounced around and around until it landed on the number three. The woman gathered up Ylena's two coins and the coins from everyone else at the table. No one had picked three.

Quinn patted her on the back. "Oh well. That's the second lesson." He leaned closer and winked. "There are only two lessons." He pulled out another coin. "Want to try again?"

She laughed. "I think I understand those two lessons. Do you do this all day?"

"Sometimes. Or at least until I run out of money." He laughed. "This gambling is a bit too dependent on chance for me to enjoy it, though. Want to see the kinds of games I enjoy?" His open face was so earnest that she couldn't help but agree.

He led her to a new set of tables. The people in this area were more reserved, and the games seemed to last longer than the woman spinning a wheel. He sat down in an open seat and gestured for her to join him. "This game is called Fifths. The gentleman here is going to shuffle those cards and deal us in." He put two blue coins in front of him on the table and then looked at Ylena with a slight frown.

"Maybe he should only deal me in this time. Until you figure it out."

She laughed. "That's definitely best!"

The serious-looking man in a suit shuffled the cards and laid some down in front of Quinn and the other players at the table. Ylena thought the cards seemed religious. There were symbols with plants, flowing water, animals walking on their hind legs, and other pictures that appeared to represent each Virtue. But other than that, she couldn't follow what was happening at all. Quinn and the other players would occasionally signal the man in the suit to place another card in front of them. When a player groaned and leaned back, the man would calmly collect their coins and continue. Eventually, only Quinn and one other player remained. Quinn added another two blue coins to the table, and the other player followed. The man in the suit nodded his head and flipped over one more card. The other player slapped his fist on the table.

Quinn turned to Ylena with a grin. "Wasn't that exciting?" he asked.

"I don't even know what happened. I'm assuming you won?"

He scooped up a handful of blue coins off the table. "Yes, I won. But I'm not doing a good job teaching you how fun this is." He adjusted his glasses as he thought. "I thought starting with the practical would be most instructional, but maybe you are the type of student who needs to know the philosophy first. Come with me to the bar." Ylena was still suspicious of any place that had a bar, but they both ordered a drink and sat down at a small table.

Quinn's voice settled into the tones of a teacher. "I'm assuming you've realized that Grotto Instinct is below Temple Knowledge." She nodded. "The Grottos like to take each of the Virtues and turn them to their complete opposite Vice. Instead of gathering Knowledge, this Grotto believes that it's best to follow your Instinct, trust your gut. Your Instinct might tell you to place all of your coins on the number nineteen. And your Instinct might be wrong."

He shuffled a deck of cards while he spoke. "There are seven different suits in a deck, one for each of the Virtues. And each suit has seven different numbers. There are multiple kinds of games to play, but let's start with a simple one called Thrice." He dealt two cards to each of them, one face up and one down. "The goal is for you to get a number as close to the dealer as possible. I have a three of Order and you have a five of Purpose. I'm taking one more card. Now you get the choice: take one more or stay with what you have."

Her facedown card was a seven of Purity. He still had two cards, and she couldn't guess what they were.

"The game gets more complex when you have more people around the table. You know what's in your hand, and you can see the face-up cards. You might see a few other things: a sigh of relief or biting a lip in worry. But there is still so much that is hidden. So many secrets." He tapped his upside down card and grinned. "What am I hiding that I don't want to reveal? Does my confident expression mean that I am guaranteed to win? Or maybe I'm bluffing and want to trick you into making the wrong choice. Or does it mean I've had too much to drink and would feel confident about anything?"

She looked at him with narrowed eyes. "I'll stay."

He rubbed his hands together with glee. "Let's reveal the secrets." She flipped her card over to show that together she had twelve. Besides his three of Order, he flipped over a six of Perfection and a two of Harmony. "Not bad! It's hard to say what the others at the table would have been holding, but it's likely you would have won at least part of the pot."

After the lesson and a glass of some sort of fruity drink, she felt ready to get back out to the tables. Instead, Quinn put one of the yellow coins on the table. "Would your decision have been any easier if this had been at stake?"

"I don't even know how much that is worth, so I'm not sure."

"It's worth about a dozen of those fruity drinks. A blue one is worth about one hundred of those."

Her eyebrows shot up. "In the last game, you had four blue coins on the table!"

"I know! That was fun! It was nice that the Warden gave us the coins. I rarely get to play with so much."

She remembered the Warden spinning the medallion across his fingers. She wasn't sure she would call him nice. It also made her suspicious. "I've been in the Underneath long enough to realize that this place probably isn't as fun as it seems on the surface."

Quinn's face turned serious. "You're right. There is never a sure bet. You always have to consider the risk you are taking." He put a blue coin on the table next to the yellow. "If you are really confident, this might seem reasonable." He set down another blue coin. "You might do the math again and realize you are sure this is a good bet." He took his entire coin purse out of his pocket and put it on the table. "You might think there is no way you could lose." He emptied his pockets and added a watch, a pocket knife, and an ornate key to the pile. "You can put your complete faith in your Instinct. And you can lose it all."

"Why would anyone risk all of that?"

"There is an emotional payoff when your Instinct is correct. Some people love that feeling so much that they play endlessly just for a few moments of that bliss. But the other reason is that, for most people, winning a big payout is the only way they can ever hope to earn enough to go Upstairs."

"How often does that happen?"

"Rarely, but often enough that people believe it is a possibility. It's a lot more likely for those people to bet everything they have and then end up working for the Warden for the rest of their lives." He put all the coins and personal items back into his pockets. "I know that's depressing, but trying to win a big payout isn't the only reason to go to the casino."

"I thought that was why we are here?"

He took a stack of the colorful coins and handed them to Ylena. "I think you are prepared to go out on your own. That will make it much easier to accomplish the other purpose. Gathering information!"

"I've seen the way Wilder gathers information, and I don't think I can do that believably."

"I don't think you will have to work nearly as hard as Wilder. I suggest you go sit down with a drink at one of those tables playing Thrice. Sit by a guy and occasionally look at him with wide, innocent eyes." He pointed at her. "Yes, exactly like that! Then, say something vague about the Spectacle and see if he has any secrets to reveal. If not, repeat that pattern with others until you find something or run out of coins."

"Where will you be?"

"I'll be back at the Fifths table, gathering information of my own."

They split up for several hours, and Ylena won and lost coins in almost equal measure. Luckily, she never had to buy any of her own drinks again, because there was always a guy willing to buy one for her. She discovered that there were rumors going around that the Spectacle was going to be the Underneath's pinnacle of debauchery. That didn't seem like a shock to Ylena, but it was interesting to know just how many people were looking forward to the event. She received multiple invitations to meet people at the Spectacle and a few invitations to continue their conversation somewhere more private. Thankfully, she was sober enough to still have her wits and a few coins by the time Quinn came to find her.

25

Quinn chattered happily as they left the casino together. "Everything fell into place so precisely today! Some days, I feel like I can visualize the pattern of the cards before they land. It's so exhilarating!"

She looked at him with curiosity. "Do you believe that Instinct is more important than Knowledge? I thought a scholar like you wouldn't believe in Instinct."

He turned to walk backward in front of her while he talked. "I knew you were interested in philosophy! While most of the people in the Underneath believe the Virtues are the opposite of the Vices held in the Grottos, I believe they are intertwined and that both are necessary. I think the reason that I almost understood the pattern of the cards today is because of all the Knowledge I have gathered. And the Knowledge I have gained is inspired by the Instinct I have to understand patterns. Does that make sense?"

"That's interesting. I'll need to think on that a bit." His words looped around in circles, but she felt just a step away from understanding.

"Most people aren't interested in discussing philosophy

with me. I think I have read every philosophy book available in the Underneath, but I rarely get to discuss it."

"Are there a lot of libraries in the Underneath?"

He shook his head. "No libraries. I've heard those exist Upstairs, but down here, books are only purchased at a high price. Or stolen. I've gotten a few that way." He grinned.

She imagined the massive library filled with books that she'd had access to up in the City. It seemed like such a waste to have books sitting around when brilliant people like Quinn couldn't get to them.

They rounded a corner and stepped into a crowd of people gathering around the wall of the cave. A man shouted, "Any other takers?"

Quinn asked a woman at their side, "What's the bet?"

"He bet he can climb up to that ridge faster than anyone else. There is only one other challenger so far."

He thanked the woman and pulled Ylena aside. "So, you've climbed mountains?"

She chuckled. "Since I was a baby."

"Is this wall more challenging than a mountain?"

She studied the texture of the wall. "There could be a few challenging areas..."

"But would you win? What does your Instinct tell you?" His grin was contagious.

"I'd win."

Quinn's eyes lit up, and he nodded. "Fantastic. Next lesson. Bluffing." He whispered as he pulled her closer to the front. "Answer all those questions exactly the opposite of what you just did. And when in doubt, imagine what Wilder would say in this situation and say the opposite." He winked.

"Excuse me, sir?" Quinn called to the man at the bottom of the wall. "My sister here thinks she would like to try climbing!"

The man's focus zeroed in on Ylena. "Oh, really? Do you have much experience climbing?"

"Um ... not much?" Did that count as the opposite of what she had said?

He smirked at her. "So, you think you can climb this wall?"

"It looks like it should be easy, right?"

He chuckled. "You think you can beat me?" He flexed his muscles and purposefully looked down at Ylena from his considerable height.

She bit back a retort and reminded herself: opposite of Wilder's confident swagger. "Maybe? I'm a little nervous, but I'll try my best." She gave him the innocent eyed smile Quinn had suggested earlier.

She saw the moment when she had caught him like a fish on a line. "I'm sure you will, young lady! So, are you prepared to put money down to prove that?"

Quinn fumbled in his pocket for coins in a clumsier way than he had been earlier. He dropped several coins on the ground and scrambled to get them. "Is this enough?"

The man tried to hide his glee unsuccessfully. "Oh yes, that will be fine." He snapped his fingers, and a slick-haired woman came up and took the coins from Quinn.

Quinn squeezed Ylena's arm and whispered in her ear, "Good luck!"

She nodded and walked over to a place at the bottom of the wall. Besides the big man, there was a scrawny man already waiting. She looked up and took a moment to mentally plot out her handholds and footsteps. She turned her head to look at the big man and opened her eyes wide in what she hoped was a fearful expression. He chuckled and cracked his knuckles.

The slick woman counted them down, then blew a whistle. Ylena jumped into the lead quickly, and as she moved, she studied the next few moves ahead to find her path. She glanced at the two men a few times but then realized she should focus on climbing. She let her mind move into the peaceful place she found when she climbed the mountain.

Her arms and fingers and legs were tiring when she risked another glance at the two men. They were far below her, so she took a moment to look down at the crowd. She was curious what Quinn's face would look like to see her so high.

She saw him talking to Lady Erenne.

She almost lost her hold. Lady Erenne ... High Priest Erenne was taking to Quinn. He had a cheerful expression on his face, and when he looked up and saw Ylena watching him, he raised his arms in a cheer. The High Priest studied Ylena with dark eyes, then pulled her cloak over her hair and walked away. Ylena tried to follow her movement through the crowd, but she noticed the two men closing in on her position. She cursed and started her movement upward again.

She hurried up the last stretch of wall. A few stone handholds flowed strategically into position thanks to an angry tear drying on her cheek.

She reached the ledge and heard a cheer from the crowd far below. The men below her had stopped climbing and were staring at her with angry expressions on their faces. She started down the wall as quickly as she could without revealing her unique skills.

When she reached the bottom, she saw Quinn collecting money from the slick woman. Before she reached him, she saw him collect money from several other people in the crowd.

She wanted to ask him about Lady Erenne, but he pulled her out of the crowd before she could speak. When they had cut through several side streets, Quinn leaned against a wall while he laughed. "Oh, Ylena, you were terrific! I wish the others had been here to enjoy that. You are a quick study!"

"Who were you talking to back there?" She didn't join him in laughing, but he didn't notice.

"You have to be more specific. I had side bets going with half the crowd!"

"It was a tall woman with dark hair. She was wearing a cloak. You were talking to her when I stopped close to the top."

"Oh, her. I don't know who she was. She was just one of the many odd people you find around here! She said something about how you look like her granddaughter. Why? Do you know her?"

"No ... She looked like someone I used to know. But I was mistaken."

He straightened up from his position on the wall. "We should get moving to meet with the others. I don't want any of those people back there to sneak up on us. Plus, I learned some information, and I want to share it with everyone at the same time!"

He smiled and hurried down the alley without noticing the troubled look on Ylena's face.

26

———

Quinn led Ylena to a run-down building that looked like every other building in the neighborhood. They climbed three flights of stairs, and he knocked on a door painted with flaking red paint. The door cracked open enough to reveal Rev's single blue eye before it flung open wide.

"Quinn, have you corrupted our dear Ylena even more tonight?"

"I have! She is a quick learner." He gave her a sweet grin as they walked inside.

They entered a dreary room with an unsteady table and several mattresses scattered on the floor. Strange artwork and scribbled lines covered the walls. "What is this place?" she asked.

"This is one of our safe houses," said Tayeh from her seat at the table. "It's always good to have a place you can regroup."

Ylena looked at a crudely drawn picture of male anatomy on one wall. "It's … charming."

Rev laughed and pulled Ylena to a seat at the table. "It

helps if you focus on the people, not the decor." She set out several plates of food on the table.

Wilder stood from his seat on one of the mattresses and joined them at the table. "So, how did it go at the casino?"

Quinn emptied his pockets and dropped handfuls of coins onto the table. "We did pretty well."

Rev and Wilder laughed while Tayeh started counting the coins. "Did you win all this, Quinn?"

"Actually, Ylena and I worked together to win most of it. She turned out to be a fairly good hustler."

"Thank you, I guess ..." The others seemed to take it as a compliment, but she wasn't so sure.

"The two of you were more productive than we were," said Wilder. "We only learned one thing that was notable. A couple had a baby that manifested the Gift of healing, and before they took the boy up to the temple, they had a visit from one of the Warden's cronies. They asked the couple a lot of questions, but eventually, they told them to take the child to the temple. The woman who told me the story had been drinking a considerable amount, so I'm not sure about its authenticity. The woman doesn't know that the Wardens kept back some children this year to remain in the Underneath, and I didn't want to let her know it appeared that her child wasn't chosen."

Ylena imagined Wilder comforting the woman as she told him the story. She couldn't imagine how painful it must have been for the woman to give up her child, which helped soothe the slight tingle of jealousy.

"Besides all our hustling, I learned something, too." Quinn leaned forward in his seat with excitement. "The Wardens are pouring massive amounts of money into this Spectacle, and no one is sure why. They say that it will be the largest event ever held in the Underneath, but the fact that the Wardens are working together is enough to make some people suspicious."

"I don't understand why that is so strange," said Ylena. "Upstairs, the High Priests always work together. They also constantly scheme against one another and are suspicious, but they work together."

Quinn fell back into his teacher mode. "The High Priests have a structure in place that ties them all together in a balance. But each Warden is actually more closely tied to the High Priest in their respective temple than they are tied to each other. It's one reason that I'm not sure how long the High Priests can keep their doors locked. Their balance Upstairs depends on their power down here. That's one reason that the death of the High Priest in Purpose threw everyone Upstairs and Underneath into chaos."

Ylena finally connected the dots that the death of the High Priest of Purpose is what brought her grandfather into the City several months ago. By following him, she got herself involved as well. She thought back to seeing Lady Erenne earlier. Lady Erenne was now High Priest Erenne. Had she been the one to kill the previous High Priest? Did she start the entire process?

"I learned something, too." Rev drummed her nails nervously on the table. "Since no one is sure when the doors will open again, the price of food has gone up. Tonight's dinner cost three times as much as it did a few days ago. There are so many people who could barely afford to eat as it was. I don't know how they will survive."

"Do you think the Wardens have a plan for that?" asked Ylena.

"The Wardens don't care what happens to the poorest people in the Grottos," said Tayeh. "They might actually convince some of those people to do jobs for them they wouldn't consider before. I think the Underneath is about to get a lot more dangerous."

They ate the rest of their meal in a thoughtful silence. As they were cleaning up, Quinn made a curious sound.

"What is this?" Quinn was studying a piece of paper.

"Honey, that came out of your own pocket, so I'm pretty sure it's yours," said Rev.

"It's not mine. Someone must have slipped it in my pocket."

"If it would have been me, you would have noticed," said Rev with a wink.

"They must have done it while I was playing cards. Or maybe when I was watching Ylena climb?"

Ylena remembered Lady Erenne talking to him and asked, "Can I see that?"

I have information about the little ones with the gifts. Meet me at the casino tomorrow night.

When she saw the handwriting, she knew who had written the note. The real question was, why? And how much could Ylena trust her?

They passed the note around, and each took turns studying it.

"No way," said Tayeh. "We have no idea who wrote this."

"I think we should go," said Quinn. "This is exactly the kind of information we've been looking for, and it basically dropped into my lap!"

"It didn't drop into your lap, honey," said Rev. "A pro placed this in your pocket. The fact that they were so good that you didn't notice makes me even more suspicious."

The three of them looked at Wilder to see his opinion, but he turned to Ylena. "What do you think?"

She was surprised that someone asked her opinion. "I'm curious to know what information they have to share. I think it's worth taking a risk." She would go tomorrow night even if she had to sneak out on her own, but she would feel safer if the others joined her.

Wilder smirked. "Quinn, you definitely taught Ylena about risk and gambling. I guess we are going to meet our mysterious source tomorrow night."

27

T he next morning, Ylena and Wilder headed to their rehearsal at the Den. Ylena decided that she would not embarrass herself again by asking the Maestro stupid questions. She was glad to learn about his past, but she couldn't help but feel like a silly child around him.

When they entered the room, a young man stood up from his seat at the table. He was almost as tall as Wilder but a slimmer build, and his head was shaved as smooth as the Warden's had been. "Good morning! I'm Wyatt. It's a pleasure to meet you."

"It's nice to meet you, Wyatt! I'm Ylena, and this is Wilder. Where's Maestro?"

Wyatt shrugged. "He's not here yet. I guess we can relax for a while!" He smiled and sat back down.

Ylena and Wilder joined him. "So, Wyatt, where are you from? And other than looking like the Warden, how did you get recruited for this role?" asked Wilder. He had his usual smile on, which helped to downplay the blatant information seeking.

"I grew up here." Wyatt's smile was equally charming,

but Ylena couldn't tell if it was equally fake. "I've been performing my entire life, so when the role came up, I was excited to get the part."

"Yes," said Wilder. "It's definitely an honor."

"I don't know much about the actual performance space," said Ylena. "Are we going to have time to rehearse in the Heart of the Grottos all together?"

"Yes," said Wyatt. "I've heard we will have time for a dress rehearsal the night before. I'm looking forward to performing with the others cast as Wardens."

"Have you met any of them before?" asked Wilder.

Wyatt shrugged with a laugh. "You know how the Wardens don't really get along."

Ylena smiled and realized that he didn't answer the question.

"Sorry I'm late!" said Maestro. "Are you kids playing nice?"

"Of course!" said Wyatt. "Just learning a little about each other."

"That's good, I guess. Let's begin, shall we?" Maestro took his usual seat at the table while they got into place.

In the Spectacle, each of the Little Wardens would perform an individual song about their Grotto, and that would make up the bulk of the show. There was also an opening scene and an ending scene they would hopefully learn before their dress rehearsal. Ylena and Wilder knew the position they ended in from the previous Grotto performance, and they prepared to stand around some more.

"Is that seriously the best you two can do?" asked Maestro.

"Excuse me?" asked Ylena.

"You two are the Goddess and Companion, but you always stand next to each other like awkward neighbors. No matter your beliefs, the story of the Goddess and

Companion is a beautiful, tragic love story. I could use a bit more of that from you."

"Like what?" asked Ylena.

"Haven't you ever been in love?" Ylena and Wilder both froze in place, and he sighed. "Okay. Imagine that you are best friends. You each have strengths and weaknesses that complement each other, and you rely on the other's thoughts so much that it feels like you share one brain. The thought of losing the other half of your soul is terrifying, and yet most of the time, you live your life together like you have all the time in the world."

Ylena knew that Maestro was instructing her for the role, but she listened to his words, fascinated about what it meant for her life. What would it mean to have that sort of relationship? She had never really talked to anyone who was in a committed relationship before. She wanted to ask him a lot more questions, but Maestro didn't seem like he was interested in having a deep conversation with her. Instructions based on her role seemed like the best she would get.

"So, think about that and let it reflect on your face. And I don't care if you won't touch each other. At least stand close enough that you could touch if you wanted to."

Wilder remained frozen in place, but Ylena relented and took two steps closer to him. They weren't touching, but they were close enough.

"That will do for now. Wyatt, you can begin your solo. I'm sure you are fabulous, but we need to give these two plenty of time to rehearse not looking awkward."

28

"So, how are we going to find who we are looking for if we don't know who it is?" asked Rev.

"They know me," said Quinn. "We just have to wait until they find me. Maybe I should go play more cards until they show up?" His face lit up with a smile.

"That's not a bad idea," said Wilder. "You could earn some more money while you are at it. Since food is becoming more expensive, we will need it."

They walked over to the Fifths table, and Quinn took a seat. The rest of them gathered around to watch. After Quinn won a hand, Ylena started getting restless. She looked over to the bar and saw Lady Erenne calmly sipping tea.

Ylena spoke as casually as she could. "I think I'll go get a drink."

"Bring me something when you come back!" said Rev. She was focused on Quinn, so she didn't see the too calm expression on Ylena's face.

Ylena walked up to the bar and ordered a drink. She sat on a barstool next to Lady Erenne without looking her in the eyes.

"It's good to see you, Ylena."

Ylena glanced at her with a raised her eyebrow, then turned back to her drink.

Lady Erenne took another sip of her tea. "They have excellent tea in the Underneath. Have you tried it?"

When Ylena still didn't respond, she said quietly, "I didn't want any of them to die, Ylena. If I could have stopped it, I would have."

"It's kind of hard for me to trust anything you say, considering how many lies you've told me."

"It's true. I have lied to you. But not as often as you might believe. I actually tried to get the High Priests to keep the rest of the cast alive, if only to question them about where you had gone. But in case you hadn't noticed, the High Priests' reactions are slightly … extreme."

Ylena snorted. "That's a bit of an understatement. It's also strange that you reference the High Priests like you aren't one. I never got to congratulate you on that promotion. That could be because I didn't even know you were a Priest."

Lady Erenne sighed. "My time at Temple Purpose is complicated. The previous High Priest and I had some disagreements."

"And you murdered him?"

Ylena didn't think Lady Erenne would answer, but she said, "Not intentionally. But I am relieved he is dead."

Ylena's eyes widened, and she turned to stare at her. "I can't believe I ever trusted you at all."

"He was a terrible man, Ylena. Even among the High Priests, he was the worst."

"So now you have taken his place. Are you going to do a better job than him?"

"Well, I honestly couldn't do much worse." She drank her tea with a smug look.

"I can't believe that everything you had me do was just so you could become High Priest."

Lady Erenne set down her tea. "That was never my goal. Think about it. Why would I need you to be in the Pageant in the first place? Why would I have taken you to see your father's grave? I already have others who spy for me. Why would I need to train you instead of using them?"

"I have asked myself those same questions since the night that almost everyone I knew was murdered. Why?" Tears sprang to her eyes, but she turned away so Lady Erenne couldn't see.

"I know it doesn't make sense, dear." She reached out and touched Ylena's hand. "Trust that everything will work out in the end."

Ylena looked at Lady Erenne's red lacquered fingers resting near her wrist with Pim's tattoo. She closed her eyes, and the tears fell down her cheek.

Ylena climbed onto the dark stage, snowflakes falling around her. She touched Pim's cold wrist. She sucked in a harsh breath and swiped at the tears in her eyes. Her fingers slid across Pim's cold forehead as she prayed harder than she ever had in her life. But her prayers were met with silence. "I'm sorry. I'm sorry. I'm so sorry, Pim."

She opened her eyes to see Lady Erenne's horror-stricken face. Ylena's low voice was rough with a barely contained sob. "There is no way to make that work out."

Lady Erenne compressed her lips and nodded. "You are right. I'm sorry, Ylena." She wiped a tear from her eye, and Ylena tilted her head in thought.

"Your hair isn't turning white," said Ylena.

Lady Erenne looked at her with narrowed eyes. "You have always been clever and yet not very good at keeping secrets."

Ylena assumed that Caed's information about the Priests

no longer being bonded to the City was common knowledge, but maybe she shouldn't have revealed what she knew.

Lady Erenne shook her head. "He didn't mention that he had seen you, but I'm not surprised."

"Um ... he?"

Lady Erenne stood. "Good night, Ylena."

Ylena watched her walk away into the crowd.

29

"Here's your drink." Ylena handed Rev a glass of beer. "What did I miss?"

"Quinn is winning a lot of money. No sign of whoever wrote the note." Rev was close to Quinn's side, cheering him on.

"How long should we wait?" asked Ylena.

Rev shrugged. "Don't know. Now that I've got a beer, I don't mind staying longer." She smiled and yelped as Quinn won his current hand.

Ylena walked the few steps to where Tayeh and Wilder lingered. "Any sign of our contact?"

"Since we don't know who it is, it's hard to say," said Tayeh with a frown.

"At least I found a few people I know to be part of the Spectacle," said Wilder.

Ylena looked around the open room and realized they might wait for a long time and for nothing. The flashing lights felt too bright, and there were so many people and so many sounds that she felt suffocated.

"I think I'm going to wait outside for a while." At Wilder

and Tayeh's expressions, she added, "I won't go far. I'll be right outside."

She walked out the door and sat on the large stone steps in the purple glow of the crystal. She leaned back against a giant statue of an animal she couldn't identify and closed her eyes. Sharing that memory of Pim had drained her more than any other Gift had. Her emotions were raw, and her thoughts were fuzzy.

A baby was crying. She didn't know who would have a baby in a casino, but she could hear the baby's hiccupping sobs just a few steps away. She looked around corners and down alleys and along roofs, but she didn't see the child anywhere. The cries reminded her of the sound of the little children from the nursery she visited with Caed. Those babies had powerful Gifts, but they were still so small. Caed was so good at comforting them ...

If only she could find this child, she might help. Why was the baby so sad? Tears were dangerous for children that young because they didn't know how to control their Gift. He must be so lonely and confused. She'd felt like that when she first discovered her Gifts. She climbed the wall to get a better view of the cave so she could see where the baby was hiding ...

"Ylena." Wilder's hand was on her arm.

She lifted her head from the statue and blinked in the bright glow. "There was a baby crying. Did you hear it?"

Wilder shook his head. "I think you were dreaming." His smile was kind as he offered her a hand to stand.

"A dream?" She couldn't shake the sound of the child's cries.

"I don't blame you. It's been a long day. We didn't have any luck finding the contact, and I thought I'd come find you so we could all leave together."

"It felt so real ... I guess I'm more tired than I thought ..."

She still felt unsettled, but she ran her hand through her black hair and straightened her clothes to feel more put together. As she adjusted her cloak, she heard a sound. She pulled a piece of paper out of her pocket. "What is this?"

There are children hidden in the Underneath. The Wardens are the only ones with the path to reach them.

"What is it?" asked Wilder.

Ylena handed him the note. "I don't know how this got into my pocket."

"The contact must have put it in there while you were asleep."

Ylena shivered at the thought that she might have been that unaware, but she also wondered if Lady Erenne had put the note in her pocket back at the bar.

Wilder handed the note back to her. "Let's go find the others. We need to figure out what this means."

Once they gathered together at the safe house, they passed the note around and tried to guess what it meant.

"This note tells us nothing," said Tayeh. "We already knew there were children hidden down here. And we also knew the Wardens are behind it. This is a waste of our time."

"I think there is more to it." Quinn was studying every inch of the paper. "It says the Wardens are the path. Other than our brief meetings with each Warden, we haven't really been studying the Wardens' behavior. I think we need to do some reconnaissance to see where the Wardens go."

Rev was fidgeting with her blond hair. "We've known all along that the Wardens are up to something. The significant fact about this message is that someone out there knows that *we* are up to something. Who wrote this note?"

They considered this in silence for a while until Wilder spoke up. "Whoever wrote this has one of three things in mind. One, they want to see the Wardens fail and want our help. Two, they want us to overstep and get ourselves killed. Or option three, they want both. I think we have to see where this leads."

The nodding was unanimous.

"Let's get some sleep tonight and head to the next Grotto tomorrow. We'll figure out the Wardens' secrets soon."

DESIRE

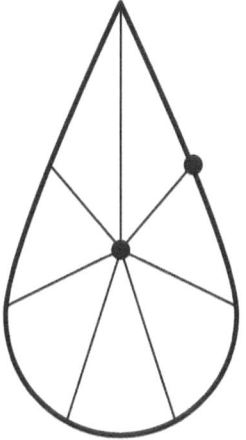

30

_____

Their walk to the next Grotto was quieter than usual. Ylena wasn't sure why the others weren't as talkative, but since she had a lot to think about, she didn't mind. She kept replaying the conversation with Lady Erenne. High Priest Erenne. Besides Ylena's continued anger and feelings of betrayal, she was now anxious as well. Caed knew High Priest Erenne? Since he was a Priest, Ylena guessed that would make sense, but Lady Erenne's words made it seem like more than that. Were they working together? Ylena felt her trust in Caed drop again.

Their crew stepped out of the connecting tunnels into the next Grotto. Wilder, Rev, Tayeh, and Quinn all gave each other a significant look that Ylena didn't understand. Rev pulled her aside while the others walked ahead.

"Um ... okay .... why are you all acting weird?" asked Ylena.

Rev cleared her throat and seemed embarrassed for the first time since Ylena had met her. "Remember how you asked us to warn you when there was something about a Grotto that you should know?"

"Yes. I would have appreciated a warning about what alcohol was. What are we getting into here?"

"If you remember your Upstairs geography, you will realize this Grotto is below Purity, and, well ... they definitely go in the opposite direction with it." She shifted her weight uncomfortably, and Ylena tried to wait patiently. "This is Grotto Desire, and one way they celebrate that Vice is in brothels. A lot of brothels." At Ylena's confused expression, she continued. "Brothels are establishments you can patronize to pay for sex."

"Oh." Ylena's eyes opened wide. "I appreciate the warning. I won't be forced to ... participate, will I?"

Some of Rev's usual spark came back. "No, but I am sure you will receive quite a lot of offers."

"I think I understand. So, is that it?" Ylena blushed more than anyone she knew, but even so, this conversation didn't seem serious enough to warrant the strange behavior from the others.

"I know you grew up on a mountain with just your grandfather ..." said Rev tentatively.

"Yes ... and?" asked Ylena.

"We just weren't sure if anyone had ever really explained to you what sex is?"

Ylena stopped walking. "First off, yes. After I had my first period, Grandfather had a woman who visited the mountain sit me down for a very long talk. Now that I think about it, it's possible that woman was from this Grotto. Her descriptions were definitely ... thorough." Ylena shook her head to clear away the images. "But second, what do you mean by 'we'?"

"We were worried that you might be surprised—"

"You all discussed this? Together? About what I may or may not know?" That was when she blushed.

"We thought maybe I would be the best one to explain—"

"Thank the Goddess for that! If I had to have this conversation with one of the others ..." Ylena rubbed her forehead.

"I don't know if it helps, but none of the others offered." Rev stifled a laugh. "Now that we've resolved that, let's go catch up with them."

When Ylena and Rev met up with the others, they all turned to look at her with questioning faces. She blushed again. Rev nodded her head, and they all sighed in relief.

Thankfully, they stopped staring at her and continued walking. Which was not surprising since there was a lot to stare at in this Grotto. Scantily clad men and women stood in open doorways and hung off balconies. They called out a variety of services they offered. Ylena realized she would have picked up on what this Grotto was all about pretty quickly even without Rev's warning.

She was grateful that Wilder was walking at the head of their crew, because he seemed to attract the most attention. The more calls he got, the more pronounced his smile and swagger became. He gave winks to men and women alike, and a few times, he even turned around to walk backward and make eyes at someone he found interesting.

Ylena had been the object of that stare so many times; she knew how powerful it could be. She saw the way he stared at a woman who had shockingly blue hair and realized she hadn't seen him look at her that way since they had been in the Underneath. She wasn't jealous about that. Not jealous at all. It was just a curious fact she noticed.

She was relieved when they made it past the brothels. They crossed the open area surrounding the purple crystal and were soon standing in front of the Warden's Den.

Wilder motioned them to come close. "I think we should split up for a while. Quinn and Tayeh, the two of you can scout around the Den and see if you notice anything unusual. Then, wait and see if you can find where the Warden goes." The two of them nodded seriously. "Rev, will you go to Vivi's and see if she has room for us?"

"Are you sure I should be the one to ask? She seems a lot more willing to do favors for you." Rev gave him a wicked grin.

Wilder struck a cocky pose. "I'm sure she would. But I'm a little preoccupied at the moment, so it's up to you to figure out how to convince her."

Rev bowed her head. "Challenge accepted."

"And what are you and I doing?" asked Ylena.

"The usual. Walking into a Warden's Den and hoping we make it out alive."

Ylena and Wilder walked down the long hallway to the Warden's door. Two beautiful men who weren't wearing much more than muscles stood guard. The men gave them appraising stares, and one opened the door.

They entered a room covered with billowing fabric, lush velvet, and thick fur. Gorgeous men and women seemed to be the decor, draped elegantly over every couch and chair. The men and women looked up expectantly at Ylena and Wilder. She felt them analyze each part of her body.

As she shrunk back, she noticed a man stand from his seat among a pile of lovely people. He strode toward the two of them with a confidence beyond what she had ever seen from Wilder. His pants were exceedingly tight, and he wore a long jacket with no shirt underneath. His long, blond hair was perfectly tousled, and he ran his fingers through it to tousle it even more perfectly. Ylena had met many beautiful people in the City, but he was one of the finest specimens she had ever seen.

Wilder offered the usual introductions before Ylena even realized she was staring at the Warden with her mouth open.

"I'm sure you will find a lot in this Grotto to contribute to the Spectacle." The Warden brushed his fingertips down Wilder's bare bicep, and his smile was so flawless she couldn't think. "The two of you will make a lot of friends here. You are both so ... fresh." He traced a soft finger along Ylena's cheekbone. He parted his lips and took a breath in. "Would you like to join us for a while? We have plenty of room for more."

A few of the beautiful people on the couches licked their lips and patted a space on the couch for the two of them to sit.

"We appreciate the offer, but we really must continue our preparations for the Spectacle. Enjoy your day." Wilder took Ylena's arms calmly, but his grip was firm as he pulled her back out the door.

31

"That was more overwhelming than I imagined," said Ylena.

"I knew what to expect, and I have to admit I found it overwhelming myself." He rubbed a hand over his face.

They turned down the hall to meet with Maestro. When they entered the room, they saw him sitting in his usual seat. Draped lazily across the table was a beautiful younger match of the Warden. His wavy, blond hair was playfully pulled back, and his flowing shirt was mostly unbuttoned. Maestro was watching him with a skeptical raised eyebrow.

"Now, Maestro, you know that I have been trained by the best. I know how to perform."

Maestro responded in a dry voice. "Yes, Connor, I'm sure you do. But I'd still prefer if we take some time to rehearse the scene." He spotted Wilder and Ylena with grateful eyes. "There you are! Let's begin. Now."

Ylena and Wilder walked over to their places on the side of their imaginary stage and got comfortable.

Connor turned to face them. "No, no, no, that won't do at all." His buttery voice glided over them. "My song is much more ... interactive than the others. This Grotto is a lot more fun when you can have multiple performers." Maestro groaned and rubbed his forehead.

Connor pulled Ylena and Wilder by their hands into the area that was marked as center stage. "Now, stand here while I sing."

Even though he said that it was going to be interactive, Ylena and Wilder didn't need to do much more than stand there and admire him. He must have spent every one of his seventeen years in training his voice and his physique, because both were phenomenal. He stepped close to Ylena and teased a few more of the buttons of his shirt loose. Her eyes opened wide, which made his perfect lips curl into a delicate smirk. After serenading Ylena, he stepped up to Wilder.

Wilder was much taller than him, but Connor didn't appear intimidated at all. He sang a particularly graphic line of his song and ran a finger slowly down Wilder's chest. Ylena could swear she felt Wilder blushing. She smiled and took a particular sort of glee in the rest of the performance.

Ylena had blushed during most of the songs the Companion sang to the Goddess. Wilder had seemed to enjoy the effect his words had on her and on every other girl in the room. But Connor's song was unlike anything Ylena had heard before. She didn't have time for blushing because her mind was trying to work out the logistics of the maneuvers he was explaining. When he realized he was having more of an effect on Wilder than Ylena, Connor focused his attention on him. By the end of the song, Ylena was biting the inside of her lip to keep from laughing.

"Wow," said Maestro drily. "That was really something."

"Thank you, Maestro. If you ever need a personal performance, I'm always willing."

"That will not be necessary, Connor."

"Your loss." Connor stepped back up to Wilder. "I think you and I could benefit from a bit more practice, don't you think?"

Ylena's lips twitched as she tried to hide her smile. "Connor, you shouldn't tease poor Wilder. I'm pretty sure he comes from Purity Diocese, and you know how they are." Wilder shot her an irritated glance.

Connor tapped his lips with a long finger. "I've heard conflicting opinions on that. But I'd like to conduct my own research."

"Um … well, Ylena and I really need to be going. Thank you both for your time." Wilder pulled Ylena from the room.

She was chuckling under her breath as they walked out of the Den.

"I'm glad I could amuse you, Ylena." Wilder's dry comment made her laugh even harder.

"It's just that you have always known what kind of power you have with your smile and your voice and …" she gestured toward his entire body "… and your everything." A little of his smirk came back. "It was nice to see you squirming from the attention of a dreamy boy for a change. It's a little overwhelming, isn't it?"

"So, you're saying I'm a dreamy boy, too?" His full smile was back.

She punched him playfully on the arm. "That's it. I'm going to tell him you need to rehearse."

"No, thank you!" He laughed.

"Well, I can't blame you for being overwhelmed by his attention. He's extremely good looking. It's easy to fall for a dreamy boy's tricks." She winked.

He stopped walking. "Ylena, I have never tried to trick you like that. You know that, right?"

"Oh yes, you have!" She laughed. "From the first

moment I saw you, you have smiled that sweet smile and recited every line of dialogue like you wrote it personally for me! You've been trying to get a reaction from me from the very beginning."

"Yes, I have. But it has never been a trick."

She opened her mouth to respond but wasn't sure what to say.

"I could use some coffee. Do you mind if we stop for a drink?" asked Wilder.

She sighed in relief at the change in topic. "I'd love some coffee. I only drank tea on the mountain, but I'm grateful that Pim taught me the value of a good cup of coffee."

Wilder gave her a sad smile but didn't comment. She knew he still blamed himself for Pim's death, and she still didn't know how to tell him it was actually her fault.

"This sign says coffee. That's good enough for me!" He pulled the door open and ushered her inside.

The cozy coffee shop was similar to one Ylena had seen Upstairs. A long bar stood against one wall, and comfortable couches and small tables were scattered throughout the room. They placed their orders and took a seat at a table in the corner.

Ylena studied Wilder's face. "Are you excited to be here? Your face changes from confident to nervous from moment to moment."

He looked down at the table self-consciously. "You can see that?"

"I know that your confident, flirty look sometimes hides another feeling, but I'm not always sure what."

"You are clever for someone who didn't grow up here. Yes, I have conflicting feelings about Grotto Desire. I love the passion and the unrestrained beauty. I love the honesty of admitting what you desire and being confident enough to get it."

"I have never heard words that describe you more." The words fell out of her mouth before she could catch them. She thought he might become insufferably cocky, but he turned introspective.

"I also hate Grotto Desire. Too many of those men and women hanging off the balconies are using their performance to gain attention. The lustful eyes of a stranger across their skin can numb the feeling of loneliness. Those words describe me, too."

Ylena wasn't sure how to respond, but a man delivered two cups of coffee to their table, so their conversation faded.

They had taken several sips of their coffee when Ylena said, "Thanks for sharing that with me, Wilder."

"I kept enough secrets from you when we were Upstairs. I figure it's time for me to be honest."

She opened her mouth to reply when a woman came over to their table. "Sorry, I was on a break, loves. But I'm ready now." She licked her lips playfully as she unbuttoned her shirt.

Ylena's eyes opened wide, and Wilder tried to hide his smile behind his hand. "That's my fault for not warning you, Ylena. Even the coffee shops around here come with a show."

32

"If the coffee didn't wake me up, that performance surely did." Ylena gulped the last of her coffee and looked only at the woman's face. "Thank you for sharing all of your ... skills."

The woman laughed and looked to Wilder. "Does she always blush so prettily?"

"Always. It's adorable." He winked as Ylena made a face at him.

The woman turned back to Ylena. "I always appreciate a visible reaction to my performance, so I thank you for the blush. It's a bit like candy to most of us in this Grotto, and I'm sure others will try to take a bite." She blew Ylena a kiss and walked away with a sway of the hips.

Wilder started scribbling on a piece of paper. "I'm going to invite her to join the Spectacle. I think she's fun." He hurried over to the woman and handed her the paper with the information.

Ylena watched him with a flat stare. "Yes. Fun."

The woman gave Wilder a warm smile and a kiss on the lips. Wilder swaggered back to the table.

Ylena rolled her eyes. "Can we go now?"

"I hate to warn you about this, but you should know that a coffeehouse stripper is one of the tamest shows in this Grotto."

Ylena groaned and rubbed her warm cheeks. "Great. Well, I'm just going to learn to accept it. No more blushing. I'm going to look at all of these naked bodies and pretend they're boring."

"That would be a waste of perfectly good naked bodies!" He laughed. "But seriously, blushing is proof that you are alive. Savor the rush of blood for the blessing of life that it is."

"I never thought of it that way," she said.

"If you want more Grotto Desire theology, talk to Rev. That's about all I know." He opened the coffee shop door to usher her out. "Now, get that blush ready, because we are headed to Vivi's."

On the walk to Vivi's, they received several more offers of entertainment from the men and women they passed. Since it was just the two of them, Ylena found herself as the subject of their attention more than she liked. And several ambitious people said they were skilled enough to take on the pair of them.

Wilder slowed down in front of a bright pink building with white balconies. Two girls from above squealed, "Wilder!" and then disappeared inside.

He smirked and opened the door. Ylena tried to will her body into calmness and followed him inside.

They entered a cozy living area with warm lighting. Women in extremely short, lace dresses lounged on comfortable couches. Shirtless men straddled chairs at intimate tables. A woman wearing a long, sparkling dress leaned against the fireplace and raised an eyebrow at them as they entered.

"Wilder!" The two young women from the balcony had made it down the staircase, and they were soon curled along Wilder's sides. Ylena realized they were twins. They both had the same dark hair, golden brown skin, and long, fluttering eyelashes.

"We haven't seen you in ages!" squealed one.

"Did you miss us?" asked the other.

Wilder smiled at them both warmly. "Sorry I haven't been back for a while, and yes, I've missed you. I'd like to introduce you to Ylena. Ylena, this is Kira and Kara."

The twins sized her up, and Ylena was afraid they would see her as competition like at the school in Rivalry.

"She's cute," said Kira.

"Yes," said Kara. "But even though there are two of us, it will still be double the price for you both."

Wilder covered his laugh with a cough. "That's a fair proposition, but unfortunately, we are here for other types of business today."

"I'm curious to know what kind of business that is." The woman from the fireplace had joined them. Her blond hair was piled into curls onto the top of her head. The glittering dress she wore was a structural marvel. Ylena couldn't figure out how the woman's extremely full bust was not falling out of it.

"Hello, Vivi," said Wilder. When the twins saw the look Vivi focused on Wilder, they uncurled themselves from his sides and slid away.

"You sent Rev ahead of you to try to sweet-talk me?" The woman's voice was as smooth as a purr. "You know you only have to crook your finger, and I will obey."

Wilder smirked. "I appreciate the sentiment, but we

both know you don't obey. You won't do anything you haven't already decided to do."

"Well, it's a good thing I've decided to do anything you can dream of asking."

The two of them were standing close, and Ylena felt distinctly out of place. She was considering backing out of the room when Wilder noticed her.

"Vivi, I'd like to introduce you to Ylena. Ylena, this is Vivi, the owner of this fine establishment."

"It's nice to meet you," said Ylena.

Vivi's blue eyes focused on her, and once again, she felt like she was being measured. "The pleasure is mine. So, where did the two of you meet?"

"We were in the Pageant together Upstairs," said Ylena.

"Ah, yes," Vivi purred. "Wilder is quite the performer. An artist, really. Don't you agree?" Vivi's eyes were seeking a specific answer, but Ylena wasn't sure what it was.

"Um ... yes, he is a very good singer."

Vivi's eyes narrowed and then relaxed. She seemed to shake herself like a bird settling its feathers. "So, Wilder, what exactly are you up to? Rev mentioned the upcoming Spectacle."

"The Wardens have asked us to gather performers for the show. I was hoping some of your employees might be willing?"

"You know that my people are always willing."

He chuckled. "Yes, they are that. Beyond looking for performers, we are also seeking any information that seems ... curious. I know your people are also very good at discovering secrets."

Vivi stepped closer to Wilder and rubbed the fabric of his shirt between graceful fingers. "Yes, I have taught them how to uncover all the places people like to keep hidden."

Ylena was feeling out of place again, but Wilder rescued

her. "Ylena, maybe you want to go find Rev? Vivi and I should discuss this further."

She wanted to get out of this awkward conversation, but there was a part of her that didn't want to leave Wilder alone with this woman.

"Rev is upstairs in the second room on the left." Vivi said the words for Ylena, but she never took her eyes from Wilder.

"Okay. I guess I'll see you around, Wilder." Ylena walked up the stairs. Wilder didn't watch her go.

33

Ylena arrived at the second door on the left just as a guy was leaving. "Thanks for the help, Rev! You're the best!" He wore tight leather pants, and his unbuttoned shirt flowed behind him. He squeezed past Ylena in the doorway with a grin. "Hey, sweetheart! Are you sure you are looking for Rev and not me?"

Rev called from inside with a laugh. "Leave her alone, Spencer! She's mine."

Spencer looked Ylena up and down and then walked down the hallway. He glanced behind him to see if Ylena was still watching.

She was.

"Get in here!" said Rev. "Stop getting distracted!"

Ylena closed the door behind her and examined the room. There was a small vanity covered with powders and perfumes and a wardrobe which showed the signs of Rev's scavenging. She was lying on the monstrosity of a bed that took up most of the room, wearing a silk robe with feather trim. She flopped onto her stomach when Ylena entered.

"We will share this room for the next few days. What do you think?" asked Rev with a wave of her hand.

"The bed is big enough that hopefully I can avoid you pawing all over me at night," said Ylena with a laugh.

"Don't be too sure about that!" said Rev with an evil grin. "These paws are extremely skilled." She waggled her fingers. "Come sit over here and tell me how your morning has been."

Ylena unlaced her boots and made herself comfortable on the bed. "I met the Warden. He was stunning."

Rev got a dreamy look on her face. "I've seen him a couple times, and he really is magnificent." Her face turned more serious. "Completely gorgeous, but just as depraved as the rest of the Wardens. The beautiful people he keeps with him aren't there by choice. Some of them enjoy the perceived power of being close to him, but once he chooses someone, they belong to him until he tires of them." She sighed. "Anything else?"

"I experienced my first coffeehouse stripper."

Rev hid her face in a pillow to laugh. "I guess I should have warned you about that, too. People in this Grotto really only wear clothes to have the chance to take them off."

"Then, we came here. Wilder and I were propositioned by twins." Rev nodded as if that was completely normal. "Wilder and Vivi had a conversation that I was obviously not a part of."

"Vivi made it clear that the only reason she was giving up the use of one of her rooms was that I promised that Wilder wasn't far behind. That's nice of him to spend some time entertaining her."

"Oh, I'm sure he's really entertaining her by now."

Rev's blue eye perked up. "Interesting ... Do I detect some jealousy?"

"What? No. Of course not. He's free to do as he pleases. It makes no difference to me."

Rev made a humming sound. "Don't be embarrassed at

feeling a little possessive. Wilder is a shameless flirt, and this Grotto brings that out in full force. You had him to yourself for the Pageant, so I'm sure it's difficult to see him in his natural habitat."

"It's not that. At least, I don't think it's that." She scratched her head and sighed. "It's complicated."

"Relationships always are! Tell me about it." Rev sat up and rested her head on her hands on the pillow in her lap.

"When I first met Wilder, I could barely speak when he smiled at me," said Ylena shyly.

"Wilder has that effect on a lot of us. That's nothing to be ashamed of."

"We spent a lot of time together, and I enjoy performing with him. It's just that ... there's Caed."

Rev slapped her hands down on the pillow. "There's another guy? Why haven't we talked about this yet?"

She shrugged. "Because it's complicated?"

Rev rolled her eye dramatically. "Tell me about Caed."

"He's a Priest."

"Okay ... yeah ... that is complicated," said Rev.

"He's a Priest that doesn't believe in the Goddess," Ylena said. Rev settled into the pillows like she was preparing for a long story. Ylena sighed and continued. "He taught me to dance. He figured out I had a Gift before I did." She kept it at just the one Gift for this story. "He could have had me executed before I even knew what was happening, but he accepted me for who I was. He introduced me to his mother."

Rev slapped her hands on her mouth. "You met his mother?"

"Yes. She takes care of the children in the temple nursery, and we went to see her and rock the children to sleep."

Rev's blue eye focused on her. "And you've kissed him?"

Ylena thought about kissing Caed in the room filled

with the white roses that he helped her bring to life. Her voice was a rough breath. "Oh, yes ..."

At this, Rev lowered her head down on to the pillow, and Ylena could see her shaking it back and forth.

"What?" asked Ylena. "You said relationships are always complicated. Is this bad?"

Rev raised her head with a sigh. "It's not bad. It sounds lovely. I'm only worried that you will break Wilder's heart."

"Me? I will break *his* heart? He's off somewhere alone with Vivi. I think he's doing just fine without me."

Rev shook her head. "Wilder might play with Vivi, but it's nothing serious to him. I don't think he's ever had one honest conversation with her. Have you ever had a meaningful conversation with Wilder?"

"Yes, quite a few."

Rev nodded with a frown. "Exactly. There's something between you. I've seen it for a while now, and I was happy about it. I didn't know there was someone else. Does he know?"

Ylena looked a little embarrassed. "The two of them were a bit competitive. My friend Pim said they were like two bulls in the same pen."

Rev rubbed her fingers through her blond hair in frustration. "Ugh. Yeah, this is complicated."

"Wilder saved my life." She thought back to how quickly he reacted when he thought she was in danger from being revealed. "I didn't ask him to. He just did it."

Rev looked at her with a calm expression. "Ylena, you have a choice to make. You have to decide what it is you want. I can't tell you what to choose, but I beg you—when you decide, make that choice clear. If you choose Caed, tell Wilder honestly and then let him go. Don't linger over this decision, or you will hurt one or both of them, along with yourself. This is the perfect Grotto for this moment. Figure out what you desire. Decide, and do it quickly."

Ylena was uncomfortable with the idea of declaring her feelings about either of them. "This is Grotto Desire. I'll just choose them both. That's seems normal here!" She tried to keep her voice playful but failed.

Rev raised an eyebrow but didn't laugh. "If you hadn't told me they were like two bulls in a pen, I might have suggested you offer them that option. But that's not what they want, and I know it's not what you want. In fact, I think that you already know your choice but are too afraid to be honest about it. The longer you wait, the more painful it will be. And if it's Wilder's heart you are going to break, you better do it quickly. I like you a lot, Ylena, but if you continue to pull him along with no intention of choosing him, I will honestly be furious with you."

Ylena nodded in understanding. Rev patted her hand kindly and left her alone in the room with her thoughts.

34

Ylena stayed alone in their room for several hours. She didn't want to venture downstairs to be propositioned by anyone. And her conversation with Rev disturbed her. She knew that Wilder and Caed had both been possessive of her, which was annoying. But also flattering. She had told them both to stop their strutting behavior, but she had never tried to be honest about her feelings.

Admitting what she desired required a level of vulnerability she wasn't sure she was ready for. And telling one of them she wasn't interested would mean giving up that attention, and something inside her craved that. Since the day her grandfather left her alone on the mountain, she had felt lonely and out of place. The attention from both Wilder and Caed made her feel wanted in a way she never knew she needed. Pushing one of them away felt like cutting off a part of her personality she had only just discovered.

She was fidgeting on the bed when Rev flew into the room in a rush. "Time to get dressed! We are going out!" She hurried over to the closet and began flinging clothes onto the bed.

"Where are we going?" asked Ylena.

Rev threw some sparkly clothes at her. Ylena obediently put them on.

"Remember that coffee shop?" Rev asked.

"It will be difficult to forget."

"This is like that combined with the circus."

Ylena tried to understand that combination. The circus performers were already scantily clad. She sighed and continued to dress. She needed Rev's help to lace up her corset but realized she should have put on her stockings first because it was hard to bend over and still breathe.

After they had both dressed, Rev dug through the jewelry and scarves and shoes until they were both glittering and draped and yet still barely covered.

"Are we watching or performing in this?" Ylena said jokingly.

"Who knows what will happen?" Rev said with a delighted giggle. That response didn't comfort Ylena.

Ylena's heels were higher than any she had worn before, so she had to walk carefully down the staircase. She was at the foot of the stairs before she noticed Wilder. He was dressed in tighter pants than she had ever seen him wear, and his loose shirt was open enough to show his tattoo on his muscular chest. She looked into his eyes and realized he had noticed her looking at him. He was pleased.

He took her by the hand and spun her in a move they had done together in the Pageant. "Wow, Ylena. You always look fabulous, but today, you look like pure Desire."

"Thanks, Wilder." She lowered her head and bit her lip. Then, she caught Rev's narrowed eye. She covered herself with her feather wrap. "So, where are we going?"

"To Ecstasy Theater."

"It's a theater?" she asked.

"Yes, but the performances are quite different from anything we did at the Pageant. Shall we go?" Wilder offered

Ylena his arm. She took it with a hesitant look at Rev, but luckily, he offered his other arm to her. He looked at them both with a smile and said, "This is nice. I mean, you aren't twins, but ..."

Rev and Ylena both swatted at him, and he laughed.

Ylena appreciated having Wilder's arm to hold on to as they approached Ecstasy Theater. She still wasn't that secure walking in her heels, and when she craned her neck to stare at the beauty of the theater, she felt even less steady. The theater was another building shaped from the stone by Priests. There was no way to get those flowing lines of architecture without literally liquifying the stone. The theater was graceful curves lit with glowing crystalline along the edges. They walked up the steps and entered the shining doorway.

Instead of stone benches like in the amphitheater Upstairs, the audience sat at individual tables. Wilder whispered in the ear of an usher, and she led them forward to a table for three close to the front.

"Wilder!" exclaimed Rev. "How did you get us such great seats on short notice?"

"Vivi pulled a few strings." He said with a smile.

"I bet she did," said Ylena under her breath. Wilder didn't hear, but Rev gave her a serious look.

The lights dimmed, and Ylena was grateful to be in the dark. A single spotlight raised on a singer at center stage. It reminded Ylena of the scene in the Pageant when she started with the same lighting. The similarities soon ended.

The singer had a lovely deep voice that traveled through the theater. Her long dress was covered in ribbons and jewels that sparkled in the spotlight as she moved.

And she *moved.*

The music pulsed in a hypnotic fashion, and her hips followed in a steady rhythm. Her hands traveled along her body in ways that she seemed to enjoy. Her smile was captivating, and Ylena could feel herself and the entire audience pulled forward in their seats.

The woman continued to sing while slowly pulling off each of her long gloves. Each note of her song was tantalizing, and each move was intentional. She slowly unlaced the ribbons running up her right thigh. She dragged the ribbon out as she held a long note, and a long, shapely leg sprang into view. As she calmly sang, she unlaced the ribbons along the front of her dress until it seemed like the top was only staying on by a magical force. It fascinated Ylena. While the woman in the coffee shop was exuberant, this woman was truly an artist.

She stared directly at the crowd as she pulled the ribbon on her dress so ... slowly. Ylena held her breath, unsure how this was going to end. The woman gave the ribbon a firm tug while spinning in a glittering twirl. When she ended, her back was to the audience and her dress was on the floor. She turned her head to the audience and blew them a kiss before the stage went dark.

The crowd erupted in cheers, even from Ylena. Before anyone had time to catch their breath, the lights came back on. The woman and her dress were gone, but the stage was full of dozens of dancers in matching outfits of sequins and feathers and bare skin. Ylena watched them dance with rapt attention. It had been so long since she was in a dance lesson, and she wanted to learn every move.

35

When they arrived back at Vivi's, they found Tayeh and Quinn waiting for them in the hall-way. Tayeh had her arms crossed and stared at them angrily. "You never considered that Quinn and I would also like to go to the theater?"

Rev looked embarrassed. "Sorry, Tayeh. We weren't sure how long you would be, and we got the tickets and—"

Tayeh cut her off. "You owe us."

Wilder joined Rev in bowing his head in a penitent manner. "Um ... are you so mad you won't tell us what you discovered?"

Tayeh snorted, but Quinn seemed happy enough to explain. "We'll tell! We learned that—"

"Not here," said Wilder. "Upstairs."

They all piled into the bedroom. Ylena and Rev had to gather sparkly, lacy undergarments from every surface before there was enough room for everyone to sit.

Quinn dove back in. "We watched the Warden's Den for most of the day, which was extremely boring. Beautiful people go in and out, but the Warden doesn't seem to leave much. We took turns watching and asking around."

"I talked to a few people I know in the area," said Tayeh. "I was careful not to reveal what I was looking for, but it's common knowledge that the Warden doesn't leave his Den other than for a few trips to Ecstasy Theater each week. That's where he scouts out his new conquests. I got that answer so many times that we both decided there wasn't much use sitting outside his Den for several days."

Rev looked thoughtful. "Maybe this Warden is different from the others? Do we know if the other Wardens travel more than that?"

"We met several of the Wardens outside of their Den, so we know they get out sometimes," said Quinn.

Wilder frowned. "I wish we would have known to follow the Wardens in the other Grottos."

Tayeh snorted. "Following Wardens is not a habit I would take up without good reason."

"Can we say for sure this is a good reason?" asked Ylena. "We don't really know where that note came from. Maybe someone is trying to send us on a pointless search?" Ylena was sure it was Lady Erenne who had given her the note, but she didn't trust her motives at all.

"Maybe," said Wilder. "But it's the only lead we have. I think we need to make plans to break into one of their Dens."

Tayeh laughed. "Are you insane? I know the entrances all look unguarded, but I've seen warriors flood out of that place at a loud sound out front. Their fighters are all armed to the teeth and bored and looking for a challenge."

"I know, but it's the only lead we have," said Wilder. "The only other option we have is to ignore this and wander into the Spectacle. We'll be at the mercy of the Wardens and whatever plans they have for us and everyone in the Underneath."

"Yes," said Tayeh firmly. "Just like we always are. Why should it be any different now?"

"We're together," said Rev. "That's what's different. And Ylena and Wilder have legitimate reasons to walk inside the Wardens' Dens. That is very different."

"Everything in the Underneath is different now," said Quinn. "The crystal spires used to glow with an amber light, and now everything is purple. Nothing looks right anymore." Ylena had never seen the Underneath when it glowed amber, but she remembered how strange it felt when the City lit up in a new color.

"Quinn is right," said Wilder. "I think the glow of the crystal is affecting everyone down here. Haven't you noticed how people seem a bit more on edge than usual?"

"That could be from the rising cost of food," said Rev. "If the High Priests don't open their doors and start sending food down here again, people are going to starve. We rely on the Priests to make enough food for all of us."

Ylena wanted to tell them that the Priests couldn't use their Gifts anymore, but she didn't know how to say it. Plus, she wasn't sure what that would accomplish other than causing a panic.

"I honestly hope the Wardens are planning something drastic," said Tayeh. "We have to get the doors back open."

"I'd rather hear about their plans now instead of waiting for an announcement at the Spectacle," said Wilder. "I want to take action. If you'd rather sit this one out, Tayeh, I totally understand."

Tayeh grunted.

"So then we are all in agreement?" asked Wilder. "We are going to sneak into a Den and figure out what the Wardens are planning."

❧

They stayed up late discussing strategy, but eventually, they were too exhausted to continue. Tayeh and Quinn laid out blankets to sleep on the floor in their room. Ylena tried to convince them she should take the floor considering she had slept on a stone cave floor her entire life, but they both gave her a look that said they were tougher than her, and she had to agree with them.

Wilder, however, left the room and said he would find them in the morning. Rev hinted that the only way Vivi let them have this room was that she got to keep Wilder to herself in her own bed. Ylena tried to not let Rev see any expression on her face about that.

The next morning, Ylena looked significantly more tired than the two that had slept on the floor. It did not comfort her when Wilder came downstairs looking even more exhausted than she felt.

"Anyone else in the mood for coffee?" he asked with a yawn.

Ylena snorted. "Is there anywhere to get coffee that doesn't involve a woman's breasts near my face?"

Rev smirked. "Sure! There is a nice coffee shop where you can instead see plenty of men's—"

"No, thank you!" said Ylena quickly. "It's just so early! Isn't there any place that's calm in this Grotto?"

"I think I know a place," said Wilder. "I can't guarantee that everyone will be fully dressed." Ylena sighed and rubbed her forehead. "But it is probably the most peaceful place in the Grotto."

Wilder convinced them all to bring extra clothes with them, and when they arrived, Ylena realized why. People lounged in bubbling tubs filled with scented water and smiled while shivering under cool showers. Some were completely nude, but others wore thin clothing that would dry quickly. The courtyard of Temple Purity above them was filled with water statues and waterfalls, and she wasn't sure what their Priests would think about these mostly nude people savoring the pure water.

Wilder led them over to a seating area next to a pool filled by a small flowing waterfall. It was loud enough that their voices wouldn't carry, but not so loud they had to yell. Wilder waved at a server who brought them coffee. Her dress was sheer, but at least it was a dress.

They each broke off into separate conversations while they drank their coffee. "Thank you, Wilder," said Ylena gratefully. "This is very nice." She sipped her coffee and closed her eyes to the peaceful sound of the waterfall.

"I remembered you said you grew up under a waterfall," he whispered in her ear. She opened her eyes but didn't move her head. He was very close. "I know this has been rough on you. The Underneath is stressful even for those of us who have grown up here. I think you are handling it very well." His smile was kind, and she didn't know how to respond.

She felt Rev's eye boring into her from her other side. She leaned forward in her chair, away from Wilder, and addressed the group. "Excellent coffee, huh? None of you prefer tea?" Ylena remembered Lady Erenne drinking tea at the bar. "I heard the tea down here is great."

Tayeh said, "No one in the Underneath drinks tea for breakfast. Who told you the tea was good?"

It frustrated Ylena that her offhand comments would get her in trouble again. Luckily, she remembered the last time she had tea. "My grandfather had tea at his place. He gave me tea on my first night here."

"Oh," said Wilder. "They do have different kinds of tea in Delirium."

The others said, "Ah ..." and nodded meaningfully.

Wilder leaned close to explain. "You shouldn't drink any

tea in Delirium without asking a lot of questions. Most of those are even worse than what you experienced your first night at the bar."

The others chuckled quietly under their breath. Ylena wondered exactly what kind of tea Lady Erenne had been drinking and if she liked to get drunk on sugar-rimmed fancy drinks as well.

~

After their coffee, they all jumped into the pool with the waterfall. She'd learned to swim during the summer months in the pool outside her cave, but even then, the water was frigid. She hated the cold water, but Grandfather thought it was important that she learned how to swim.

The water in this pool was pleasant against her skin. She floated on her back for quite a while until she felt a touch on her arm. She dropped her feet to the bottom of the pool and found Wilder standing next to her.

"I was worried you were falling asleep. I wasn't sure if you could float in your sleep." His smile was sweet.

She laughed. "I never tried before. I've never been swimming in water I didn't want to immediately jump out of." She looked around the pool and realized the others had gone. "Where did they go?"

"Tayeh and Quinn had some things they wanted to pick up after our conversation last night. Rev has some of her own contacts in this Grotto that she wanted to check in with. When she realized you and I didn't have anywhere else to go, she almost decided not to leave. I guess she was jealous that the two of us could swim a while longer."

Ylena made a non-committal sound. She knew Rev was worried about leaving Ylena alone with Wilder. Rev would not think this was a good decision. Standing alone in a warm pool, next to Wilder, in water that was shallow enough that his entire bare chest was out of the water, her own chest at the waterline with nothing but a sheer top …

"Ylena, I want to thank you."

"Thank me? For what?"

He bowed his head and frowned. "You've been so kind to me, despite what I did. I knew there could be unexpected consequences when I poured the babies' tears into the basin, but I did it anyway. There wasn't another way I could save those kids' lives, but I'm sorry all the same. I don't expect you to forgive me for that decision, but I am honestly grateful that you have been so sweet to me despite that. You are a good person, Ylena, and I'm glad to know you."

Ylena's cheeks turned red, but this time, it was from shame. "Wilder, you aren't to blame for their deaths. I forgive you for walking out on the Pageant, and I know that none of it was your fault."

"That's kind of you to say." He looked down at her, and there were tears in his eyes. "You don't have to pretend like it wasn't my fault. But your forgiveness means more than you know."

"But it wasn't your fault—"

"I don't regret putting their tears in, but I do regret hurting you. It's the same with the death of the Priest. I knew I had to kill her to save your life, and I would do it again. But it has torn me up inside." His voice dropped to a whisper. "Her name was Alys. I see her open eyes some nights as I fall asleep."

Ylena was struck silent. Why was he telling her this? Rev said he had never had an honest conversation with Vivi in his life, and yet, here he was, baring his soul to her.

"Wilder …" Her voice was rough, and she had tears in her eyes.

He leaned toward her with a soft questioning look. She closed her eyes, and a tear dropped into the pool.

A spout of water at the far end of the pool rose and then crashed down in a splash, shattering the moment. Wilder turned around to see what caused the sound. She sighed in relief.

"Did someone fall in?" he asked.

"We should check."

They swam to the far end of the pool and couldn't find anything. Ylena said, "I guess one these pipes must have had some air in it or something." She shrugged. "We should find the others."

"You're probably right. We still have plenty of opportunities to talk before the Spectacle. I always enjoy talking to you, Ylena."

He stepped out of the pool, and Ylena watched the water pour down his bare back. She felt like the worst person alive.

36

W hen they made it back to Vivi's, Tayeh and Quinn were already in the room, sorting through some items they had picked up. Ylena was glad Rev wasn't back yet, because she needed some time to prepare herself. She knew the second Rev looked at her, she would know Ylena was guilty of something. Ylena looked at Wilder and realized he was staring at her with a small smile. She hurriedly looked away.

"So, Quinn, what do you have there?" She had to look at anyone except Wilder.

"This is a set of lock picks. I use them to get into places that people don't want me to go," he said happily.

"Will you teach me?" She didn't know why she would need that skill, but she needed a distraction from Wilder's eyes.

"I'd love to!" He reached into a different bag and pulled out a collection of locks. "These are for practice. Take this one." He handed her the largest lock that had a glass back. "You can see how the inner workings fit together and figure out how to move the lock picks."

It took her several tries, but she eventually got it. "You

are a quick study! Try to find the trick to each of these locks. Each one is unique, but once you recognize the patterns, they will make more sense."

Ylena was still practicing on the locks when Rev came in. She looked frazzled, which was not usual for her.

"What's wrong?" asked Wilder.

"I talked to a friend who delivers the food that gets sent down here from the Priests. She said that there is no more food coming and that the reserves are almost out."

"We expected as much," said Wilder. "The Wardens must hope that holding the Spectacle at the same time the food runs out will motivate people to join behind them for a revolution. They are counting on us being desperate."

"She also said that the Wardens are still getting the same amount of food delivered to their Dens, despite less food going everywhere else."

"That's also not that surprising," said Tayeh. "The Wardens are terrible. It's expected."

Rev rubbed her hands through her wild looking hair. "She also said the Wardens get way more food delivered than their number of guards should need."

"Of course," said Tayeh with a grunt. "Terrible people."

"No. Listen. A lot more food. A lot." Rev's voice was firm.

Ylena whispered. "That's where they are hiding them. The children. They have a nursery for the babies with Gifts inside the Dens."

Quinn nodded. "It's the path." At everyone's questioning look, he said, "The note. It said, *The Wardens are the only ones with the path to reach them.* The path is through the Den."

"It makes sense." Wilder narrowed his eyes at Rev. "What doesn't make sense is why you look like you just ran all the way here."

"Well, when she told me that, I immediately suspected it

was the babies." She avoided looking at Wilder. "I may have done something a little rash."

Quinn looked interested to hear what she had done, but Wilder and Tayeh both crossed their arms and glared at her.

"I tried to sneak into the Den." She said the words in a rush.

Wilder and Tayeh started yelling at her, but Quinn asked excitedly, "What happened?"

"Not much. I tried to distract the guards enough that I could sneak into the door in the long hallway, but they didn't fall for it, and I ended up running through the City, trying to hide from a whole squadron of guards who followed me out." She slumped onto the bed with a sigh.

"I can't believe you would be so stupid!" said Wilder. Ylena had never seen him this angry before. "Not only could they could have caught you, now you've set them all on guard and it will be impossible for us to get in! You ruined all of our plans because you thought you could handle this on your own!"

"But Wilder, it's babies! I had to—"

"The babies are fine for now!" he roared. "The Wardens cared enough about them to send me Upstairs to bond them to the City and keep them safe for an entire year. They would have been fine for one more day while we prepared to do this together!" He paced across the room angrily.

"I'm sorry, Wilder. I was stupid. I ruined everything." Rev hid her face in the bed.

"Maybe not," said Ylena. "It's true that we can't sneak into this Den anymore, but we still have one more Grotto to go. As far as I've seen, all the Dens are the same. Is that true?"

Wilder slowed down his pacing. "That's true. They are all the same on the outside and with their one long hallway to each Warden's personal lair."

"Then Rev ruined nothing. In fact, it might be easier since we have a natural reason to walk right into the next Warden's Den." She thought about the dangerous looks of the gorgeous Warden. She said cheerfully, "And maybe the next Den will be even safer than this one!"

They all turned to stare at her with incredulous looks. She assumed she would figure out later what dumb thing she had just said.

Ylena had to hide how excited she was that Rev had made a mistake. She had been dreading the moment when Rev realized that not only had Ylena not declared anything one way or another with Wilder, but she had left the situation purposefully confusing. She had too many other things on her mind to make huge life decisions about the guys in her life. Everything needed to stay the way they were with no changing.

Rev was avoiding eye contact with Wilder, who was still upset with her, so she missed several of the glances he sent Ylena's way. Ylena was also trying to avoid eye contact with him, so she focused more on picking the locks.

At some point, Tayeh left to go pick up some food and bring it back to their room. Vivi didn't want them eating in the common area with her people. Other than Wilder, she didn't feel like they lived up to the same beauty standards as her employees. They sat on the floor, eating one of the simplest but most expensive meals Ylena had eaten in the Underneath.

"I wonder how Grandfather is doing," she said aloud. "Does he have enough money to afford to eat?"

Quinn had a bite of bread in his mouth, but he asked, "What does he do for a living?"

Ylena thought for a moment. "I have no idea what he does here. All the work we did to grow our own food on the mountain doesn't seem that useful here."

"Maybe it will be," said Tayeh darkly. "If we can't get any food from the Priests, we will need to figure out some way to grow our own down here."

"That's all he did on the mountain? Grow your own food? I thought you mentioned traders that came back and forth?" asked Rev.

"Yes. There were always people who brought us food we couldn't grow ourselves in exchange for some things we grew. Mushrooms, tea, root vegetables, those sorts of things."

"That's kind of strange," said Quinn. "We can get all of those things from the Priests. Well, we usually can."

"That's true," said Ylena. "I wonder why they came to us, then?"

"I'm guessing because it was one less way to be indebted to the Priests," said Tayeh.

"If your grandfather gave them a better deal with fewer strings attached, I'm sure there are many people in the Underneath who are grateful to him." Rev gave her a comforting smile. "I'm sure he will be fine."

"Thanks," said Ylena. "You're probably right." She was glad to see Rev smile at her again and not just glare.

After they had eaten and finished making their plan for the next Grotto, Wilder stood to go. "Well, I guess I should get going. Umm ... Ylena, can I speak to you outside a moment?"

Rev's head popped up, and her glare was back.

"Sure ... okay." Ylena followed him out the door. She couldn't figure out if it would be better for Rev to see their conversation or not. She pulled the door closed behind her, and even though they were in an open hallway, their conversation suddenly felt very personal.

"Look, Ylena, I just wanted to explain about Vivi ..."

"You don't have to explain!" she said quickly. "You are free to do whatever you want. Vivi is beautiful, and she clearly enjoys your company." Her words seemed a little too rushed to be casual.

"I want you to know that it is just a business transaction for me. This is what I have to do for a safe place to stay in this Grotto. I'd be lying if I said that it was the worst price I'd paid for a safe room." Ylena could tell he was trying to keep his confident smirk to a minimum, but then his expression changed as he studied her face. "But now I'm wondering if a safe place to stay is worth the cost." His voice dropped to a whisper. "I could cash in the medallion I won from the Warden. It would pay for at least a few nights somewhere safe, and I wouldn't have to ..." He nodded toward Vivi's room.

She widened her eyes. "You shouldn't do anything you don't want to do." She wasn't sure if she meant selling the medallion or spending the night with Vivi.

"It's rarely as simple as that. But I'm willing to make things complicated. If that's what you want." His eyes were asking her a question that she wasn't prepared to answer.

A laughing couple stumbled up the stairs and ran past them. Their door clicked shut on a giggle, and Ylena took a step back and said, "I should get back inside before Vivi gets mad at me for lingering out here."

Before she knew what was happening, he leaned in and kissed her on the cheek. "Good night, Ylena."

He walked down the hallway to Vivi's room. In typical Wilder fashion, he looked back to see if she was watching and smirked when he saw that she was.

She took a deep breath and scrubbed her cheek with her

hand before she walked into the room. She thought Rev might see his kiss imprinted there.

Rev was staring at the door, waiting for her to enter. Quinn and Tayeh were sitting on the floor, looking anywhere but at the two of them.

"Did you have a friendly chat?" asked Rev innocently.

"It was fine." Ylena busied herself tidying up some of her things.

"Not awe inspiring or heartbreaking, either one? Just fine?" asked Rev with a pointed stare.

"Yes, just fine. That's all it is. Just fine."

"Ylena, I told you—"

"Yes, I know what you told me," snapped Ylena. "I'm not ready. I can't do what you want."

"If you hurt him—"

"Are you jealous?" Ylena knew it was a cold-hearted distraction, but she would take what she could get.

"I care about him, Ylena. And I also care about you."

"If you care, then stay out of it. Let me deal with it."

"You're not dealing with it. That's the problem. You are avoiding it. You can't run from this, Ylena."

"Watch me." Ylena grabbed her cloak from the back of a chair. "Don't wait up."

37

Ylena had never felt such an overwhelming need to escape before. She could see Rev's eye glaring at her, no matter how far from Vivi's she walked. Rev acted like it would be such a simple thing to decide. Ylena had barely made any decisions for herself the whole time she had been in the City. Why should this be any different? She wished there was a way someone could make the decision for her so she didn't have to hurt anyone's feelings.

She didn't realize where she was walking until she stood in front of the spa they had visited earlier. It was closed, but the lock was one of the really simple ones she had just learned about, and Quinn had given her his old lock picks. She wandered through the empty building until she made it to the pool with the waterfall.

The room was lit with a soft glow of the few crystalline lamps still on. She took a deep breath and listened to the peaceful sound of the water. There was a smooth stone floor in front of the pool, and she lowered down to do some calming stretches. She swung her head in slow circles and let the motions soothe her. Her mind drifted to the moves of the woman with ribbons on her dress, and she moved her hips to the rhythm of the song in her mind.

She pulled off her cloak and her boots and then removed her shirt as well until she was only in her fitted pants and lace undershirt. The tears from her angry walk had dried on her cheeks, and she hummed the rhythm from the music at the theater. She spun the notes around in a circle until they repeated in an endless loop. She twisted their harmony into the loop and added in a clap for the accent on the offbeat. When the music was pulsing to her liking, she began to dance.

She combined the moves she had learned for the Pageant with some moves she had watched the feather clad women do. The movement brought her pleasure, and she smiled. She felt powerful and strong, two things she rarely felt lately. She had missed the feeling of joy that dance brought her. Other than her one combative dance with Kieran, she only danced during their uninspiring rehearsals, and she hadn't realized how much she'd missed it. She couldn't believe that before the Pageant, she had never danced in her life. It seemed like she was created for this—the rhythm, the beat, the movement.

A few more tears had trickled down her sweaty cheeks, although she couldn't quite say why. She was happy in the midst of her music when she felt someone watching her.

There wasn't any thought. She just reacted.

She bent down to the pool and plunged her hand into the water. The water shot up and surrounded the watcher, then it drug him under the water. She could see the man struggling at the bottom of the pool. When she focused on the water, she could trace the lines of his form as he tried to pull himself to the surface to breathe. She realized she could pour the water into his lungs if she wanted.

Then, she realized it was Caed.

She used the water to deposit him on the side of the pool. He had stopped struggling and lay in a wet heap on the stone. She gasped and wiped her hand across her eyes as she ran to him. She pulled the water from him drop by drop until the droplets hovered above them, sparkling in the air.

He wasn't breathing, so she pulled his shirt open and placed her hands on his still chest. She pushed breath and movement into his chest. She willed his heart to beat and his blood to flow. Even more tears fell onto her hands as she waited for him to respond.

He rolled over with choking breaths. She leaned back on her heels and covered her face with her hands. What had she just done? She had almost murdered Caed with a Gift of the Goddess. Again. It came to her so easily. What was she becoming?

Caed stopped choking, and Ylena raised her head to find him sitting up and taking careful breaths. "I realize ..." His voice was rough, and he talked slowly so he wouldn't cough. "I snuck up on you again ... That was a poor decision ... on my part ... I apologize."

She slid from her crouch and sat down with a sob. "I almost killed you. Why are you apologizing to me?"

"Maybe that's ... exactly why I'm apologizing." His voice was still strained, but she could see a playful twinkle in his eye.

She covered her face with her hands. "I'm becoming someone I don't like, Caed. What is happening to me?"

He took her hands in his own and scooted closer to her. "You've got some things to work out." She looked at him incredulously, but he pointed at the water droplets glistening above them. "But you still are creating beautiful things like you always have."

She swirled her hands through a few drops overhead

and flung them back into the pool. "Those drops were in your lungs. I'm beginning to think you are right. The beauty of the Goddess's Gifts might not be worth the risk."

He opened his mouth to respond but then closed it without a word.

She studied his face for lingering signs of damage and ran her fingers through his hair until it was as messy as always. He smiled at her caress until she touched his white lock of hair and asked, "So, High Priest Erenne, huh?"

His breath escaped in a rush. "She mentioned she spoke to you. She was a little perturbed that I talked to you first."

"Well, no one told me I should keep your hair a secret."

"Did you tell your friends?" She realized he meant Wilder and the others, and he looked worried.

"No. I didn't."

He visibly relaxed at her answer. "Did you tell them you had seen me at all?"

"No. I wasn't sure I wanted to answer questions about why I have a Priest friend."

He got a smug look. "A Priest friend? Is that all I am?"

His question seemed a little too close to the declaration Rev had told her to make, so she slid away from answering. "It doesn't really seem worthwhile to have a Priest friend who doesn't tell me anything important. I've learned more valuable information from Lady Erenne, who has been using me since my first day in the City, than from you."

His smug look faded. "That's fair. I'm used to doing this on my own or with people like High Priest Erenne, people I need to work with but don't trust. I'm not sure how to work with someone like you."

"How about you start by telling me one thing you haven't told me yet?"

"Like what?" he asked.

"I assume you have a lot of things to choose from. Just pick something."

"I joined a fight club."

"That's what you were doing in Grotto Rivalry?"

He nodded. "I think they are using the fight clubs to recruit. I want to find out where those fighters end up."

She looked off into the distance to consider the possibilities, but he brought her back by saying, "So, what secrets are you considering?"

"What do you mean?" she asked sharply.

"Do you mean to tell me you don't have any secrets you would like to keep from me?"

She thought about how they were planning to break into a Warden's Den and realized she couldn't tell him that because he would be too worried. She thought of one thing she could talk about, and it was likely he already knew.

"We think the Wardens are planning to announce a revolution at the Spectacle."

Caed nodded. "High Priest Erenne and I have both made the same prediction. They are clearly planning something. The question is what."

She felt guilty for revealing something so obvious, so she gave him something else. "Wilder poured tears of Gifted babies from the Underneath into the basin the night of the Pageant."

Caed nodded again. "I suspected that when you told me he poured something in." It irritated Ylena that she again told him something he knew. He continued, "We just don't know if the ceremony actually worked for them. If it did, those babies and the ones from the temple nurseries are the only ones in the entire City with Gifts they can safely use."

"The ceremony worked," she said.

"You've seen the children?" He leaned forward in anticipation.

"No, I haven't. But a Warden told me that the children's hair reverted to its natural color. I guess she could have been lying, but it seems like those children are part of the plan. Bonding them to the City was the first step."

"That is very interesting. Anything else you want to tell me?" he asked with a grin.

Her mind raced through other secrets but tripped over her conversation with Rev about Wilder and Caed. "I think you are the one with the most secrets. You owe me a lot more information than I owe you."

He grinned. "How about this? I'll answer one of your questions if you answer one of mine."

She raised her eyebrows. "Any question I want?"

He leaned back on his palms and nodded.

She filtered through all the questions she had ever asked him or ever wanted to ask. A lot of the questions, like "What is behind the doors guarded by Sentinels?" were eventually answered through no help from him. Now was her chance. What did she want him to answer?

"How did you meet Lady Erenne?"

He sighed. "That's a really long answer."

She settled into a comfortable position. "I expect a complete answer. You are the one who made the deal, so you had better talk quick."

"I told you once that I had two brothers and a sister killed by a High Priest." She nodded but didn't speak. She had no idea this is where the story would start. "All three of them were killed by the former High Priest of Purpose. I don't know if you've heard, but of all the High Priests, he was the worst."

"I heard that." She had heard it from Lady Erenne, but she wasn't sure she believed how any of them could be any worse than what she had seen already.

"I'm not saying that he was the worst because he was the

one who killed my brothers and sister. He did bad things. Horrible things. With children." Ylena's eyes widened. Caed's face hardened. "It happened for years, and no one could stop him. The other High Priests turned a blind eye. And if anyone confronted him, his Sentinels killed them. That's what happened to my siblings. They gathered together a group of a dozen Priests to confront him. He got word that they were coming and killed them all."

Ylena covered her mouth with her hands.

"After that, no one had the nerve to confront him. I tried to find ways to stop him or to gather up enough other people to join me, but everyone was too scared. He was so powerful. I was spinning in my anger and frustration until I met Priest Erenne. I stumbled upon her one day in the courtyard drinking tea. She heard I was looking for a way to stop the High Priest. She seemed nice. I thought she was going to talk me out of it. Instead, her face turned fierce, and she told me she was dedicated to taking him down."

Ylena tried to picture the two of them talking in the courtyard. It seemed like a strange combination of her worlds, and she couldn't picture it.

"She asked me to gather information for her. I had connections she didn't have, and I could track his movements. And the movements of the children." He rubbed his hands through his hair. "I told Priest Erenne all the information she needed to know to confront him. I don't know exactly what happened between them, but the night that I heard he was dead, I slept better than I had in years."

"She told me she didn't intend to kill him but that she is relieved he is dead."

Caed's face twisted into a grimace. "I would have gladly killed him if I would have had the chance. I'm just happy I could do anything at all."

"And you've been working with her ever since?"

"That seems like a second question, and you haven't answered my first yet." He smiled a wicked grin, and Ylena tried to think what kind of secret he might ask her to reveal.

"Fine." She tried to sound more confident than she felt. "You actually did a good job answering for once, so ask away."

"Where did you learn to dance like that?" His eyes twinkled with mischief.

"What?" she snapped.

"Before you tried to murder me, you were dancing. Where did you learn those moves?"

She stood up with a huff. She straightened her clothes and realized she was wearing significantly less clothing than usual.

He stepped closer to her with a graceful prowl and spoke in a smooth voice. "Are you refusing to answer? Do you have some other dance teacher you don't want to tell me about?" His teasing voice tickled across the bare skin of her shoulders.

"I've learned quite a few things during my time in the Underneath, thank you very much. But if you must know, I watched a performance at Ecstasy Theater. I'm a quick learner."

He brushed his thumb gently down her bare arm. "Yes, you have always been that. Your skill has always impressed me."

She smiled at the compliment. Her hand reached for one of the remaining floating water droplets. She reminded the drop how it was part of the enormous collection of droplets still in the pool and convinced it to talk to those other droplets until the drops scattered like stars throughout the dark room.

The sparkling droplets hovered until they fell one by one around the two of them. One droplet fell on Ylena's cheek and merged with the dried tears. Another drop landed on Caed's neck below his ear. Ylena watched the water trail down the side of his neck and slide down his collarbone. She watched it trickle down his chest and then beyond the buttons Ylena hadn't pulled apart in her struggle to heal him. She looked up into his eyes and raised her eyebrow, knowing exactly where the wandering drop of water had gone.

Caed's eyes widened, and he gave a delighted laugh. He pulled her into a kiss as the rain poured down.

CHAOS

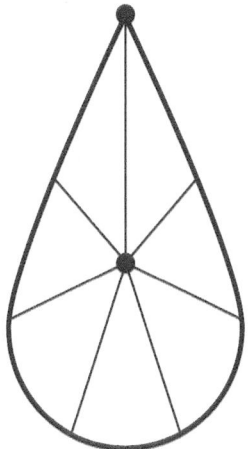

38

Ylena tiptoed over the sleeping forms of Quinn and Tayeh and gently climbed into the bed next to Rev. She had dried off on her walk back to Vivi's, but her thoughts were still dripping with a warm rain.

When she woke, Rev had already left their room. She stretched with a contented sigh. Even though she had some more bad dreams about a crying child, she was savoring the euphoria of her rain-soaked kiss with Caed.

"You're in a good mood this morning," said Tayeh.

"I guess I am." She smiled and brushed out her hair. It had dried in a wild mess.

"You left here pretty upset last night. To be honest, I wasn't sure if you would come back."

She stopped brushing and turned to her. "Of course I came back. I'm not walking out on anyone." She started brushing her hair again so she could avoid Tayeh's eyes. "Rev and I had a disagreement, that's all. I'm sure we will work it out."

"Good. We are leaving soon for the next Grotto, and we don't have time for bickering." Tayeh walked out and closed the door.

Ylena tried to not let Tayeh's sharp tone ruin her good mood. She touched her lips several times as she was dressing, just to remind herself of Caed. She packed up her things and headed downstairs to meet with the others.

The four of them were chatting at a table in the front room, and when she approached, they all stopped. Wilder gave her his wide smile and appeared to be the only one who was happy to see her. Rev gave her a flat out glare, and the other two seemed distinctively uncomfortable.

Ylena decided to use a lesson she learned from Pim. If there is something disturbing that you can't fix, pretend that it doesn't exist. And smile.

"Good morning!" she said. "Are we ready to go?"

"We are!" said Wilder. "We are going to stop for some coffee and food on our way. Does that sound good to you?"

"That sounds wonderful! Lead the way!" She really was in a terrific mood, so her cheeriness was only partially fake.

She followed Wilder out the door, and the others lagged behind.

"You seem in a good mood this morning. Are you that happy to be leaving Grotto Desire?" he asked.

"Actually, I've loved it here. And I didn't blush nearly as much as I expected!"

He laughed. "I'm glad you enjoyed it. I'm actually fairly glad to be leaving. Spending that much time with Vivi is exhausting."

She blushed. "I can imagine."

"Not because of that!" He seemed embarrassed. "I meant emotionally exhausting. Vivi is very possessive, and she is always analyzing our conversations, looking for subtext. It can be tedious."

"I'm surprised she wasn't waiting downstairs to see you off this morning."

"We got in a fight last night."

"Oh?" She was curious, but afraid to ask more.

"I told her I wasn't interested in continuing our ... business arrangement. She wasn't pleased." He sighed. "I thought she might kick us all out onto the street, but I think she was embarrassed that everyone in the house would know why."

"I see," she said awkwardly.

"Yes. So, that's done." He exhaled. "Now, we get to move on to a different kind of danger," he said wryly.

"What is the next Grotto like?"

"It's ... rough."

"Okay... In what way?"

He rubbed a hand over his thick curls. "Imagine Grotto Rivalry. Except with a lot more sharp weapons and no rules to the fight. Grotto Chaos is intense. I'm not looking forward to it."

"I see. Will we have a safe place to stay there?"

"Safety isn't possible, so I'm not sure what we will find. I haven't been back for a while. I try to avoid this Grotto whenever possible." He was silent for a moment. "It's where I was born. And where I was when my father left."

Ylena tried to imagine Wilder as a young boy growing up in a place like that. "I'm sorry. I wish we didn't have to go."

"Me too. But it's good to know we have a plan once we get there. It's possibly the most dangerous Den to sneak into, but it will be nice to focus on the plan instead of the memories."

She gave him an encouraging smile, and they walked in comfortable silence until they stopped to eat. They bought food from a small food stand and ate while sitting on the ground at the entrance to the tunnel that led to Grotto Chaos.

While they ate, the silence of Rev's anger toward Ylena

wasn't as noticeable. Wilder finished eating and then gave them all last-minute reminders.

"Ylena, once we exit the tunnel and enter Grotto Chaos, you must be completely aware of your surroundings. There are a lot of followers of the Vice of Chaos, and they will do things to shock or hurt or even please you, with literally no rhyme or reason. Be on your guard at every moment. And if you get into trouble?"

"I run." She said this with a confident look at Tayeh. She didn't respond.

"Yes. You run," said Wilder. "That also goes for Quinn." He nodded cheerfully. "And depending on the circumstance, that could go for you, too, Rev." She nodded once. "Tayeh and I will try to give you a head start. Don't waste it by trying to help us. You will only make it worse. Got it?"

Ylena and the others nodded obediently.

"When we arrive, we are first looking for a somewhat safe place to stay, and we will only go to visit the Warden and the Den when we have that. Try to keep a low profile. We don't want the Warden to know that we roamed through the Grotto before stopping in to say hello. So, are we ready?"

They stood together and headed into the tunnel.

She exited the tunnel and got her first look at the Grotto, immediately feeling ill at ease. The shapes of the buildings were just ... off. They were tall and crooked, spread apart and built on top of each other, painted different colors for no discernible reason. Her eyes couldn't focus on one wrong thing. Everything was a mess, and it hurt her head.

They walked among the buildings, and Ylena noticed how the people acted strangely. She saw people laughing wildly or screaming, but sometimes, they were by themselves. She found it troubling but wasn't sure why.

Rev spoke to her, seemingly against her will. "Remember what I told you in Grotto Peculiarity? In that Grotto, some people have such an extreme devotion to Peculiarity that they glorify those who are different, even if it harms the person they are idolizing. A similar thing happens here. People whose minds work differently are worshiped as paragons of Chaos. They sometimes benefit from being revered, but most of the time, it just means they don't get the help they need."

Ylena appreciated the explanation and started to say so, but Rev moved back to her place by Tayeh. Ylena tried to pretend it didn't hurt.

She considered Rev's explanation and thought about the people she had seen in the healing center Upstairs. Even the Priests couldn't heal afflictions of the mind. She remembered her conversation with Walter, the man who said he was over two hundred years old. He was in the room when Wilder killed Priest Alys. He told unbelievable stories and filled notebooks with his own secret language. She didn't want to imagine what might have happened to him if he lived in Grotto Chaos.

Ylena tried to not let herself get distracted. She had to be on guard for the people that would randomly run out in front of them, circle their group, and then run off. And for the woman who walked up calmly and tried to rip Quinn's bag off his shoulder. Tayeh smacked her on the back of the head and sent her running off. They had only walked a few blocks, and Ylena felt exhausted.

Wilder stopped them in front of a crooked building that was two-and-a-half stories high. "Wait for me around the corner. I will come get you if this is where we will stay."

The four of them waited for him in awkward silence.

Ylena wanted to say something but didn't know where to begin. She didn't think there was anything she could say to Rev that would make her happy, so she stayed silent.

Wilder came around the corner, and they looked to him with hopeful faces. He just shook his head and continued walking.

They followed him to several places, all of them odd in their own way. Sometimes, he barely made it inside the door when he came back out. On their fifth stop, he was gone for so long that the four of them starting shuffling their feet anxiously when he finally returned.

"This will have to work," he said.

"That's not exactly a glowing review," said Tayeh.

"No. It's not."

They followed him toward the tall, narrow building. There were no windows and only one door. Quinn started to walk in, but Wilder shook his head and pointed him toward the back. There were no windows on the back side either, just a ladder running straight up the building that stopped next to a door three stories off the ground.

"Wow," said Rev. "That is unique enough to belong in Peculiar."

Wilder sighed. "I'm not really looking forward to climbing up and down each day, but I hope it discourages some of the lazier criminals."

"And the ambitious criminals?" asked Ylena.

"There's no stopping them. Let's go check it out."

39

The room was just that. A room. There was no furniture. The only sign that this might be a place for people was a tattered sheet stretched in the corner, partially hiding a chamber pot. Ylena grew up in a cave, and this was austere compared to that.

They each claimed a section of the small room and set down their things. Then, they sat and stared at each other.

"Can't we just try to break in to the Den right now and be done with this?" said Rev. "I'm not really having fun right now."

"I didn't realize we were supposed to be having fun," said Ylena.

"Some of us are having more fun than others," said Rev with a fake smile.

"This is not fun for me! I just want to move on with my life!" Ylena's voice was strained.

"Okay ..." said Wilder. "I think we could use some space to clear our heads. Let's divide up and take care of some things before our attempt at the Den. Ylena and I can go scout out the Den—"

"Absolutely not," said Rev.

Tayeh jumped in. "I thought I could take Ylena to do more training. Fighting in Chaos is different from anywhere else, so I think it would be helpful."

"I can scout the Den with you, Wilder," said Quinn. "I watched the last Den, and I have to warn you, it's pretty dull."

"I'll gather supplies," said Rev. "I'm not hauling any furniture up that ladder, but maybe I can find each of us a blanket."

"Sure," said Wilder. He looked disappointed, but it was a good plan, so he didn't complain.

Tayeh and Ylena were the first to leave the confined room. They made it to the bottom of the ladder, and Ylena sighed with relief. She was slightly disappointed that she didn't get to go with Wilder. He was the only one actually talking to her at the moment. However, she felt warning bells going off with each serious conversation they had.

As she followed Tayeh in silence, she wondered if maybe the danger was all in her head. Maybe it was just Rev overreacting. Wilder had always been a flirt, and that didn't seem likely to change. Rev had known Wilder for a long time. She was probably feeling jealous that Ylena spent so much time with him.

Tayeh opened the door to a gym that looked pretty similar to the one they went to in Rivalry. She saw a punching bag in the corner, which looked promising. She definitely had some anger to get out today. Instead, Tayeh led her toward a ring where Ylena could hear the clash of metal.

"Sword fighting," said Tayeh. "It's not the most practical of skills unless you are planning on fighting one of the Warden's minions at some point."

Ylena watched the two men in the ring step back and forth with intricate footwork. The swords looked heavy, and the muscles along their bare arms and back stood out with every swing.

"I don't think I can learn that in a day," said Ylena.

Tayeh grunted. "Obviously. I just wanted you to see it so you know what the Wardens' guards are trained to do."

Ylena nodded and settled in to watch. The match finally ended with a multitude of bruises and quite a bit of blood. After they left the ring, two women without swords entered.

They fell into a fighting stance, and Ylena saw a blade glittering in each of their hands. Their footwork was even more complex than the men's. They spun and kicked their legs, trying to attack as they also had to defend. Ylena knew it was much more complicated than she could even understand.

She didn't see what happened, but the women suddenly stepped apart from each other. One woman had blood pouring from a wound on her arm. It was gushing out faster than any of the wounds the men had taken, and she dropped to her knees with a dazed expression. The other woman looked concerned but unsure.

Tayeh clicked her tongue. "That's bad. It wasn't even intentional." She shook her head. "That woman is going to die because of the other's sloppy work."

"She's going to die?" asked Ylena.

The woman was blinking her eyes slowly and swaying on her knees. No one else was moving.

"Yes. There's no chance of fixing a wound like that."

Ylena jumped over the barrier that blocked off their fighting space. She touched her hand to her eyes as she ran.

She made it to the woman just as she fell over onto her side. Ylena gripped the woman's forearm and pressed her tear into her skin.

They both gasped. Ylena leaned back as the woman blinked her eyes and sat up slowly. "What happened?"

"Um …" Ylena looked over at Tayeh, who had her arms crossed, looking at her with a furious expression. "You fell over, and I helped you up. Glad you are okay. See you later. Bye."

She finished her awkward spill of words and ran out of the ring. The standing woman looked between Ylena and the woman on the ground in confusion. Tayeh grabbed Ylena by the arm and dragged her out of the gym.

"What happened to keeping a low profile? We aren't supposed to be here yet. How many people with the ability to heal do you think are currently in the Underneath right now?"

"I couldn't just let her bleed to death!"

"Yes, you could! We have more important tasks to handle than healing some random woman in a random gym! How many people in this Grotto do you think are bleeding out at this exact moment? None of them are our concern right now."

Ylena stopped walking and dropped her voice to a furious whisper. "I understand we have a job to do. And I will do it. But you need know that if there is someone dying in front of me, you can be Goddess-damn sure that I am going to do something about it! My entire life is confusing and pointless right now, but that is the one thing I know I can do. If you want to keep me from healing anyone, then you need to keep people from getting hurt around me, okay?"

Tayeh listened to Ylena's speech with her arms crossed and no expression on her face. When Ylena came to the end, Tayeh sighed, then nodded.

They spent most of the day traveling to various gyms in the area. Ylena got to see more kinds of fighting than she even knew existed. They circled back to a gym close to the terrible room where they were staying and watched a pair of fighters with swords and shields.

"Do they know about these styles of fighting Upstairs? I've only seen Priests demonstrate a single style, and it's nothing like any of this."

Tayeh snorted. "Everything is so peaceful Upstairs that there is no need for fighting like this, right?"

"I don't imagine the High Priests would encourage it," Ylena said ruefully.

"Technically, all of these styles came from Upstairs." Tayeh seemed reluctant to admit it. "I'm sure there is some Priest in a back room practicing with a sword and shield, but it is just a theory up there. Once the theory came down here, it became reality."

Ylena realized that was the difference between the style she had seen from the Priests and the type the young girls in the arena did. To the girls, it wasn't a theory. It was their way to stay alive.

The men with the swords and shields cleared out of the ring with no mortal wounds. Ylena agreed she wouldn't rush to heal minor wounds, but Tayeh had accepted the fact that Ylena was serious about saving someone's life if necessary.

The next two fighters entered the ring. Tayeh groaned.

Wilder was pulling his shirt off and picking up a sword.

"You have got to be kidding me," said Tayeh. She tried to take Ylena by the arm. "Come on. Let's go."

"Why should we?" asked Ylena. "I know what Rev's issue is, but what's yours?"

Tayeh crossed her arms. "I'm not an idiot. I might not have picked up on this"—she waved her arms between Ylena and Wilder—"as quickly as Rev did, but I'm not blind."

"I'm not saying there is a this"—she waved her arms in

the same way—"but if there was, what is your problem with it?"

Tayeh narrowed her eyes. "Are you telling me you aren't going to break his heart?"

Ylena crossed her arms. "I'm not planning on it."

Tayeh grunted. "That's not a good enough answer."

"You and Rev need to let Wilder make his own decisions. He's a grown man." She turned toward the ring to watch him fight.

Ylena had danced with Wilder many times, but the smoothness of his steps in the ring was a wonder. His expression was fierce, but he still had the usual twinkle in his eye. He didn't know she was there, but she enjoyed watching him fight.

Which reminded her of the night she'd watched Caed fight. She felt uneasy at the similarities.

She told Tayeh they could leave when Wilder won the match. He thanked his opponent and went to pick up his shirt. He saw Ylena and Tayeh and hurried over.

"What are you two doing here?"

"It was our plan to train today, remember? What are *you* doing here?" asked Tayeh.

"Quinn and I scouted what we needed quicker than expected. I didn't feel like sitting in that bare little room, so I came here. What did you think?" He nodded toward the ring.

He had addressed Ylena, but Tayeh answered. "It was adequate. You can put your shirt on now."

He grinned but complied.

40

The three of them headed back to their room together. Although Ylena grew up climbing, she found the ladder leading to the door floating on the side of the building really disturbing. She came inside and found Quinn and Rev already there.

Wilder followed Ylena through the door, which earned the usual glare from Rev. When Tayeh followed, she got her own glare, apparently for letting it happen.

"Thanks for picking up some blankets." Wilder either appeared to be blissfully unaware of Rev's mood or was trying to play nice.

Ylena walked over to the blanket that was folded neatly by her things. It was utilitarian but warm. "Thank you, Rev."

"You're welcome," she said grudgingly.

"So, how did your scouting go? Are we all set to do this tomorrow?" asked Tayeh.

"Yes, everything is as we planned," said Quinn.

They each occupied themselves in their own way for a while, but eventually, the silence became oppressive.

"Are we really just going to sit in this sad room until tomorrow morning?" Ylena asked. "Isn't there anything fun in this Grotto? A circus, casino, or some kind of show?"

The others looked at each other like they were struggling with a silent decision amongst themselves.

"There is something," said Tayeh. "The question is whether it is advisable to go the night before we have an important task."

"I feel like we could use a fun group activity," said Wilder. "What could possibly go wrong?"

Tayeh groaned. "You did not just say that."

Quinn spoke in his usual optimistic tone. "No matter what we do, none of our inappropriate behavior will stand out amongst all the other degenerates."

"No inappropriate behavior!" said Rev. "I already screwed up one of our opportunities. We can't lose another one."

"It will be fine," said Tayeh. "And maybe it will be a chance to get out any pent-up frustrations."

Rev rolled her eye but nodded, which meant they were going. Ylena didn't know where, but she was excited to go.

The decision to leave their room meant an outfit change for most of the group. Changing in the single room was a tricky proposition, but they were soon ready to go.

Ylena had followed the clothing choices of the others and was wearing a short skirt with boots and a cropped top. The others talked excitedly along the way, and Ylena tried to stay quiet so they would forget they were mad at her.

They approached another Priest-made building in the center of the Grotto. Its architecture was less chaotic than the rest of the Grotto, but it was obviously built to be intimidating. As they neared the building, Ylena heard a loud pulsing sound coming from within. The music sounded like nothing she had ever heard before. She wondered if there was anything they should warn her about but didn't want to draw attention to herself by asking.

Their crew walked in through the massive doors, and a wall of sound hit Ylena in the chest. They were at the back of an enormous crowd of people dancing and thrashing about on the dance floor. She could see a stage with performers far in front of them, but she couldn't pay attention without losing her crew moving through the crowd. They stopped at the bar at the back of the room. Ylena ordered a drink and turned to talk to Quinn.

"What kind of music is this?"

"This band is mostly punk. But later tonight, there will probably be rappers and some rock or grunge."

"I've never heard of that."

Quinn smiled. "It's probably not a style of music the High Priests enjoy. If you listen to the lyrics, you'll hear why."

She didn't understand everything they were singing, but it sounded like they were suggesting the High Priests do some anatomically interesting things.

"How is it so loud?" She had to yell at Quinn to be heard.

"That guy with the long hair and the girl with the mohawk are playing metallic guitars. The players clip their guitar into the stone frames built in the stage. The strings vibrate against a thin stone plate covered with crystalline, which is connected to those giant stone boxes. Inside, they have a thin cone of crystalline that projects the sound out here."

"It's so clever." Upstairs, the Priests in Temple Discipline could bend their music through the air to connect to every ear in the audience, but down here, they had to be more creative. The result was a sound that was metallic and distorted. It was oddly entrancing.

"Want to go dance?" asked Quinn.

She looked out at the churning crowd of exuberant dancers. She really wanted to join them but wasn't sure if that was a good idea.

He read her hesitation accurately. "It might be best if you accept my offer to dance before anyone else asks you." He didn't quite look at Wilder when he said it, but she understood.

She downed the rest of her drink. "Has anyone ever mentioned that you are brilliant, Quinn?"

He winked. "A time or two."

The music was hypnotic. The sound pulsed through the air as if Priests were churning it up themselves. She let her body obey the rhythm as the harsh melody floated across her skin. Quinn had lost her somewhere in the press of the crowd, but she didn't care. She was deep within a crowd of strangers, but she had rarely experienced such a private moment. The music was for her enjoyment alone, and she savored each note.

She frequently felt hands on her. Sometimes, it was unintentional in the press of people, and other times, she felt a hand lingering too long to be accidental. If they moved on, she let them pass, but some warranted a strategic elbow. She was preparing her elbow to swing again when the person with their hand on her back stepped in front of her.

"Caed!" She said his name loud, but it was lost in the sound.

He smiled and pulled her close. He copied the way she had been moving her hips to the music and was shockingly close to her. She was surprised but smiled with delight. She had been paying attention to the other couples in the crowd and had picked up a few moves herself.

She laughed wickedly and shook her long hair around her. She ran her finger down his chest while continuing the rocking motion with her hips. He smiled and spun her around until they were both dizzy and laughing.

She was reminded of every perfect memory she had dancing with Caed. She laughed so much a tear touched her cheek. A breeze hid near the ceiling, and she pulled it down to swirl around them. She let the playful breeze skip across his neck and then tickle behind his ear. It ruffled his hair, and the white locks stood out in sharp relief under the crystalline lamps.

She stopped dancing and gathered his hair in her fingers. Was there more white than the last time she had seen him? Had she paid attention when she had been kissing him last night? It was too loud to ask him any of those questions, and his eyes looked like he would like to avoid the answer anyway.

He looked over her shoulder and then ducked away into the crowd. She turned around and saw Quinn waving her down. She couldn't see where Caed had gone, so she followed where Quinn led.

The others were back at the bar, or maybe they had never left. She couldn't tell if the music was as freeing for them as it was for her, but the fact that they weren't on the dance floor didn't seem like a good sign.

Tayeh yelled in her ear, "I've noticed several questionable people. I think we need to leave."

Ylena looked out onto the dance floor filled with people who were screaming the lyrics, pumping their fists in the air, and thrashing about. "Everyone here looks questionable. Including us! I don't want to leave yet." She knew she sounded petulant, and when Tayeh gave her a flat stare, she sighed. "Fine. Let's go."

Ylena trailed behind the others as they walked to the door. She looked behind her several times to find Caed to say goodbye, but she couldn't see him. She hurried to catch up and found the others surrounding Wilder. His hands gripped Caed's shirt and pressed him up against the wall near the entrance. The others looked confused, but Wilder looked angry and suspicious.

"Caed." At Wilder's use of his name, Rev shot around to glare at Ylena.

Ylena tried to keep her face as neutral as possible, but she knew that she usually failed at that.

"Wilder," said Caed. "What a pleasant surprise! When was the last time I saw you? Oh yeah, it was when you walked off stage and abandoned Ylena and the rest of the cast to die." Caed's voice was casual as if he wasn't currently pressed up against a wall.

Wilder narrowed his eyes and gripped Caed's shirt tighter. "What are you doing here? Ylena doesn't need a Priest like you lurking about."

Caed's eyes widened in surprise. "Ylena is here?" He connected eyes with her. "Hi, Ylena. It's nice to see you. You look good." He grinned, and even though she knew he was acting, her heart still sped up.

"What are you doing down here? I thought the High Priests closed the doors?" said Wilder.

"I have connections."

"Does the Warden know you are here? Maybe I could do her a favor and drop you off for a visit?"

"No!" said Ylena. She hadn't meant to speak, but now that she had, she tried to interpret all the reactions. Quinn and Tayeh were still confused. Wilder seemed to have forgotten she was there. Caed was frowning like she was ruining his fun. And Rev was analyzing her as usual.

"We can't take him to the Warden. We have other important things to do tomorrow." After she said it, she realized how silly it was for her to speak up. Wilder would have never spoiled their plan just to hurt Caed.

She was fairly certain about that.

"You think I should just let a Priest freely wander around in the Underneath?" asked Wilder.

"What's he going to do down here? He is probably just here to dance anyway. Let's just ignore him and focus on what's important."

Wilder frowned and released Caed's shirt. "Have fun dancing, Caed. Ylena and I are leaving now. Together."

She knew he said it to hurt Caed, but she couldn't look at him to apologize without giving away her true feelings. She followed Wilder and the others outside as Caed watched them go.

Ylena decided that the less she said about what just happened, the better. When no one spoke for several blocks, she thought she might avoid any complicated questions.

"Is someone going to explain what in the Abyss that was all about?" asked Tayeh.

Rev looked directly at Ylena, but luckily, Wilder spoke as he stalked down the street. "Caed is a Priest we worked with during the Pageant. He was just supposed to be our dance instructor, but he was always putting his hands all over Ylena. He said that I couldn't be trusted, but he was sneaking into the Underneath for unknown reasons even back then. I don't trust him at all."

Ylena wanted to say something to defend Caed but realized all of those things were technically true. She wasn't sure what she could say to change Wilder's mind.

"What's he doing down here in the same Grotto as we are?" asked Tayeh.

"Yes," said Rev with a scowl. "That's exactly what I was wondering."

"Who knows?" said Wilder. "Priests make plans like the Wardens do. They only care about themselves."

"Does this change our plan for the Den tomorrow?" asked Quinn.

"No." Wilder's voice was sure. "We continue with our plans. I won't let Caed ruin what we have here."

Ylena avoided Rev's glare and walked in silence.

41

___

Sleeping on the bare floor in the terrible room did not prove restful. Ylena always slept on a stone floor in the cave, but her time sleeping in beds had apparently made her weak. She couldn't get comfortable the entire night, and anytime she drifted off, she had more dreams of the crying child. She hoped that if she could find where they were hiding the babies with powers, the dreams would stop.

They woke early and went through the awkward maneuvers of getting ready in the same room. After talking through their plan one more time, they split up to their different tasks. Ylena and Wilder walked to the Den together, and the guards let them in to see the Warden.

She was lying upside down on a couch, her feet propped up on the back. Her dark hair hung down over the edge onto the floor. She appeared to be counting something.

"Welcome, young friends!" she said. She jumped up and grabbed their hands to bring them to the couch next to her. "How are you enjoying the Grotto?"

"Very well, Warden," said Wilder.

"Good to hear!" The Warden's voice was cheerful, but Ylena knew not to trust it. "The Spectacle is almost upon us. Are you prepared?"

"Yes, Warden. Everything is going well," said Wilder.

"So, what are your thoughts about the Spectacle? Be honest." Wilder opened his mouth to answer again, but the Warden turned to Ylena. "I would like to hear from you, dear."

Ylena realized that the best way for her to dissemble was to tell the truth. "I think the Spectacle will be thrilling. I'm sure people will talk about it for years to come."

"Quite right!" said the Warden. "I can't wait to hear all about it!" She shooed them off of the couch and flipped upside down again. "Goodbye!"

The two of them exchanged looks and then walked out of the room, passing the guards standing outside the door.

Before they walked into the door leading to the rehearsal space, Wilder said to the guards, "My friend, Quinn, will come by soon to drop off a prop he picked up for our performance. Will you send him back to us when he arrives?"

The two guards grunted and continued their watch.

Their rehearsal went about the same as usual. They stood in place for a long time while dealing with the particular quirks of their costar. The Little Warden of Chaos was very similar to her namesake. She had a dreamy expression on her face most of the time, but it occasionally turned sharp as a knife. Ylena, Wilder, and Maestro all trod carefully around her.

"That was quite the moving performance, Moya."

Maestro looked ready to be finished for the day, but Ylena and Wilder had other plans.

"Maestro, can we run this song one more time?" asked Wilder. "I'd like a bit more rehearsal."

Moya looked at him suspiciously. "You need more practice standing there?"

"We have a small dancing portion—" began Wilder.

"Can we rehearse how the Spectacle ends?" asked Ylena. She had to keep them all in here rehearsing. "I'd love to find out how this ends."

Maestro shrugged. "Sure. Why not? It's very short, but a little extra rehearsal is probably a good thing. Are you willing, Moya?"

She giggled and clapped her hands. "That sounds like so much fun! I love that scene."

Maestro dug into his folder of paperwork and pulled up two pieces of paper for Ylena and Wilder. "Okay, let's run through the lines of the song, and I will show you where to stand."

Goddess: This City is mine.

Companion: The City and its people are Yours.

Goddess: I am pleased with everything in the light of the sun.

Grottos: But Goddess, what of the Underneath? Are we not Yours? Do you hear our cry?

Goddess: The Priests belong to me and care for my people who live Above. You are not mine.

Grottos: Then we will rule ourselves.

Our Vices will guide us.

Our Wardens will lead us.

And one day, we will rule Your children.

Ylena shook her head as she tried to understand the words. "This says the Goddess doesn't claim the people in the Underneath. Is that true?"

Maestro gave her a snide look. "I can't exactly ask her, can I?"

"I guess not," said Ylena. "But some people down here worship her, right?"

Moya's accusative eyes roved across Ylena's face. "Even though I'd love to find out what heretical teachings you've been listening to, I think I will keep my focus on the script. I suggest you do the same." Her sweet voice stood in harsh contrast with her threat.

Ylena turned to Wilder to see what he would say, but he was ignoring her and focusing on Moya.

"This script is terrific. Where should we stand to deliver these lines?" He had turned his smile onto Moya, and it seemed to distract her as well as it always did.

"Great question, Wilder! The two of you will stand at center stage, and all of us that are playing the role of Wardens will surround you. It will be quite menacing and delightful!" She clapped her hands in excitement.

"That does sound delightful," said Maestro. "I hadn't heard that plan yet, but it sounds as good as any other. Go ahead and try it."

Ylena and Wilder stood center stage and recited their lines. Ylena felt guilty saying something that she felt must be wrong, but she honestly didn't have any proof to say that it was true. If the Goddess built the City a thousand years ago and the High Priests built the Underneath around two hundred years ago, then that means the Goddess wasn't really involved, was she? And if she actually had been involved in building the Underneath, what did that say about her as a Goddess? Ylena wasn't sure what to believe.

They were still running the lines when Quinn walked in. Ylena had been so distracted that she forgot they were in the middle of their plan.

"Hey, guys!" Quinn's cheerful voice rang across the room. "Sorry to interrupt. Can I ask Ylena a quick question?"

Wilder looked at Ylena. "Why do you need Ylena? Don't you mean you have a question for me?" The plan was for Wilder to leave with him for the next step, not Ylena.

"Nope! I need Ylena. But thanks!" Quinn stepped out into the hallway. Ylena shrugged and followed him out.

42

"Quinn!" she whispered. "This isn't the plan—"

"Come on. There isn't time." He led her up the stairs quickly. "Rev is distracting the guards outside, but even she eventually tires of that."

At the top of the stairs was a hallway that matched the long entrance downstairs. There were small rooms off either side.

"These look like the rooms of all their guards," whispered Quinn. "It looks like they might have as many as a dozen guards roaming around here at any time. I'm guessing they normally hang out in the training room below when you aren't in there rehearsing. Some are in their rooms now, so we have to be quiet."

They hurried down the hallway past the rooms and made it into a dining area. There were tables and benches throughout the room, and at one end, they saw a child-size table. The toddlers were just around the age that they should be able to sit at the table and feed themselves with limited assistance. Ylena had seen all the babies Mims was taking care of, and she couldn't imagine that many babies in the care of the Wardens.

Quinn didn't stop to look at the table, but continued to another door further in the room. "I've unlocked every door but this one. I can hear people inside, but I can't understand what they are doing."

"What can I do?" she asked.

He pointed at the rough stone that made up the high walls of the room. "Climb that. Each of the rooms I entered had a type of ventilation grate along the top, and I think you can peek through it into the next room if you can get up higher."

Now she understood why he'd asked for her and not Wilder. She followed him into the room on the right of the closed door and started climbing the wall. It was rough, but it was smoother than a lot of the stone along the walls of the cave. She had to backtrack once because she was hurrying and didn't want to show Quinn how she could shape stone. And for once, she hadn't been crying recently. She made her way to the top and peeked through the grate. Holding the position was straining all of her muscles to their limit, but she had to know if there were children inside.

There were no children. Just more guards. She was frustrated at all of this work for nothing when a guard blew a handful of poison dust into another guard's face. Ylena almost lost her grip on the wall. One guard was killing another! What was happening? Had they unfortunately timed their mission at the same time as an internal conflict?

The guard who breathed in the dust was clutching her throat and rolling helplessly on the floor. Ylena wanted to help, but she knew she could never make it in time. She had seen how fast that dust could work. That woman would be dead in seconds.

The woman stopped clutching her throat and pulled a

vial out of her pocket. She popped the top off and poured it into her mouth. Her legs stopped thrashing, and her eyes returned to normal. She was still panting, but at least she was breathing. Then, the woman smiled.

Ylena almost fell off the wall again. What was in that vial? Was it something everyone knew about? And the biggest question of all, did Wilder know this existed when he left them all alone to die by the Sentinels?

Ylena had the benefit of tears to help her on the way down, although she tried to be subtle to not show Quinn. He didn't see the handholds, but he saw her tears.

"What was ...? No, never mind. Tell us later. Let's go." He followed her back down the hallway and down the stairs. He stopped in front of the door to the rehearsal space. "Think of a good reason you are crying. You can't hide it." And with that, he hurried back out the door.

When she entered the room, she realized he was right. She couldn't hide it. She saw Wilder's face and was immediately suspicious of him and couldn't help but see Pim dead on the ground.

He hurried to her side and whispered, "Ylena, what's wrong?"

She obviously couldn't talk about it in the room, which he should realize. She turned to see Moya and Maestro staring at them in curiosity. She needed a reason that Quinn made her cry.

"Quinn says he doesn't love me anymore." She covered her face with her hands because she knew she wasn't a good enough actor to pull it off.

"He said what?" said Wilder.

"He doesn't love me! Don't make me say it again! Can we just go now?"

"Oh ... um ... yeah, that's probably for the best. Are we free to go, Maestro?"

"Sure." He rolled his eyes at what he assumed was more of their relational drama. "I'll see you in the final Grotto."

Wilder nodded and helped lead a weeping Ylena to the door. Once the door closed, she stopped crying and carefully wiped her tears.

"What is it, Ylena?"

"Not now." She pushed open the door that led into the long hallway.

Rev stood between the two male guards who had both turned inward to stare at her. She was wearing clothes, but barely, and she was leaning back against the wall in a pose that accented all of her best features. She was playfully biting on the tip of her finger in a way that drew even more attention to her bright red lips. The taller guard leaned in to whisper in her ear, and she giggled and put her hand on his chest.

"You boys are just the best! Thank you for entertaining me. You made the wait so pleasurable!"

Wilder rolled his eyes so the guards couldn't see.

One guard realized they weren't alone. "Hey, where's the little guy?" It took Ylena a moment to realize they meant Quinn. He was taller than Ylena, but compared to the bulky guards, he was little.

"Oh, you mean Quinn?" Rev pointed at him from where he stood at the door, and he waved. "He's such a quiet guy that it's easy to forget he's been here the whole time!" Her sparkling laugh entranced the guards again, and they forgot any suspicions before they had time to take root.

"I'll come back and visit soon, okay?" she said with a wink and followed Ylena, Wilder, and Quinn out of the Den.

Outside, they met up with Tayeh. "How did it go in there?"

"I'd rather not discuss it until we are back in our room," said Ylena.

"How did it go out here?" asked Wilder.

"Pretty boring. There were only two people who were going to walk inside. One woman looked scared, and I told her the Warden was in a foul mood and that she should come back after lunch to see if that helped."

Wilder chuckled. "And the other?"

"That one was way more fun! He didn't believe me when I said he should come back, and then I told him it was too full in there and he should wait until someone else came out. He still didn't listen, so I twisted his arm behind his back and led him around the corner to the alley before I beat him up there. I assume he either ran home or is hiding and scared I'll come back for him." She chuckled darkly.

"That was more productive than me," said Wilder. "I literally stayed in rehearsal the whole time. Ylena got to have all the fun."

"The plans changed?" Wilder nodded, and she grunted.

They made it back to their room and began climbing up to the third floor. Wilder and Ylena were the last two to go up when she turned around from the ladder to talk to him.

"I have to ask you this now," she said. "Depending on your answer, I don't know how I will react, and I don't want the others to see."

"What is it, Ylena? What did you see?" Wilder was studying her face with concern.

"I saw a guard blow Sentinel dust into the face of another guard."

Wilder's face was horrified. "I'm so sorry. You shouldn't have had to see that again."

"Before the guard died, she pulled a vial from her pocket and drank it. And she lived." Ylena stared at his face and tried to detect any signs of guilt, but she saw none.

"What does that mean? Do you mean they've found a cure?" His face was hopeful.

"I was wondering if you could tell me."

"How would I tell you? I'm just now hearing about this ..." His face fell. "Oh, you thought I already knew."

She still stared at him with hard eyes. "So, you are saying you didn't know? Not at all?"

"No! If I would have known, I would have brought some for my own safety."

She growled. "Thanks for being honest. Once again, you've proven that you would have walked away no matter the consequences." She turned to begin the climb up the ladder.

He pulled her around by the arm. "Ylena! I didn't know! I don't know how that information would have changed my decisions, because it's honestly something I never considered." His voice dropped to a whisper. "I have apologized to you multiple times about my part in the deaths of Pim and the others, and you said you didn't blame me. I know you still do, and I wish you'd be honest about it."

She wanted to yell at him about their deaths, but she remembered again that she was the one to blame. Why was it so easy for her to forget and try to blame him? The image of him walking out the theater door was burned into her mind, and anytime she remembered Pim's death, that was the image she saw. She started to speak when they heard a voice from above.

"Everything okay down there?" asked Rev.

"We're fine," said Wilder.

Ylena didn't answer but began the long climb up.

43

O nce Ylena and Wilder made it inside, she told the others what she had seen. They were all just as shocked as Wilder.

"I'm not surprised they have kept this so secret," said Quinn. "The High Priests use that dust as their number one form of attack. People down here have tried to discover how they create it for years, but no one has ever figured it out. Finding a cure makes their weapon meaningless."

"This is a much bigger advantage than the babies with Gifts," said Wilder. "They can use this cure right now."

"Maybe they plan on revealing this at the Spectacle?" said Tayeh. "It would definitely encourage people to join a revolt if they knew the High Priest's poison dust wouldn't immediately kill them."

"Can you imagine what this means?" said Rev. "We could storm the doors right now. We could all get out. This could happen soon. It would mean the liberation of every person in the Underneath."

They sat in silence and considered her words for a moment. Ylena tried to imagine what it would be like if every person in the Underneath suddenly walked out into the City. It would certainly be more crowded, but the City had a lot of space that wasn't being used. The excessive executions, plus the fact that their Priests couldn't bear children, meant that the City was underpopulated. But even with all that space, how would the two groups of people react to one another? Ylena didn't really care what happened to the High Priests, but what about the Priests who were just trying to survive in the City like everyone else? Would they lump in all the Priests with the evil High Priests? And what about the fact that the Priests couldn't even use their Gifts right now? Would that make them useless?

Her mind was spinning with questions with no answers. Everyone else seemed lost in their own thoughts until Rev spoke.

"Should we go find some dinner? If we are leaving here in the morning, I'd like to stop by the one excellent restaurant in this Grotto."

They all agreed and were quickly out the door and down the ladder. On the way, Rev explained why the restaurant was so good.

"They take their love of Chaos and use it to blend some truly fascinating combinations! A lot of places around here try that, but this is the only place I've found that actually succeeded at making something edible."

They arrived at the restaurant and easily found a table for all five of them.

"It's usually a lot busier than this," said Rev. "I guess the high price of food is getting out of hand."

A tired server came over to take their order. He said, "We have potatoes with a mushroom wine sauce."

"And?" said Tayeh.

"That's it. That's what we have." He shrugged.

"I guess we will take five orders, please." said Rev.

The server asked for the payment in advance, and Quinn counted out the sizeable sum. When the server left, Quinn said, "My gambling winnings are running low. If the food situation doesn't change soon, I'm going to have to go back to Instinct and try to win some more."

"Let's wait to see what happens after the Spectacle," said Wilder. "By then, we could live in a completely different world."

Their food arrived, and even though it was simple, it was delicious. They ate in silence as they each considered what the Spectacle would bring.

On their walk back to their room, Rev pulled Wilder and Tayeh into a conversation about the weapons they saw in the stores they passed. Ylena expected it was a move to keep Wilder away from her, but she was too introspective to be upset.

Quinn caught her staring at the three of them and fell back to walk alongside her.

"It won't always be this hard."

"I don't know what you mean." She switched her attention to the weapon dealers' shops.

"If you talk to him, it won't be as bad as you think."

"I talk to Wilder a lot. That's what Rev says the problem is."

"No. You aren't talking about the right things." He sighed and ran his fingers through his hair. "Can I tell you an embarrassing story? Will you promise not to laugh?"

Ylena chuckled darkly. "I embarrass myself painfully all the time. I promise I won't laugh."

"You know I went to the same school as Wilder and Rev." She nodded, and he continued, "I remember the day that the headmaster brought Wilder to the school. Looking back now, I realize he was scared and malnourished, but even then, I thought he was the most magnificent creature I had ever seen."

Ylena's mouth dropped opened, but she closed it before Quinn could see.

"He's only a year older than me, and at that time, I was just starting to realize what all the swirling emotions meant. I fell for him so hard. In many ways, he's exactly the same now as he was then. Kind, quick with a smile, and clever enough to realize precisely how charming he can be. He could have used that charm on me, and I would have done anything he asked. But he never did. He was always so kind."

He smiled as he lost himself in the memory.

"So, you eventually grew out of it and became friends?" she asked.

"No. It wasn't that easy. Wilder noticed my obvious mooning over him, and he came to talk to me. Who knows? Maybe Rev is the one who talked him into it. But he sat me down one day and said, 'Quinn, I like you a lot, but not in the same way that I think you like me. I want to be your friend, and I want to be clear. A friendship is all it will ever be. I'll understand if that makes it too painful to be around me, but if you can settle for friendship, I will be here.'"

Ylena's heart caught in her throat. She whispered, "What did you say?"

"At the time, I thought my world had ended. I just nodded and let him walk away. But after a few days of avoiding him, I realized that my life was better with him in it, and I was willing to settle for friendship. Over time, that initial heartbreak went away, and we've been friends ever since. Would you ever have guessed if I hadn't told you?"

"No. I honestly wouldn't. I never picked up on any of that between the two of you."

"Because we are friends. Truly. Now, don't get me wrong. Wilder is even more attractive now than he was when he was younger." He smiled. "However, I moved on and found someone who could reciprocate my feelings. If Wilder hadn't said those hard words to me, I might have wasted my heart on him for years. It was one of the most loving things he ever did for me."

They walked in silence for a while.

"Thanks for sharing that, Quinn. I think I understand what I have to do."

44

They each began climbing the ladder to their room for the last time. The other three had already climbed inside, and Ylena motioned Quinn to go first. Before she put her foot on the rung of the ladder, she heard a cry.

"Do you hear that? It's the child I've been hearing in my dreams."

Quinn called something to her from high on the ladder, but she couldn't hear. The child's cry was too loud. She wandered around the side of the building but couldn't see him. The purple glow from the crystal was bright enough that she should have been able to see him based on how loud his cry was. But she couldn't find him.

She ran down several streets trying to get closer to the sound of his cry. He sounded lonely and afraid, and she had to find him. She pulled herself to a stop when she arrived at the Warden's Den. She stood in the bright area around the crystal and considered how she could get inside the Den to get him out.

His cry was getting more frantic. He was young enough that he could only say a few unintelligible words, but it was clearly a cry for help. Tears poured down her face, and she considered dissolving the stone of the entire Den to get him out. She took a step forward but was pulled back.

"Ylena! Wake up!" Wilder stood like a human wall in front of her, and she couldn't make it to the Den.

"I'm awake!" And as she said the words, she actually came awake. But she wasn't so sure if she had been sleeping a few moments ago. She shook her head and tried to clear her mind of the child's cries.

"You can hear me?" asked Wilder.

"Yes, of course I can hear you."

"You couldn't a minute ago. I've been yelling at you to stop for several blocks."

She blinked her eyes, and the child's cry faded away completely. "Several blocks?" She looked around and realized how far from their room she had run. She saw the other three coming around the corner to join her and Wilder near the crystal.

"Quinn saw you wander off saying something about a child crying. He called for the rest of us, and we followed you here. What was happening?"

She rubbed her head and tried to piece it together. "I heard a child crying. He was so frantic. It was loud, like he was close by. I felt like he pulled me here."

They looked at the Den in front of them. "We know the children have to be in there," said Rev. "Your mind must be trying to make sense of that. Grotto Chaos can mess with anyone's head."

"But it was so real. I felt like he was trying to talk to me."

"You could tell the baby was a boy?" asked Quinn.

"Yeah ... somehow ..." She felt like she could almost picture him in her mind.

"You probably should try to get some sleep. Maybe that will clear your head," said Wilder.

She nodded, and they started the walk back to their room. She was worried that she would still hear the child in her dreams.

They only made it a few steps when several things happened at once. A Sentinel leapt from a doorway and stabbed Tayeh in her stomach. Another Sentinel whacked Wilder in the head with a large staff, and he crumpled to the ground. A third Sentinel joined him to pick up Wilder and drag him off. Ylena examined the situation and ran to Tayeh, who was kneeling on the ground. Ylena still had tears in her eyes from searching for the crying baby, and she touched Tayeh's bloody hands where they gripped her stomach.

She didn't notice the Sentinel who had raised the end of his sword to knock her on the head until Rev and Quinn tackled him and ripped the sword away. Ylena and Tayeh both gasped as the Gift did its work. Rev and Quinn were still wrestling the Sentinel when Tayeh picked up the sword.

Seeing the three of them were back in control, Ylena ran in the direction the two other Sentinels carried Wilder. She glimpsed them several blocks ahead and guessed they were running to the stairway that led Upstairs. The streets were laid out in a chaotic pattern, and sometimes, her shortcuts took longer than she expected. She hoped the same was true for the two carrying Wilder.

The Sentinels paused in an alley to shift Wilder's limp form between them. Ylena found a man selling shriveled up potatoes out of the back of a cart. She tossed him a coin and grabbed a potato from the cart as she ran by. At the entrance of the alley, she sank down to her knees. Her tears fell freely as she set the potato on the ground. Roots shot from the potato and branched down the alley, slithering like snakes along the stone. The Sentinels didn't notice until the vines began creeping up their legs. They tried to swat the roots away, but they tangled up their legs and fell over. The more they fought, the tighter the vines wrapped around them. She saw Wilder lying crumpled on the ground, and her eyes narrowed as she wound the vines even tighter. She looped a vine across their eyes and one across their mouth to quiet their screams.

She let go of her hold on the roots and ran up to Wilder. She gently turned him over and began checking him for wounds.

"Wilder! Can you hear me? Wilder!" She wiped a new tear from her eye and took his face in her hands. She closed her eyes and reached out to find what there was to heal. He was so still, and her panicked fingers reached for any sign of life.

She gasped at the same time he did. He blinked his eyes like he couldn't focus on her face. "Wilder, can you hear me?"

"Yes," he whispered. "You're bleeding."

"I'm not hurt. You are." She was crying again.

He wiped away her tears and showed her the blood that was mixed in. "This isn't yours?"

She pulled her hands away from his face and realized she was covered in blood. She had wiped her hands across her face to gather the tears. "It's Tayeh's blood. But she's okay."

She heard Rev, Tayeh, and Quinn run down the alley behind her, but she continued to search Wilder's face to make sure he was okay.

"Who did this?" asked Tayeh.

Quinn touched the vines that were tightly wrapped around their assailants. "Maybe it was that Priest we saw last night."

Wilder shook his head. "No, Caed is from Discipline, not Order." He looked at Ylena. "Did you see who did this?"

"No," she looked at the vines so she wouldn't have to look him in the eyes. "I found them like this when I came around the corner."

"There must be another Priest lurking down here," said Rev. "Why would a Priest try to stop Sentinels? Why wouldn't they help take you to the High Priests?"

"Not all the Priests follow the High Priests," said Ylena a bit too defensively. "In fact, the High Priests murder Priests just as easily as they do anyone else."

Tayeh grunted. "Whoever did it might still be around. I don't want to wait and find out if they were trying to help you or grab you for themselves. I suggest we get out of here."

"I agree," said Wilder. He stood and didn't seem to suffer any lasting effects. "In fact, I suggest we grab our things and head out tonight. I'm not falling asleep soon, and I'd rather be finished here."

Everyone agreed, and they began their walk to the final Grotto.

DELIRIUM

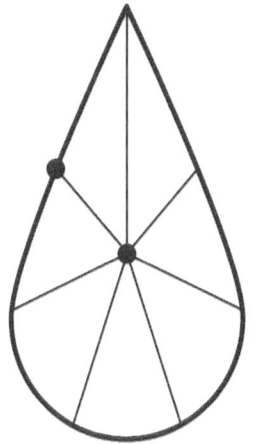

45

They arrived in Delirium in silence and exhaustion. No one could think clearly about the best place to go, so Ylena took them to the only place she knew they would be safe.

She knocked on the door and smiled when a familiar face answered.

"Grandfather!" She grabbed him in a hug. "I'm so glad to see you. Can we sleep here tonight?"

Grandfather took in the sight of all of them, some still covered in blood, and opened the door. "Are you hurt? Do you need me to call an apothecary?"

Ylena didn't know what that was, but Wilder answered as he walked in. "That's unnecessary, Brynn. We are all familiar with Ylena's Gift, and we are fine."

Grandfather studied their faces as they each settled their blankets down on the floor of his living room in exhaustion. He must have realized they were well enough for the moment, because he soon turned off the light and went back to bed himself.

Ylena felt like her eyes had barely closed when they were

suddenly open again. Grandfather tried to be quiet in the kitchen, but considering it was all one large room, he was unsuccessful. She noticed the others were stirring in their blankets, but she got up to join Grandfather in the kitchen.

"Tea?" he asked her quietly.

"Coffee," she said with a smile.

He got an odd expression. "Oh, yes, of course. Coffee." He took the coffee down from the shelf. "I forget you aren't the same little girl I raised on the mountain."

She sighed. "I feel like I left our home on the mountain two lifetimes ago."

He gave her a sad smile. "It was peaceful up there, wasn't it? I spent most of my life here in Delirium, but it is still strange to be back."

"Do you want to go back to the mountain?"

"I don't think that's an option for me anymore. The Wardens were happy when I was being useful up there, but now they've found other jobs for me."

She was going to ask more when Wilder joined her at the table.

"The food shortages have got people on edge in other Grottos. What about here?" asked Wilder.

Grandfather chuckled darkly. "If people in Delirium are on edge, it's because that's what they've chosen. There are still plenty of options to make everyone feel completely relaxed."

Ylena remembered seeing some people passed out on the street on her first night here, and she finally understood why. "That's what this Grotto celebrates? Being so relaxed you eventually pass out?"

"For some people," said Grandfather as he continued to prepare the coffee. "You can find many things to eat, drink, or smoke that will make you feel relaxed or excited or unconscious. The sellers here have quite the variety." Ylena couldn't tell if he was proud or sickened by the idea.

He brought the coffee over to the table and poured them each a glass. "We also have apothecaries who have cures for stomach aches or muscle pain, things like that. But since they sell basically the same things, that line gets blurred."

When the others woke up, they each took turns in the small washroom trying to clean up.

"Tayeh, you lost a lot of blood," said Quinn. "We are all covered in it!"

"I can't believe I'm still alive. Ylena, I owe you a debt. I should be dead."

"I'm sorry that I healed you without asking." Ylena gave her a fake stern expression. "I told you not to let anyone get hurt around me!"

Tayeh gave a wry smile. "Yeah, sorry for that. I'll try to keep a better lookout for guys hiding in shadows with swords."

They finished wiping off all the blood and dressed in clean clothes. Ylena and Wilder had to meet with the Warden again, and the others decided to split up to see what they could discover. But before they left, Quinn pulled Ylena and Wilder aside.

"I drew a map of the Den based on our time in there yesterday. Something felt strange about it, but it wasn't until I drew it that I figured it out." He handed them the map. "Here's the long hallway we enter. The doors in front lead to the Warden. To the right, their assistant. To the left is the rehearsal space that has a staircase leading up to their sleeping quarters, dining hall and the small training rooms. But I think there has to be more on the other side of the room you rehearse in. I don't know how to get in there, but it makes sense that they would have built a room there to match the space upstairs."

Wilder studied the map. "So, there is a large room hidden between the rehearsal room and the outside wall of the building?"

Quinn nodded. "Too bad we don't know a Priest from Purpose. They could just melt the stone of the outside wall, and we would be in."

"Yes, that's too bad," said Ylena slowly.

"What are you thinking?" asked Wilder.

"Oh! Nothing. Um ... But last night, when I heard the child crying, they really were on the other side of that wall."

Quinn nodded. "It's very possible."

"Maybe we can listen near the inside wall during our rehearsal today? I haven't noticed anything, but maybe there is a hidden door in the room somewhere?" said Wilder.

"Maybe," said Quinn. "It's also possible that it only has a staircase that leads down from above. That would definitely make it more secure."

Wilder clapped him on the back. "Excellent work, Quinn! You're the best!" Quinn beamed at the praise as Ylena and Wilder headed out the door.

Ylena and Wilder walked into the Den of the Warden of Delirium together for the second time. The first time Ylena had been here felt like a blur. She had arrived in the Underneath the night before, and her whole body had been frozen with grief. She still felt the sadness try to drown her some days, but she was surprised to realize that her mind was clearer than it had been before. That made her feel good, but also guilty.

The guards opened the door, and Ylena and Wilder walked inside.

"Welcome back, young ones!" said the Warden. "Come join me again!"

They sat on the couch in front of the fire like they had before. The Warden was in a bright red dress, and her lipstick was a perfect match. "I trust you've had an eventful time touring the Grottos."

"Yes, Warden," they answered in unison.

"Good. Tell me, will the show be magnificent?" she asked in a conspiratorial whisper.

"Yes, Warden," said Wilder. "The rehearsals are going well, and we've gathered amazing performers from each Grotto. I think you will be pleased."

"I'm sure I will! I look forward to hearing about it!" Wilder made a strange face, but she continued. "You should also gather our best apothecaries to have on hand just in case they are needed."

"Of course, Warden. I'm sure they will make the event more ... festive."

She clapped her hands. "Yes, exactly! I think the Spectacle is exactly what we need right now!" She stood up, and they followed. "Off you go! Get to practice! We want everything to be perfect!"

46

Ylena and Wilder headed across the hall into the training room for their last rehearsal in a Grotto. Maestro was seated at his usual place at the table, but the girl who would play the Warden hadn't arrived.

They sat down beside him, and Wilder asked, "Are you worried about what is going to happen at the Spectacle?"

"Of course not," said Maestro. "I think the Wardens will be so pleased to have shared such beautiful art with the masses that they will become kinder, gentler rulers."

"Okay ..." said Wilder. "I'm picking up on your sarcasm."

"Of course I'm worried!" He lowered his voice even though they were the only three in the room. "Why are the Wardens so excited about throwing this big celebration for everyone? It's extremely out of character, and I don't trust it one bit."

Ylena spoke up. "We thought that maybe they are preparing to make an announcement about a revolt against Upstairs and are trying to get everyone motivated."

Maestro looked at her with a flat stare. "The Wardens have never tried to 'motivate' anyone before, other than by terrifying us into doing whatever they please. There's no need for them to throw a party. They could just say, 'We are storming the temples next week. Lots of you will probably die, but if you don't do what we say, then you definitely will die.'"

"I agree," said Wilder. "So, what are we going to do about it?"

"What are 'we' going to do? 'We' won't be doing anything. I have no idea what they are planning, so I have no idea what to do. I don't know if it's safer to have Pierce stay by my side during the Spectacle so we will be together, or to tell him to stay as far away from the Spectacle as possible. And I have no actual reason to trust either of you, so 'we' will just do our own things, okay?"

"You don't trust us?" asked Ylena. "We are stuck in this just like you! Why wouldn't you trust us?"

"Both of you just came from Upstairs. I don't trust anyone from Upstairs."

"But you came from Upstairs," said Ylena.

"Yes. Exactly. I know how conniving I was, along with everyone else in the City. I'm not sure who I trust less: the Wardens or anyone from the City."

Wilder snorted. "Thanks for making that so clear. We'll just figure everything out on our own."

Maestro opened his mouth to retort, but a tall, red-haired girl glided into the room. "This is delightful! I'm so excited to get started!"

Maestro nodded his head listlessly. "Yes, Daena, this is thrilling. Let's begin."

Daena had a clear, alto voice that resonated through the room. Ylena realized she wouldn't be able to hear anything from the next room unless she pressed her ear up to the stone, and even that was questionable. While she stood waiting in her pose with Wilder, she had plenty of time to examine the far wall. There were no outlines of a door, and Ylena felt that if a door into the next room existed, it came from above.

On the last note of Daena's song, Ylena spun wildly and tossed the clip from her hair against the far wall. She touched her messy hair. "Oops! I guess I need a better hairstyle for the show!" She gave a self-deprecating smile. "I'll go grab that."

Maestro rolled his eyes, and Daena gave a fake smile that barely covered her disdain. Ylena hurried over to the wall where the clip landed and made a show of looking for it. The others quickly got bored and ignored her.

As she felt around for her clip, she tried listening through the stone for any sounds of crying babies. She "found" her clip and started slowly putting it back in her hair. The crying child she heard in her dreams filled her thoughts, and she allowed a tear to roll down her cheek. She casually rested her hand on the wall, like she was taking a breather. A thin thread of stone liquified and spread out in a narrow line as she bore a hole under her palm. She was about to look inside when Maestro called.

"Ylena, are you okay over there? You are acting a little odd today."

She straightened up quickly, and the stone flowed back into the hole. "I'm fine! I just felt out of breath for a moment." She reluctantly walked back to the group. "We've been rehearsing so hard, you know!"

Daena looked at her with a baffled expression. "You spend almost the entire number just standing there."

"Um ... yeah ... that's true. I guess I'm out of shape after the Pageant." Wilder rubbed his forehead to hide his expression at her lame explanation.

"Well, since I don't want to overly tire you, Ylena, how about we call it a day?" said Maestro. "I think we are ready for our dress rehearsal tomorrow. I guess we will just see what happens?"

Ylena didn't feel very inspired by that vote of confidence.

~

"It was pointless," she said to Wilder as they walked back to Grandfather's house. "There is no way to hear anything through the stone. The only way we can get into the room is if we go up the stairs like I did with Quinn before. Maybe we could get back in and try that?"

"No. It's too late. It doesn't matter at this point." His face was resigned, and he walked with slumped shoulders.

"Why are you saying that? Don't you want to know what they are doing with those children?"

"Of course I want to know. I just know that it doesn't make a difference. They are raising those children to balance the power between the Underneath and Upstairs. Plus, they have the cure for the poisonous dust. They have what they need to start the revolution."

"But what if they are harming those children? Why do I keep hearing the boy crying? He's terrified!"

He stopped walking. "Ylena, we don't know for sure that the cries you heard are real." She frowned. "I know they seem real, but no one else has heard anything. And think about it. These children are the future food producers for the Underneath. Don't you think the Wardens are protecting them with everything they have? That's why they are in the safest place in the Grotto. They are probably eating better than anyone here. It's time for us to move on and find something that's in our control." He started walking again.

"There's something in our control?" she asked. "I'm really curious what that is."

He smirked. "I admit, our options are limited."

She raised an eyebrow but didn't respond.

47

Ylena and Wilder returned to Grandfather's house to find everyone else gathered in the living room. By their expressions, it appeared their day was equally unsuccessful.

"No, we couldn't hear anything." Wilder flopped onto one of the ragged chairs. "I think we need to resign ourselves to the fact that whatever happens at the Spectacle will be a surprise to us as well."

"We didn't learn anything about what's going to happen either," said Rev. "We learned that the Wardens have not only been selling the Spectacle as the biggest party the Underneath has ever seen, but also telling them that their attendance is required. They want every person in the Underneath to crowd into the Heart of the Grottos for this event."

"I don't think the Wardens will even attend." Wilder's statement caused everyone to stare.

"Why do you say that?" asked Quinn.

"The last two Wardens have said that they can't wait to hear how the Spectacle goes, like they won't be there. When the Chaos Warden said it, I thought was just because she is a bit … chaos. But the Warden of Delirium said it, too. I think it means something. They don't want to be around for whatever is going to happen."

"What a Goddess-damn mess." Tayeh shook her head.

Ylena tried to stay quiet because she knew she was not the most liked person at the moment, but she finally spoke up. "I feel like the Spectacle could turn into something awful. Wilder and I have to be there, but the rest of you don't. I think you should stay somewhere safe and hide."

The group broke out in multiple angry protests at the same time.

"Absolutely not!" said Rev. "I will be there—"

"You think you can handle that on your own!" said Tayeh. "I have to be there—"

"You need backup, and I have to learn their secrets!" said Quinn. "I'm going—"

"Calm down!" said Wilder. "I think Ylena makes a good point. There's no reason for you to all be at risk."

Rev gave him a hard stare. "Wilder. You asked us to join you on this little adventure. Are you seriously trying to turn us back now at the very end?"

Wilder hesitated, but Ylena jumped in angrily. "That's what I'm afraid of! That this will be the very end! I can't handle this again. I lost everyone, do you understand that?" She looked Rev in the eye. "I can't lose you like I lost Pim." Her breath caught on a sob. "I know you are mad at me right now, but I can't handle the thought of losing you. Any of you. Please. Just stay home." She hid her face in her hands to hide the tears.

She felt someone settle next to her on the floor. Rev's arms wrapped around her, and her soft voice caused Ylena to cry even harder.

"Ylena, you won't lose us. That's why we are going. Because we are sticking together. No matter what."

She didn't look up, but she spoke into Rev's blond hair. "But what if something happens? Surely a Spectacle in the Underneath is going to be more dangerous than a Pageant. What if I lose all of you and I'm all alone again?"

"You won't ever be alone, Ylena. Even if something happens to one or all of us. You aren't ever truly alone." She stroked Ylena's hair until her breathing calmed.

Ylena pulled away from Rev and wiped her tears with her hand. She held up her wet fingertips and said to the silent group, "Anyone have a stomachache or a hangnail they need healed?"

They smiled comfortingly, while Quinn pulled a hand-kerchief out of his bag. She wiped her face and took a deep breath. "Okay. You will be there."

They all nodded.

"Then I guess that's settled. We will all be there. We have no idea what will happen or how to prepare. And we have nothing to do but wait around until something terrible happens."

"Everything was true until that last bit. I think we have something to do," said Rev. "We're going out."

There was a lot of scrambling to get dressed into the proper clothes for "out." Ylena never quite understood what that was, but Rev threw her a couple things, and Ylena put them on obediently. She pulled her tear-stained hair up into a ponytail, and with the short skirt and the sparkly top, she felt a little more alive than when she started.

She imagined the large structures in the other Grottos and asked if that was where they were headed. Wilder chuckled. "There is a large, Priest-built club in the center of Delirium, but I think we will go somewhere slightly less ambitious tonight. I think we are all too emotional to walk into a place as intense as that. We actually need to wake up tomorrow morning."

She laughed but realized he was being serious. They didn't have far to walk before they arrived at the small shop that glowed with a warm light from within.

They walked up to the bar, and Ylena took a seat. Rev sat down next to her and turned Ylena to face her. "Okay, I need you to listen closely. Bars in Delirium are like the ones in Indulgence and also much, much worse." She pointed at a menu that had some teas and mixed drinks. "Teas like this and this are fine. They aren't as strong as the alcohol you had before and are nice and calming. Teas like this and this ... avoid them at all costs. At least if you want to wake up in the next few days."

Ylena looked up from the menu. "Thank you, Rev."

"Well, I didn't want a repeat from the Central Tavern. That was our fault for not telling you, but now you know exactly how dangerous this can be."

"Yes, but also ... Thank you."

Rev caught her eyes and understood her meaning. "You're welcome."

Ylena tried a sweet berry tea that Rev suggested. A woman sat in a corner, plucking the strings of a guitar and singing a gentle melody. The scent of flowers hung in the air, and she breathed in calming breaths.

Tomorrow, they were heading to the Heart of the Grottos for their dress rehearsal. The next day was the Spectacle.

The similarities between the Spectacle and the Pageant were enough to set her on edge. Upstairs, she had traveled from temple to temple, learning and becoming more than she had been before. But then, in the final moment, it had all fallen apart. Was that going to happen again? Were they all going to die?

She tried to think about Rev's words. She was never alone. It was a comforting thought, but she wasn't sure she believed that. When she had fled the Pageant and run to the Underneath, she had been more alone than she had ever been in her life. Her whole life shifted and started over. She wasn't sure she could handle that again.

She noticed Rev was no longer next to her. She looked toward the woman playing the guitar and saw Rev dancing with Wilder. They were smiling and seemed peaceful. Tayeh and Quinn were sitting on some low couches playing a game with colored stones on a checkered board. She finished her tea and wandered further into the bar.

Obviously, she found Lady Erenne sipping tea.

48

Ylena shook her head. "I need to stop being surprised to find you."

Lady Erenne smirked. "That wouldn't be any fun, now would it?"

Ylena joined her at the small table. "So, what do you want from me now?"

"I wanted to see how you are doing."

"Seriously? You are taking the time to check on me now? You didn't see how I was doing after Pim and the others were murdered, but you are asking now?"

"I admit to slightly poor timing."

Ylena raised an eyebrow.

"I'm here now, and I honestly do care, Ylena."

"The Spectacle is two days from now, and I think it's highly possible that everyone I've met down here will suffer the same fate as everyone from the Pageant. Is that what you want to know?"

Lady Erenne frowned. "I'm sorry, Ylena. I didn't know this is where we would end up."

"Tell me just one thing."

"What one thing?"

"Anything. One thing that went according to your plan. You dragged me into all of this. Tell me one thing that has gone the way you hoped."

"I hoped you would fall in love with this beautiful, terrible City."

Ylena caught her breath. "Maybe I have. But why do you care?"

"Because I love it, too. And it needs more than I can give it. I hoped you would be someone who could join me in caring for it."

Ylena felt a stirring in her heart at the words. After her teardrop shut down every crystal spire in the City, she apologized with more tears. She apologized for breaking such a beautiful City, and all the spires relit. She looked at Lady Erenne to see if she knew the extent of her words. Ylena wasn't ready to share that much information.

"I'm not sure I can care for the City like you do. I haven't killed any of its High Priests yet."

Lady Erenne's eyes flashed. "I'm willing to do whatever it takes, Ylena. I hope the other High Priests learn from their mistakes, but if they don't, I will do what is required."

"You sound just as bloodthirsty as them, so I guess you fit right in."

Lady Erenne rubbed her forehead. "Maybe I should have brought you into my plans sooner. I think that's the only reason I convinced to Caed to work with me. When I told him my plans, they lined up with his. I'm out of practice at all of this. I'm sorry."

Ylena once again tried to imagine Caed and Lady Erenne working together. They both enjoyed speaking so cryptically that she wasn't sure how they ever understood a single thing the other said.

Ylena stood to leave, but Lady Erenne said, "Please,

wait." She seemed desperate in a way Ylena had never seen before. She sat back down.

"You're going to be safe in the Spectacle, right?" Lady Erenne's dark eyes were troubled.

"Um ... as far as anyone in the Underneath can be safe. Why? What do you think is going to happen?"

"I don't know. I gave you the note about the Gifted children inside the Wardens' Dens because I hoped you would get inside and learn more. I don't know what they are planning to do with those babies or how soon they plan to do it. I won't be able to attend the Spectacle, and I'm worried I won't be able to protect you."

"Like you failed to protect me the night of the Pageant?" she sneered.

"Yes," said Lady Erenne seriously. "Like I failed to protect you that night."

Ylena scrunched her forehead in thought.

"Please be careful, Ylena. I'm not sure what I would do if you got hurt because of one of my plans."

"I'll be safe. I do appreciate your concern." She studied Lady Erenne's troubled face and made a decision. "I have a piece of information to share. The Wardens found a cure for the poison dust."

Lady Erenne's eyes widened. "That is very valuable information. The poison dust is the High Priest's main method of defense."

Ylena noted that Lady Erenne still didn't include herself when she referenced the High Priests. Because of that, she decided to share her last piece of information.

"We believe the Wardens are holding the children in a secret room directly to the left of their front door. I know it's dangerous for you to use your Gift right now, but maybe there is a way for you to melt the stone enough to see inside. I tried it earlier today from inside the Den but couldn't finish before I was seen. I hope you have better luck than I did." She stood to leave.

"Thank you for trusting me with that, Ylena." She had tears in her eyes. Those would come in handy for her later if she acted on the tip.

"Sure. I hope you find them, because I'm worried they need help. I keep hearing one of the children crying in my dreams. It's haunting." She shivered.

"You heard one of them?"

"Yes. I've heard a young boy crying for days now. I'm worried about what the Wardens are doing."

Lady Erenne gave her a considering look. "There aren't any Gifts that involving hearing the thoughts of someone else. Sharing memories with Knowledge, yes. But not hearing."

She shrugged. "Maybe he is the one with the Gift of Knowledge and is sharing with me."

Lady Erenne raised an eyebrow. "Without touching you?"

"I don't know how this works, but I know I'm not crazy!"

"I don't think you are crazy, Ylena." She tapped her lip thoughtfully. "I will check it out. Thanks for the information."

"You're welcome. I—"

"Ylena!" Rev's voice cut through the peaceful music drifting from the other room.

"I'm back here!" Ylena turned to tell Lady Erenne good-bye, but she was already gone.

Rev came through the door. "Who were you just talking to?"

"Just a random person. The people around here have a lot of odd stories." She avoided Rev's eye by looking into the other room. "What are the others doing?"

"They are getting restless to leave. I came to find you."

"I'm ready. Let's go."

They walked back to her grandfather's shop in a peaceful silence. Ylena was thinking about Lady Erenne's words. She seemed to genuinely care for Ylena, although she still kept so many secrets that Ylena didn't know what to believe. How many warnings could they receive about the Spectacle while still not knowing a single thing?

She didn't hear the child's cry, but she could feel him pulling her. She could point a straight line to the Den from where she stood. The hair on the back of her neck stood up like the moment before a lightning strike. Her fingers tingled like they were going numb. She shivered and rubbed her neck.

"Are you okay?" asked Wilder. "Are you hearing the baby cry?" At his words, the others turned to look at her with various levels of pity and skepticism.

"No. I don't hear the baby. I'm okay." She felt very conspicuous out in the purple glow, like there were eyes watching her. She tried to get the group to walk a little faster to get back to her grandfather's house.

THE SPECTACLE LITURGY

The Spectacle: Act I

When the City was born, so was the Heart of the Underneath.

The Goddess built her City to take and restrict.

Bind and limit.

Restrain and control.

But the Underneath gives freedom and life.

The religion of Above was too confining, and our spirits longed to be free. Our ancestors traveled to the Underneath to seek what they couldn't find Above.

They found their true souls Underneath.

They traveled freely up and down, living in the sunlight by day and seeking their desires Underneath at night.

Until the High Priests took control.

There were no High Priests in the City, until suddenly there were. They decided amongst themselves to rule the City and to rule the Underneath. They closed all the staircases except the ones in their temples, and they locked the doors from Above.

Travel is by their consent. The doors are opened by their word.

Without the High Priests' favor, we are born in the dark and die in the dark.

There is no sun for us.

There are no stars.

And yet ...

We burn.

We burn with rage and passion.

We burn with intensity and zeal.

We burn with a fire they do not have Above.

They will not quench us.

They cannot stop us.

We bring the revolution.

THE SPECTACLE

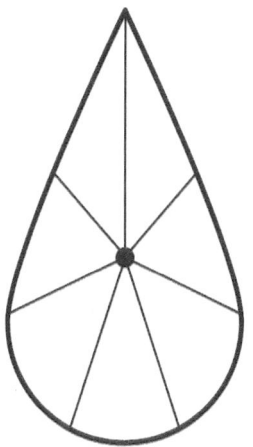

49

They woke early the next morning to begin their walk to the Heart of the Grottos. Grandfather said he would see them at the Spectacle the next day, and he sent them off full of coffee and unusually expensive eggs. Instead of walking through the tunnel that led to the next Grotto, they walked through a much smaller tunnel that led directly into the space at the center of the Grottos. The tunnels along the edges were only lit by sporadic lights and were dangerous to walk alone, but this tunnel was a whole different experience.

A thin stream of crystalline ran along the full length of the tunnel, and it was the only light. The top of the tunnel was lower than the others had been. If Wilder lifted his hand, he could have touched the stone above their head. She had never felt claustrophobic in a cave until now. They stayed together in a very close group, which felt safer but caused Ylena to feel even more suffocated. She walked for a while, studying the crystalline above her head, hoping that would help. Talking might have helped distract her, but the tunnel dampened the sound in a way that was disturbing on its own. They walked in silence and hurried as fast as they could.

After an interminable time, she noticed the tunnel was brighter than before. They walked even faster, and soon, they were in the Heart of the Grottos. The central cave was massive compared to the individual Grottos. Every time they discussed the Spectacle, she wasn't sure how the entire Underneath would be able to fit. But now that she saw the Heart, she understood. There weren't stone benches like at the amphitheater, but there was plenty of room for people to stand or sit on the ground or dance. She wasn't sure how the audience would react to their performance, but at least they had plenty of room to do it.

Wilder led them closer to the center, and Ylena was in awe. Standing directly in the center was an eighth spire. When she mentally placed the map of the City on top of the Underneath, she realized this spire reached up to end in the crystal basin at the center of the amphitheater. When she stood on stage, she never considered what was below the glowing basin. Even if she had stopped to consider it, she would never have imagined this.

The spire ran from the roof overhead down through the floor of the cave. Surrounding the spire was a round pool of crystalline. A stone ledge contained the crystalline pool, and inside were seven large, stone columns covered in crystalline flowing upward toward the City. Smaller stone pipes pulled the crystalline through various parts of the Underneath. She had once heard that every part of the crystalline was connected and of a piece, but she didn't understand that until she saw its source. She couldn't imagine the level of knowledge it took to build pipes that caused the crystalline to flow properly. It couldn't be separated from itself, and it flowed like a thick molasses, except that it always flowed upward and only along stone. Anything else was simply burned up.

She stared into the crystalline pool as it reflected the purple light from the crystal, and her eyes followed the glittering waves with fascination. She realized the others were talking, so she pulled her eyes away from the glow.

"Ugh. It really is so creepy in here," said Rev.

"Creepy?" asked Ylena. Someone had mentioned it before, but Ylena didn't understand.

"You might not feel it yet, but just wait. It's something about the air in here. It gives me the chills."

Tayeh didn't look like her usual confident self and kept glancing over her shoulder. "I've never liked it here. Today and tomorrow ... that's it, right?"

"Yes," said Wilder. "After the Spectacle, we can go wherever you want."

Quinn was the only one who didn't appear affected by the Heart. He was staring at the spire and crystalline with her same fascination. He whispered to her, "I think it's beautiful."

"Me too!" she whispered. "You don't feel what they do?"

He shook his head. "Although, I've never been here before either. Maybe it will catch up to us?"

"I hope not. I'd like to remain curious rather than end up looking as nauseous as they do."

They both laughed.

Wilder looked around. "I guess we should find Maestro. I bet he is already here."

They wandered around the perimeter of the Heart until they found him. He was directing people on where they should put giant crates of alcohol.

"I said you could set up anywhere you want except right over here. This is our dressing room area, and we don't need people coming back here all night long digging out more booze!"

"How's it going, Maestro? Where would you like us to go?" asked Wilder.

"Oh, I will tell you where to go!" He frowned and took a deep breath. "I apologize. Everyone has been extremely tedious this morning. If you'd like to set up those poles, the fabric will drape across and give everyone their own dressing room. It's not quite the same as the individual rooms at the City amphitheater, but I think it will work."

"Yes, Maestro," said Wilder. "Ylena and I brought our friends with us, and they will help, too."

Rev sighed, and Tayeh rolled her eyes, but Quinn's enthusiastic expression made up for them.

The five of them worked together to get the dressing rooms built quickly. Once they did, Maestro rolled out several large racks of costumes. "One of these belongs to each of you. Grab yours, and put the others in the dressing rooms of the Little Wardens."

Ylena found hers easily enough. The typical costume for the Goddess was white, draped fabric similar to what Lady Erenne had given her to wear for her audition. She found several tops that were draped in the traditional fashion, but she didn't know where to find the skirts. She wondered if she was missing a rack of costumes.

Maestro called them all together for another project. "Luckily, we have professionals who will build the stage pieces arriving soon. Then, the decor team will bring the drape for our backdrop and for along the stage. Unfortunately, we do not have Light Priests to run our lights, but we have some lighting trusses with stone pipes that will connect to the pool to draw out the crystalline."

"So, what else do you need us to do?" asked Quinn.

Maestro narrowed his eyes, apparently trying to guess if

Quinn was being sincere or not. "I need all of you to go over there and stay out of the way."

The crew happily followed those instructions. They unfolded a couple blankets and stretched out together. They told stories about performances from their childhood, and Ylena was happy to be included in the conversation. She relaxed on the blanket and closed her eyes as Wilder told a story about Rev.

Ylena opened her eyes and saw a small boy staring at her. His dark brown eyes were wet with tears. She sat up quickly. "Who are you?"

He didn't answer.

"Are the Wardens holding you captive? Where are you? How can I find you?"

He stared at her with eyes that clearly didn't understand all of her words. His bottom lip trembled.

"It's okay. I know you are scared. But don't worry. I'm going to find you."

He seemed to understand the tone of her voice, if not the words. He put his thumb in his mouth and walked over and sat on her lap.

She didn't know what to do. He snuggled up close to her chest, and she remembered holding the babies in the nursery with Caed. She wrapped her arms around the little boy and sang. His eyes fluttered and then closed. She kept singing while she swayed back and forth. Finally, his crying stopped, and she fell asleep with her arms around him.

Her eyes popped open. She was still lying on the blanket, listening to the crew's stories. At least, they had been telling stories. They appeared to have stopped.

"Ylena? Are you okay?" Quinn touched her arm hesitantly.

She didn't want to admit she had dreamt about the child again. "Yeah, I'm fine. I just dozed off. Why?"

"You were singing."

She sat up slowly. "I guess I can sing in my sleep. Weird."

"Do you remember what you were singing?"

She tried to recall what she had been singing to the little boy. "No, I don't remember. Why? Was it embarrassing?" She tried to laugh. The others were looking at her strangely, and it made her uncomfortable.

"Not embarrassing," said Quinn. "But I'm not exactly sure what language it was."

50

The crew didn't get to relax much longer before the Maestro put them back to work. The stage was built, and the lighting team was hanging their contraptions to focus the crystalline. Maestro had the crew organize all the props in one of the curtained rooms they had constructed.

"Set out all these props so that the Little Wardens can grab them for Act Three." He hurried off to yell at the person running the stone for the crystalline that would amplify the metallic guitars.

"I wonder what these props are for?" asked Ylena.

There was a fake vine covered with flowers, blue and white ribbons, and even a puppet in the shape of a wolf.

Wilder shrugged. "He said Act Three, but since we haven't done more than read it, who can say?"

"I'm looking forward to the Little Wardens showing up," said Rev. "I remember a particularly cute guy from Indulgence that I would like to see again." Ylena remembered that he was the one who wore the fedora and spent the entire time flirting with Rev.

"There is also a dreamy boy from Grotto Desire," said Ylena. "Right, Wilder?" She winked.

He rolled his eyes, and Rev looked intrigued.

They didn't have to wait long before the Little Wardens started arriving. They showed up with various levels of fanfare. The girl from Grotto Peculiar wandered in on her own, but the dreamy guy from Desire brought an entire harem similar to the actual Warden. Maestro rounded them all up, and soon, everyone sat along the front of the stage.

"We don't have long to rehearse, so everyone, pay attention. We will first rehearse Act One, which is about the creation of the Underneath. Each of you playing the role of a Warden should know your lines already. The extra performers Ylena and Wilder recruited in each Grotto were assigned their specific tasks for that scene. Ylena and Wilder, you have little to do except stand stage right."

"Which is basically what we do the entire time," Ylena whispered.

Maestro continued. "Act Two has each of the individual songs about the Wardens that we rehearsed at each Grotto. I assume everyone remembers their part?" They each nodded.

"Act Three is a conversation between the Goddess, Companion, and each of the Grottos. I'd like to start there today since we need to rehearse the blocking."

He clapped his hands, and everyone stood. He directed the Little Wardens into position. Some, he grabbed by the arms and physically moved into their starting position.

"This is where each of you will stand during Ylena and Wilder's lines. When the Goddess says, 'You are not mine,' you will all move in to surround them."

All seven Little Wardens crept forward, and a shiver ran down Ylena's spine.

"You will then use your props to tie them up."

"Excuse me?" said Ylena.

Maestro rolled his eyes. "The Goddess is not the hero of this story. The Wardens will tie up you and Wilder to symbolize the Wardens ruling the people Upstairs, who belong to the Goddess." He frowned. "I admit it's a little too on the nose, but at this point in the Spectacle, many attendees will be drunk or high, so I guess it's best to be clear."

Ylena stared at Wilder and tried to judge his reaction, but his face was blank.

Maestro pointed to the room with all the props. "Why don't you each collect your specific props, and let's run this scene so we can be done with it?"

The Little Wardens sauntered or skipped to pick up their individual props, which Ylena realized must represent each of the Gifts.

"Yes, Moya, that vine is yours. You will drape it around the two of them and tie them back-to-back. The ribbons are water and air. I'm not sure why the chains are for Knowledge, Wyatt, but I'd appreciate it if you drape these across their chests like this ..."

Eventually, the Little Wardens tied up Ylena and Wilder in seven different ways. She felt claustrophobic, but in a new way. The only thing keeping her calm was Wilder's warm presence against her back.

"Yes, this looks very dramatic!" said Maestro. "After you tie them up, you will recite your final lines about how the Underneath will rule, blah blah blah. Then, each of the Little Wardens strikes their triumphant pose, and the lights will fade on the Goddess and her Companion defeated. Beautiful."

Ylena caught Rev's expression from where she stood at the front of the stage. She stared at the scene with a mixture of sadness and fury.

"I think we are ready to try this with the band and see

what happens. Put on your costumes, and let's begin the Debacle!"

"Don't you mean the Spectacle?" asked Moya.

"Sure," said Maestro with a flat look.

Apparently, the costume that Ylena thought was a top was an entire dress. Not only was the Goddess defeated in this performance, she also wore less clothing than some strippers from Desire. Ylena tugged on the draped fabric to see if she could make it cover more of her, but without much success.

She took a deep breath and walked to her space in the curtained area to either side of the stage. The band was checking their sound, and it thrummed through the entire Heart.

"The Underneath has a lot of issues, but it has some very skilled seamstresses." Ylena turned at the sound of Wilder's voice. He gave her an appraising look.

She rolled her eyes, but she also gave silent appreciation to the seamstresses for their work on Wilder's costume. He was in a leather vest, tight pants, and had leather straps wound around his muscular arms.

"I'm not sure what the Goddess would think about this. It feels disrespectful," she said.

"I don't know about that. I think the Goddess was a bit feistier than some people give her credit for. If you reread the lines from the Pageant, I think you'll realize there is a valid reason you blushed so much." He winked.

She sighed. "Even so, I don't think she'd appreciate that the pivotal scene is about her defeat. And I'm still not sure why she wouldn't claim the people in the Underneath as her own. Why would she just choose the people who live Upstairs and not down here? It doesn't seem fair."

"A lot of things down here aren't fair, so maybe that's why it's so easy to believe she has abandoned us."

"Do you believe that? Has she abandoned us?"

He stared off into the distance, considering his words. "I don't believe this is what she intended. But I never had much hope that things would change. Until I met you."

Her breath caught in her chest, and she couldn't move.

"Singing with you in the Pageant changed something in me. And seeing the Underneath through your eyes showed me there is a beauty here I never realized. I don't know what will happen after the Spectacle, but for the first time in my life, I can imagine a future that's worthy of a Goddess."

A tear trickled down her cheek. "Wilder ..." she whispered.

Maestro's voice rang out from on stage. "Places, everyone! We are running everything from the top!"

Wilder smiled sweetly and walked out to his place on stage.

51

They ran through the entire show, and when they finished, Ylena felt even more unsettled than before. The Little Wardens took wicked delight in tying her and Wilder up. Their eyes were frenzied, and they tied both of them tighter each time they rehearsed. The last time through the scene, she couldn't catch her breath until Wilder grabbed hold of her hand.

When the Little Wardens finished their last song, they walked off the stage to prepare for their curtain call. Maestro called them back to help Ylena and Wilder get untied, which they did grudgingly.

Maestro conceded they were as ready as they ever would be, so he dismissed them for the night. The Little Wardens were walking back to their individual Grottos to sleep and would arrive right before the show the following night. But Ylena and the rest of the crew decided they would just sleep at the Heart. Rev and Tayeh both thought it was unsettling, but they didn't want to walk all the way back to one of the Grottos either.

Ylena headed into her dressing room to change and found Caed waiting for her. He looked her up and down and held out his hand. "I saw you on stage, but you are even more striking up close." She placed her hand in his, and he twirled her around like the small dressing room was a stage. "You don't get to dance enough in this show. It's a waste."

"Maybe you should have been the director?" she said innocently.

He laughed. "Maybe I should!" He sat down on the floor and patted the space next to him. "Tell me how it's going."

She sat down and tried to adjust her little skirt around herself. "I'm guessing you saw some of how it's going. I'm getting tied up by seven psychopaths in a blasphemous musical and can't control any of it."

"If it's any comfort, I think the show is a brilliant little piece of propaganda. It can hold its own against the Pageant for its clever evangelism."

"How can you say that? The Spectacle is disrespectful of the Goddess and false."

"Ylena, I've said this before. I do not worship the Goddess. I think the Pageant is just as false. But that doesn't mean I can't appreciate the artistry. Or the costumes." He raised his eyebrows.

She crossed her arms over her chest. "Well, it's not as easy for me to disregard the Goddess."

"I'm sorry. I don't want to disrespect what you believe."

"I'm not sure what I believe, but there has to be some purpose to it all. Otherwise, what is the point?"

He took her hand. "This is the point, Ylena. We are here. We are alive. Let's savor life now, because it all fades away much too quickly."

She frowned but didn't answer.

He stood and pulled her up alongside him. "Let's not discuss theology right now." He pulled her into a simple, slow dance. "I'd rather just enjoy this quiet moment together."

It wasn't truly quiet. Ylena could hear the musicians rehearsing and could pick out the individual laughs of most of the Little Wardens. But the cloth-draped walls made the small dressing room feel very intimate.

He twirled her around again and pulled her back into a dance that was also an embrace. She rested her head on his shoulder and tried to savor the moment like he said.

"Ylena?" Wilder's voice came from the other side of the curtain, and she froze. "Are you dressed? Can I come in?"

"No!" Her voice was too loud, and Caed smirked as he held her closer. "Don't come in. Do you need something?"

"Rev is going to get some food from a vendor that already arrived. Do you want anything specific? It's probably just some variation of potatoes and mushrooms, but I thought I'd check."

Caed rolled his eyes, and Ylena quietly smacked his arm and walked closer to the curtain. "Anything is fine with me. Thanks for asking."

Wilder was slow to reply. "Are you okay? I know the last scene is upsetting. If you want to talk about it …"

"Thank you, Wilder." She could see Caed with his arms crossed, and she stepped even closer to the curtain. "The scene disturbed me, but I'm okay. I'm going to get changed, and I'll be out in a minute."

"Well, I'm here if you change your mind. But you better get out here quickly, or Quinn might eat all the food."

She chuckled. "Okay, I'll hurry."

When she turned around, Caed was gone.

52

After a restless night spent on the stone floor, followed by a boring morning, it was finally time to prepare for the show. After they changed into their costumes, Ylena and Wilder opened the curtain between their rooms so Tayeh, Rev, and Quinn could join them. Ylena was putting on her makeup, and the others told stories to pass the time.

"Are you okay, Ylena?" asked Wilder.

"I'm fine. I appreciate all the stories. They take my mind off the performance."

"Do you have any funny stories?" asked Quinn.

"Nothing like yours. I grew up with my grandfather, and he wasn't as entertaining as all of you." She tried to make her answer lighthearted, but she felt like she cast a gloom over their storytelling.

Rev patted her hand. "Well, now that you know us, you will have plenty of stories." She got a wicked glint in her eye and looked at Tayeh and Quinn. "Have I told you about the first time I met Ylena? Wilder showed up on my doorstep with this lovely girl, and with only a couple of words, I had her blushing like you wouldn't believe!"

Ylena smiled at the memory, and they all laughed.

She finished applying her eyeliner and started fiddling with her hair. For the Pageant, she'd had people who styled her hair and pinned it into place, but she didn't know how to do it herself.

Rev scooted over to sit behind her. "I can help. Hand me your brush." She smoothed her hair back into a twist, and Ylena began to cry.

Rev put her hand on Ylena's arm. "What's the matter, honey? Am I brushing too hard?"

Ylena shook her head. "This is completely different from the Pageant, but it feels so familiar. I'm happy, but I can't enjoy it because I'm terrified about what will happen tonight. I'm afraid I will lose all of you."

Rev patted her shoulder and began brushing her hair again. "I already said you won't lose us, but I admit I feel uneasy about tonight, too. Being here with all of you is the only reason I have any peace of mind."

"I agree," said Quinn. "I don't know what will happen, but I am glad we are all together for it."

"Yes," said Tayeh. "If you hadn't convinced us to join you, I'm not sure what I would do tonight."

"This will be different from the Pageant," said Wilder. "I'm not leaving you this time."

She wiped her tears carefully to protect her eyeliner. "Thank you. I've never had a friend other than Pim, and I'm lucky to have met all of you."

Wilder stood and offered her his hand to pull her up. "It's time for us to head backstage."

"I'm not sure I'm ready."

He smiled. "You aren't alone in this. I'll be here until the end."

She hugged the others and followed Wilder backstage.

~

Ylena stood with Wilder in the wings and listened as the crowds of people filtered into the Heart of the Grottos. They came in a steady stream from each of the seven Grottos and filled in every space in the giant underground cavern. Even though the show hadn't started yet, it still sounded like a party.

She peeked out from behind the curtains and saw a party that was unlike anything she could have imagined. Each Grotto had contributed to this event, so there was plenty of entertainment before the show even started. She saw bars throughout the Heart and servers from Indulgence and Delirium walking through the crowd offering various types of beverages. She saw plenty of betting happening, but on what, she wasn't sure. There were several people with Spectacle-themed tattoos, so she assumed there were tattoo artists somewhere in the crowd. And even though they recruited plenty of dancers from Desire into the show, she still saw several freelance artists in the crowd.

"Ylena," a silky voice greeted her. She turned from her spot by the curtain to see Connor, the dreamy singer playing the Warden from Desire, standing extremely close to her. Wilder was nowhere to be seen, and she wondered if maybe he was avoiding Connor.

"I thought you might be thirsty, so I brought you something to drink." He handed her a cup, and she took it by reflex.

She looked to see what was inside. "Is this tea?"

"Yes." He leaned in even closer. He smelled like a cold mountain breeze and fresh linen. "I thought you might need something hot and soothing." His voice was smooth, and his eyes were powerful. She obediently brought the cup to her lips.

Her thoughts caught up to her body. She lowered the cup. "What kind of tea?"

"Just plain tea. But I added honey to make it sweet when it goes down." His words were slick, but she had seen the momentary flicker of uncertainty. She didn't quite know what the Goddess thought about the Vices, but she thanked her for Instinct.

"No, thank you. I'm not thirsty right now." She tried to hand him back the cup, but he wouldn't take it.

He leaned toward her, and his whisper was warm against her ear. "Please? Drink it for me?"

She stepped back and looked at him with eyes devoid of Desire, and he knew it. "No. I don't want it." She tried to put the cup in his hands, but he pushed it away. The cup crashed to the ground, spraying glass and hot tea. They both jumped back, and Maestro strode over.

"What is going on here?" Maestro studied the mess on the floor. "Ugh! So unprofessional." He called to an assistant. "Get something to clean this!" And to Ylena and Connor, he said, "Be careful of the broken glass! I don't want you cutting yourself and getting blood on the costumes."

Connor stared at the glass on the floor, and the Little Warden from Rivalry took him by the arm. Ylena tiptoed out of the circle of glass and tried to sneak away, but not before she heard what the girl said.

"Don't worry about it, Connor. She doesn't have any Gifts that can harm us. We will be fine."

She moved further backstage to get away from the Little Wardens and bent over to take several deep breaths. What had they been trying to do to her?

"Ylena!"

She straightened as she recognized the voice. "Grandfather!"

"I just wanted to see you before the Spectacle and wish you luck."

"Oh, thanks ... I appreciate that."

"What's wrong? You look upset."

"There's a lot wrong, but most recently, I think the Little Wardens were trying to poison me."

His eyes widened, and he pulled her into a quieter area. "What happened?"

"One of the Little Wardens tried to give me a cup of tea."

Grandfather waited, but she didn't continue. "And ..." he said.

"And he was really weird about it. And another one said not to worry because I don't have any Gifts that can hurt them."

"Oh." He rubbed his hand through his gray hair. "I don't think they were trying to poison you, but at least for tonight, it is still probably good you didn't drink it." He wouldn't look her in the eyes.

"What aren't you telling me?" She thought she had come to the end of her grandfather's secrets, but her breathing was speeding up and she knew something was wrong.

"The tea isn't poison. But it will stop you from being able to use your Gift."

She stared at her sweet grandfather, and even though she loved him, she wanted to scream at him.

Her breathing was shallow, and she only had enough self-restraint to say, "Explain."

He sighed. "The tea we drank on the mountain? It's the reason you lived so long without being bonded to the City."

"I didn't manifest until I left the mountain because the Gifts only are given to people who live in the City."

"No. Your Gift finally manifested again because you left

the mountain and stopped drinking the tea I made for you every day."

She whispered. "I was always like this?"

"Yes. When you were a baby, I cut my finger on a fishhook. You grabbed me with your pudgy little hand and healed me. I started giving you the tea the next day."

"But how did you find the tea? How did you know what it would do?"

His eyes turned sad. "Your mother found it."

Ylena covered her mouth with her hand. "She did?"

"She said the Goddess showed it to her." He shook his head. "Somehow, she knew that you would have a Gift. She made me promise her that as soon as I saw you exhibit a Gift, I would start giving you the tea. She knew it wasn't safe for you to go back to the City, and she knew that without the tea suppressing your Gift, you would die within a year."

Her lips twisted, trying to hide her emotion. "You lied to me. My entire life. You never told me who I was."

"I kept you safe, Ylena! The Priests and their Gifts are a curse. I would gladly feed you and the Priests tea for your entire lives if I could!"

She stared at him like she had never seen him before. "You would erase who I am?"

His voice softened. "Your Gift isn't who you are, Ylena. It's an accident from a broken system. We have to move on."

"I can't move on from myself."

He sighed. "You don't have to worry about this right now. Just perform in the Spectacle, and we will see what tomorrow brings."

She narrowed her eyes. "Do you know what tomorrow brings?"

He avoided her eyes again. "Not exactly. But I know it will be better than today."

"Oh, really? You believe the Wardens are planning something beneficial? That's who you have faith in?"

He frowned. "That's not what—"

Loud music began thrumming through the Heart. The band had started their opening set.

"I have to get into place." She turned to leave, but he caught her arm.

"Ylena, I'm sorry. I'm really sorry."

She gave him a hard look. "If you'd like to confess, you'll need to find an actual Priest who will listen."

Ylena walked to her place backstage in a daze. She thought she finally understood the shape of her history, but once again, her grandfather had been keeping a part of her life secret. She was furious and heartbroken and had no idea how she could walk on stage and perform.

Wilder ran up to her. "Where have you been? I heard there was something strange with the Little Wardens trying to give you tea, and I couldn't find you. I was worried something—" He stopped and looked in her eyes. "What's wrong? Are you okay?"

She looked up into his kind face and began to cry. He gathered her into his arms and whispered soothing words. "It's okay. We will get through this. Nothing bad is going to happen. You aren't alone."

His kind words made her cry harder. How could he say that? Nothing was okay. Bad things had already happened. Everything was broken.

He pulled her away from his chest to look into her eyes. "Will you tell me what it is? That might help."

"I just saw my grandfather. He lied to me my entire life."

"Your grandfather loves you. If he lied, it was a stupid mistake, but I'm sure it wasn't intentional."

"Wilder, he knew I was Gifted. I healed him when I was a baby. He gave me tea every day of my life to suppress my Gift."

Wilder shook his head. "There isn't a tea like that. Maybe this is a misunderstanding?"

"That's the tea the Little Wardens tried to give me tonight. They only gave up because they believe I can't do anything dangerous with just the ability to heal."

"That makes no sense—"

"Wilder! He admitted it! He said that he would rather I drank the tea every day of my life and wasn't Gifted at all! He said that the system is broken. That I am broken."

She was gulping in air but couldn't breathe.

Wilder took her face in his hands. "Ylena, look at me." She looked at him with eyes blurry with tears. "You are not broken. You have made my life brighter from the first day I met you." His gentle voice sent calm deep into her soul. "You are a wonder. A miracle. You are the Goddess's Blessing."

She closed her eyes as he leaned down to give her a kiss.

Wilder's lips were soft. His gentle hands brushed her cheeks wet with tears. The kiss was tender and sweet and nothing like her kisses with

Caed.

Caed kissing her in a room bursting with flowers.

Caed with his shirt off, dancing in the moonlight.

Caed kissing her as she made feathers bloom in stone.

Caed with drops of water falling like stars.

Wilder stepped back from the kiss with wide eyes. "I could see that." He blinked his eyes like he could still see the images. "You have the Gift of Knowledge ... You have all the Gifts."

Her eyes were wide with panic, and she couldn't answer.

His voice dropped to a whisper. "You love him."

She covered her mouth with her hands, but she couldn't block the images he had already seen.

"I thought you …" His face was a mixture of confusion and heartbreak, and she felt her heart would break in response.

"I'm sorry." She breathed out the inadequate words.

"You never told me."

"I should have—"

"This whole time … you never told me." His voice was firmer this time.

"I know. I should have said—"

"You were so angry at the secrets I kept from you. The secrets your grandfather has kept. And knowing all that, you still never told me."

"Grandfather doesn't even know I have all the Gifts. It seemed too dangerous to talk about—"

"But Caed knows."

She ducked her head. "Yes."

"You let me spill my heart to you over and over again while you were already in love with him. You could have told me at any time!" His voice was like an avalanche barely contained.

"I'm sorry, Wilder. I'm so sorry."

"I guess the Spectacle really is true. The Goddess doesn't give a damn about the people down here."

He walked onto the dark stage for the first song.

53

Ylena stood next to Wilder on the dark stage and felt the hurt and anger rolling off him in waves. Her chest constricted with suffocating guilt like she had never felt in her life. She knew the pain caused by every secret that others kept from her, and yet she kept secrets of her own. She pretended that she didn't know what the consequences of those secrets would be, but Rev had warned her. And Ylena had done exactly what Rev begged her not to. She had pulled Wilder along, knowing that she loved Caed.

She looked at Wilder in the dim light backstage. But she loved him, too. Not like she loved Caed, but she loved him. And she hurt him. Badly. And he would never forgive her.

She had lost him. Not in the way she had feared, but he was gone.

The music faded out to only the cheering of the crowd. When the band struck their loud first note, the curtain swung open. The Little Wardens began reciting the lines of the first act:

When the City was born, so was the Heart of the Underneath.

The Goddess built her City to take and restrict.
Bind and limit.
Restrain and control.
But the Underneath gives freedom and life.

Ylena forgot about her unsettled feelings about the disrespectful script. She was the Goddess tonight.

And the Goddess was the villain of the story.

But Wilder still played her Companion. Faithful. Devoted. Loving. And the more his character loved her, the more sinful she felt.

They rarely touched in their choreography because she had refused during rehearsals. She had still been angry with him about causing Pim's death when she knew all along that it was never his fault.

So, they danced side by side or held poses while the Little Wardens sang. They were close to each other, but so far away.

She looked out to the audience and saw the cavern filled with undulating waves of people. At the center of the cavern, the crystalline flowed Upstairs along a circle of seven stone columns, and a framework of stone pipes drew the crystalline into a pattern to light the stage. The lights were bright, but they weren't bright enough to keep her from seeing Rev, Tayeh, and Quinn in the front row.

From the expression on Rev's face, she could tell something was wrong. Ylena saw her following Wilder's movements with concern. His performance was as brilliant as usual, but it was obvious to Rev that something wasn't right. And based on the glare she occasionally shot at Ylena, Rev had guessed what it was.

Ylena had lost her, too. And once Tayeh and Quinn figured it out, she would also lose them.

They had to change costumes before Act Three, but Wilder avoided her backstage until the moment before they walked onto the stage together. They both recited their lines together as rehearsed, and then the Little Wardens cried out the Grottos' Lament.

Grottos: But Goddess, what of the Underneath? Are we not Yours? Do you hear our cry?

Goddess: The Priests belong to me and care for my people who live Above. You are not mine.

You are not mine. You are not mine. The words rang in her head. It was her betrayal of Wilder. Her betrayal of the rest of the crew. And the Goddess's betrayal of the Underneath.

Grottos: Then we will rule ourselves.

Our Vices will guide us.

Our Wardens will lead us.

And one day, we will rule Your children.

As the Little Wardens moved to get the props to tie them up, Ylena believed she deserved it. She moved to stand back-to-back with Wilder and wished they would leave him alone and just take out their anger on her.

When the vine began crawling up her leg, she froze in place. Moya held a plant in her hands, and vines streamed from it and twisted around her and Wilder. The crowd's cheers grew confused.

Greyson gathered a breeze and used it to blow their hair and clothes into a storm while squeezing them together so hard that Ylena struggled to breathe.

Connor held a water sculpture of a snake that writhed between his hands. He flung his hands out, and the snake slithered through the air to join the vines. At this, the crowd realized it wasn't a prop and began cheering wildly. Everyone except Rev, Tayeh, and Quinn.

Aminah held her palms straight out in front of her, and two pure white wolves ran through the crowd and jumped onto the stage to circle with growls and nip at their heels.

Daena liquified part of the stone structure that held the mechanical crystalline lights and formed the stone into a glowing circle around their feet.

Wyatt moved carefully around the obstacles and placed his hands against Ylena and Wilder's foreheads.

Through his Gift of Knowledge, Ylena saw the empty streets of the Grottos because everyone was at the Spectacle. Empty except for an army that marched toward the stairways.

The guards were armed with weapons and the potion to counteract the poison dust. And behind them marched rows of children. Not just the babies Ylena had imagined. But children and teens, several the same age as the Little Wardens. None of them were older than Ylena.

She was the oldest. She was the first. Her mother discovered the tea which saved Ylena's life. And her grandfather had sold it to the Underneath to build an army.

Wyatt released them, and Ylena gasped. She sagged in the bonds of all their Gifts and gave up. She had hoped to rescue the crying child from a life of serving the Wardens, but instead, all those children were marching Upstairs to overthrow the High Priests in the same way the Little Wardens had defeated her now.

Jerra walked up to them, and Ylena had a moment of panic, wondering how healing could be warped. She thought Jerra was one step away from murdering her and Wilder. Jerra chuckled and said quietly, "Unfortunately, I can't use my Gift to harm, but I can add to the embarrassment and drama a little. I'm thinking bright white hair to mark you like the failed Priests Upstairs. And I can heal those tattoos while I'm at it." She winked and placed her hands on their foreheads.

Ylena couldn't see her own wrist because she was tied so tightly, but she imagined the bird tattoo she got for Pim. She

312

remembered the seven-pointed star inside a tear that represented the Goddess on Wilder's chest. Jerra would not take that from them.

She reached behind her for Wilder's hand. She took a deep breath and spoke her words as a memory into his mind.

"It wasn't you, Wilder. I'm the one who broke the City, and then I brought it back."

She showed him the image of her tear falling into the basin.

"When you are free, grab the others and run. And tell them I'm sorry. "

She could feel him hold his breath as she spoke in his mind, and when she finished, he breathed out in a rush. He took a breath to speak but didn't have time before Ylena exploded in light.

She took control of the water snake and threw it against the crystalline. The water heated and hovered in a glow until she brought down a whirlwind that blinded the Little Wardens with glowing water.

A storm hurtled Jerra away from them. Wind blew Ylena's hair into her face, and she saw a few tendrils of white, but her tattoo had not yet disappeared. The Little Wardens were staring at her in shock, but Ylena's mind felt as clear as a mountain stream and just as cold.

She took control of the vines. Moya stared at the vine in her hand as it twisted up her arms and down her legs. The vines dropped their hold on Ylena and Wilder and began growing in a pattern that branched across the stage floor and crept up the curtains.

She ripped every tendril of wind from Greyson's control, lifted him several feet in the air, and then dropped him. He landed awkwardly, and she used a steady breeze to hold him kneeling in place.

She glared at the white wolves. They stopped circling her and lay down at her feet. She looked up at Aminah, and the wolves leapt up and growled at her until she had backed up next to Moya. The vines swirled up her legs and wrapped her just as tight.

She gathered up the water that hung in the air. She settled a thin sheet of moisture along the stone stage in front of Connor as he ran away. His legs slid out from under him, and he dropped. She tied him up with water ropes.

Ylena was still beside Wilder within the circle of crystalline-covered stone. She touched a part of the bare stone, and it flowed away from them, wrapping itself around Daena's foot before she could finish backing off stage.

She didn't want to touch Jerra and Wyatt to use those Gifts, so she grabbed one of the notes from the metallic guitar from where it still shimmered in the air. She wound the note around them as they tried to run, and they fell to their knees with their hands covering their ears.

Wilder still had not moved from her side, even though he was no longer restrained. She looked at him with intense eyes and whispered, "Run."

He looked at her with shock but then shook himself and jumped into the audience next to Rev, Tayeh, and Quinn. She saw them quickly head toward a tunnel through the stunned and whispering crowd. She turned to the wolves and said, "Keep them safe." They both yipped once and leapt off the stage to follow.

She took a deep breath, pulled a note down from the top of the cavern, and sang a portion of the Goddess's Aria. The notes brushed through the hair of the audience and wrapped around their hearts. She let the wind of the notes tickle their lungs and shiver down the back of their necks. She let the notes trip along the ground until the floor began to vibrate.

The people felt the vibration through the soles of their shoes, which caused them to shuffle anxiously. Some started toward the exits.

She looped the notes of the Aria until it echoed through the cavern. Then, she added the Grottos' Lament as a counterpoint. The two songs together were haunting. The crowd began backing away.

Ylena's song grew so loud that the vibrations shook the entire cavern. The crystalline pool rippled in time to the vibrating rhythm. The crowd turned and ran toward the tunnels.

ENCORE

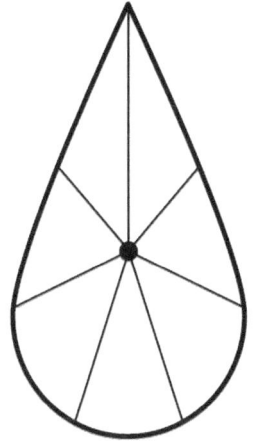

54

She sang for a long time.

She stood at the center of the Heart of the Grottos and watched the patterns in the crystalline. She grabbed note after note from the air and pulled them around her in the space until the entire cavern echoed with the Goddess's Aria and the Grottos' Lament. The notes twisted over and around each other until there was no air for anyone to breathe except for what was in her and her song.

"Ylena." Her name was a gasp.

She found Caed on his knees, struggling for air. She released the notes around them so he could breathe in her bubble of air. He took in a full breath and stood in front of her.

His hair was more white than dark, and she wondered if he had used his Gift to reach her in the center of the airless cavern. She looked around and realized it was empty. The Little Wardens were no longer on the stage, and she frowned.

"I'm sorry I wasn't here in time for everything that happened ... Although, it looks like you handled it just fine."

She thought she should answer him, but she wasn't sure how long it had been since she'd said a word, and it felt strange to talk again.

"Are you okay?" He touched her white streaks of hair. "Is this ...?"

She shook her head. She couldn't fix it herself, but she assumed any Perfection Priest could.

The child Priests ...

"There is an army coming." Her voice felt scratchy. How long had she been singing?

Caed nodded sadly. "They arrived soon after the Spectacle began. High Priest Erenne came to warn me. She apparently looked into one of the Den's secret rooms where they were holding the children. We were all surprised to learn that they had so many Gifted and that it wasn't just babies."

"It didn't surprise my grandfather. He's the one who has been supplying tea to the Wardens for years to build their secret army." Her voice was bitter and strained.

"Oh, Ylena, I'm so sorry. I had no idea."

She shrugged.

"When High Priest Erenne saw how old they were, we knew they were planning something soon. She warned me and anyone else that would listen. We are hiding in a safe house near the amphitheater. Most of the others weren't so lucky." He frowned.

"What happened?"

"The Wardens and their soldiers stormed the doorways. They defeated the Sentinels because of their cure to the poison dust and because they were armed to the teeth. All of the High Priests except Lady Erenne were captured or killed. They captured a lot of other Priests, although the Wardens are upset that the Priests' Gifts are in short supply.

But they won't mind using their last remaining Gifts until they are so white-haired they fade away."

"The Wardens will make the Priests use their Gifts even if it kills them?"

He shrugged. "The High Priests have been replaced by Wardens with an army of Gifted children. It's going to be just as corrupt as it was before."

"At least the people of the Underneath can live in the City now." She imagined what Rev was thinking tonight at her first glimpse of the stars.

Caed rubbed his hands through his hair. "Actually, the Wardens locked the doors."

"What?"

"They planned the Spectacle so that all the people would be here at the Heart while they marched their army Upstairs. Once they had secured the temples, they locked the doors again. They literally just replaced the High Priests. They didn't liberate anyone but themselves."

Ylena swayed on her feet, but Caed caught her. "I'm sorry to share such bad news."

"So, everyone I've met in the Underneath is still trapped down here? And now the City is ruled by the Wardens, who were cunning enough to plan this for years?" He nodded. "How did you get down here? And how are you getting back up?"

He chuckled. "It always has been easy to get in. Getting out is the tricky part. I figured I'd just stay down here with you until we figure something out."

She blinked. "What are we going to figure out?"

"You know, how to stage a proper revolution. The Wardens did it rather poorly in my opinion." He smiled.

She shook her head at him. "How can you be so cheerful about this? Everything is ruined. I thought I had a good relationship with my grandfather. I don't. That child I heard crying that I wanted to rescue? He's part of an army Upstairs. I've ruined the City a second time. I ruined my friendships. There's no revolution here."

He brushed her hair back from her face. "I haven't lost hope yet. Just knowing what you did here tonight gives me more hope than I've had for a long time."

"Tonight felt anything but hopeful to me."

He pulled her to his chest and wiped the tears off her cheek. His body was warm and strong where it pressed against her. She sighed against him and felt some of her tension release. Caed was here. He was safe. He was confident. Things would be okay.

He leaned down to her with an expression full of hope and desire. He sent shivers down her spine while heating the rest of her body. She pulled him closer to drown in his kiss and forget everything that happened tonight with

Wilder.

Wilder holding her face in his hands saying beautiful sweet things.

Wilder leaning down to kiss her.

Ylena kissing him back.

Caed stepped back with a gasp. He shook his head in the same way Wilder had shook his. Ylena stumbled backwards and covered her traitorous lips with her hands.

"That was tonight?" he asked.

She couldn't answer.

"He kissed you ... You kissed him?" He violently rubbed his hands through his hair. "I'm an idiot. I should have guessed. But ... you never said—" He choked on the words.

"Caed, it wasn't like that—"

"That wasn't your memory?"

"Well, it was, but—"

"I've got to go." He turned to look at the various tunnels leading out.

"Where will you go?"

"I've got to get out of here. I can't believe I came down here. I thought we ... Never mind. I've got to go."

He picked a random direction to walk away from her into the airless cavern.

"Wait! Don't go that way! Please, let me do this ..." She took the tears that had fallen and placed her hand on the stone floor. The stone around her hand rippled out in waves, then settled back down. Spiraling around the crystal and crystalline pool, a staircase took shape, step by step.

The stone flowed up and over itself until the steps reached the top of the cavern. At the top, she opened a door in the stone.

"The door exits into the area underneath the stage. I hope you can make it back to your safe house without being seen."

Caed stared at the staircase numbly. He began walking.

She ran toward him to catch up. "I'll leave it open. The staircase. I will seal the tunnels leading into the Heart, but I will leave the staircase open ... For you."

He gave her a sad smile. "Goodbye, Ylena." He walked all the way up the staircase without a look back.

55

Ylena lay down to sleep at the base of the stone staircase in the Heart. She wanted to be close to the stairs ... just in case. But part of her knew she was ridiculous. She'd ruined her relationships with Caed and Wilder. Rev, Tayeh, and Quinn would never want to be her friends again. Grandfather didn't think she should exist. All of her plans, all of her relationships, all of her hopes were ruined. Even though no one died, she lost them all anyway.

She sighed and rolled to her other side and saw the little boy. He was standing with his thumb in his mouth. He wasn't crying. Just calmly staring at her.

She sat up. "I guess you are feeling better now that you are Upstairs."

He still didn't seem to understand. He looked older than she remembered, and she felt like he should be able to carry on a conversation at his age. She wondered what the Wardens had done to him.

"I'm going to sleep," she said. "Maybe you should stop dreaming yourself here, however you are doing it, and fall asleep back in your little bed in the temple. Good night." She closed her eyes.

"Good night," he said. His voice was definitely older than the voice of the crying baby. She opened her eyes and sat up. She looked at his face again. He might be around six years old. How could she have ever mistaken his cries for a toddler's?

"What's your name?" she asked gently so she wouldn't startle him.

The boy's eyes unfocused as he considered the question. He looked at her again with a frown. "I don't remember."

She scrunched her forehead in thought. "Do the other children remember their names?"

"There are no other children."

"Yes, there are. I saw them all marching Upstairs."

His face shifted in confusion. "There's only me."

She felt a knot growing in the pit of her stomach.

"How did you find me?" she asked.

The boy tilted his head as he considered the question. "It was hard to find you when I was just born. I cried a lot." He frowned, but then his eyes lit up. "It was easy to find you once you came here." He gestured around the Heart of the Grottos.

She narrowed her eyes. "You remember being born?"

He appeared unsure but answered, "I was born when you touched my heart."

"Your ... heart?" Her eyes drifted to the purple glowing crystal that ran Upstairs into a basin in the amphitheater. It had once been a different color. "That's ... your heart?"

"Yes."

Her throat was dry, and her voice came out rough. "You are the City."

The small boy nodded in relief and smiled. He sat down

on the stone ground beside her and rested his head against her arm with a contented sigh.

*To Be Continued in *Dance with the Dawn - City of Virtue and Vice Book 3**

ABOUT THE AUTHOR

Susannah Welch lives in sunny South Florida with her brilliant husband and a magically hypoallergenic cat. She enjoys singing and dancing and showing off. She likes her stories with a little bit of drama, and a whole lot of sparkle.

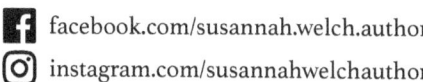

facebook.com/susannah.welch.author

instagram.com/susannahwelchauthor